The Watchers Trilogy
Awakening

KARICE BOLTON

DEDICATION

To all of the people in my life who always tell me to go for it!

Love you my dude! Jon, you are the best husband a girl could ask for...

Mom, thank you for always giving me encouragement and to my dad who is watching down over us all!

ACKNOWLEDGMENTS

I want to say a simple thank you to Amazon, Barnes & Noble, and all of the other avenues available for the indie publishing world. It allows the art of storytelling to continue to flourish in unexpected ways!

NEXT IN THE TRILOGY:

LEGIONS

BOOK 2 OF THE WATCHERS TRILOGY

BY

KARICE BOLTON

TO CONTACT THE AUTHOR PLEASE VISIT
HER WEBSITE AT

KARICEBOLTON.COM

OR
EMAIL

INFO@KARICEBOLTON.COM

OR
FOLLOW HER ON TWITTER

@KARICEBOLTON

CHAPTER 1

The screams shot me out of bed. My heart was pounding seventy miles an hour. I felt for my fleece blanket to throw off, since I seemed to be stuck to my sheets with a million gallons of sweat. I looked around my blackened room, with only the red glow of the alarm clock displaying 3:00 am to comfort me. My heart sank as I lost the battle for another night's sleep. I heard the gentle snore of my bulldog, Matilda, rattling through the air. She was used to my screams by now. I promised myself with a little whisper that I was safe. It was only a nightmare – another nightmare. That is all it was. It couldn't possibly be real that kind of terror. The dreams were coming closer together now, and worse yet, they seemed to lead to nowhere but sleep deprivation.

I commanded myself to take deep, steady breaths to calm myself. Still breathless and shaky from the last images that had blasted into my brain, I tried to rid myself of the awful scene replaying over and over-that of my demise. The mere thought of the attacks made me want to hide in my closet from the world. The black, swirling creatures were coming at me and through me from every direction. Their mouths open, displaying several sets of teeth with blood dripping from their lips waiting for me to make a mistake. This was not a world I recognized. How my mind could even create such deadly monsters I didn't know. The elements of realism spooked me beyond belief. I grabbed a tissue from my nightstand and wiped the dampness from my forehead, unsure of how much longer I could keep this up. Every night and every dream seemed to be different. They all had similar storylines, to a degree. Sometimes the unfamiliar characters reappeared to haunt me over and over again. It just depended on the night. Part of me felt as if I should know these people or at least the events that kept taking place. Why else would they keep reappearing? However, the events were so fantastical, the thought that I should recognize them made me feel even crazier for thinking it.

Fully awake now and completely disappointed in the prospect of another long and drawn out day without sleep, I trudged to the window and opened my heavy, red velvet curtains to expose the calmness of an outside world in an attempt to calm my own mind down. The snow was slowly floating down from the sky leaving a beautiful pattern on the sidewalk, illuminated only by the streetlight. The sight brought a shiver to my bones. Even though only a minute ago, I had to wipe away the wet heat of fear off my body. I couldn't keep chasing and being chased like this. I couldn't constantly go on thinking my life was in danger whenever I closed my eyes. I needed rest.

I needed sleep. Lack of sleep was only making it worse. I was sure of it.

"What is all of this telling me? I don't even know the people in my dreams!" I whined to Matilda.

She responded with her usual snorts and snores, sprawling out even more on my mattress now that I had left a larger area for her enjoyment. I flipped on my nightstand light that cast its familiar glow, attempting to move back into bed without displacing Matilda. A sigh escaped as I grabbed my latest book to read, which was ready and waiting for another night like all of the others.

I opened the book to the third chapter as my mind attempted to identify who the people in my dream were this time. Seeing crumpled remnants of humans discarded all over was never something that I could get used to regardless of it being a nightmare or not. I was getting used to seeing the swirls appear to attack me, but I was also intrigued at the thought of trying to figure out who the random strangers were who appeared time and time again. Sometimes they were the same people. Other times, a completely new set would make an entrance. I always avoided looking into their eyes because, during one of my very first nightmares, all I saw was the dull glow of death staring right back at me. I couldn't stomach it twice, and somehow my subconscious knew to never look them in the eyes, whoever they were.

Thankfully, the latest batch of characters seemed kind. As if I knew them from somewhere, although that wasn't possible. I'm sure they must have made an appearance in my other dreams. I just don't remember them. One stood out in particular. He was trying to save me, but it was too late. The black, soulless swirls got me. My nightmares never had gotten to that point before. Never did I know the conclusion to these nightmarish adventures before tonight.

This time, I saw how it ended. I didn't make it. It wasn't a painful process. I didn't feel tortured. It seemed like I should have felt the attack. I didn't. What I was left with was horrible feelings of despair and loneliness wrapping their way through every aspect of my life. My soul felt like an empty cavern as I saw myself being blown away into the wind. I remember looking back at the strangers on the ground. They were looking up towards the sky at me as I left to wherever bodiless souls go. The one guy who was so memorable was staring back at me, tears streaming down his face. He was the one who tried to save me. He risked his own life against the monsters for me. He was only a minute too late. My heart now longed for him, this figment of my imagination. I didn't know why.

I couldn't shake the images this time. They were too haunting, too real. And now I was going crazy believing that these things had some sort of significance. Lack of sleep was finally catching up with my fragile state of mind.

CHAPTER 2

The Grizzly Bear lodge was packed as usual for this time of night. I glanced around the restaurant as everyone was trickling in, partially undressing from their long day of romancing the powder. The pub was ideally situated at the base of Whistler Mountain, capitalizing on location rather than menu selection, but I enjoyed working here. It felt like home or as close to that as I could feel. I tried to shake off my long disastrous night of sleep while preparing for my shift. The images of my demise kept creeping into my thoughts. What was worse was that those images were virtually impossible. Yet, they plagued me tremendously, creating a pit in my stomach. I tried shaking the feelings of despair that kept trying to interfere with my ability to get back to my routine.

Outside the snow was gently falling, and the night barely beginning. It was early in the season, and only the upper half of the mountain was open, but it was enough to kick off the ski season in Whistler. There were the usual suspects scattered around the pub;

the guys in their twenties, who had been taking nips from their flasks all day on the mountain in between runs, attempting to quickly get their server's attention for more beer. Then there were the tables with the wives and girlfriends done up all cute, eagerly awaiting their other halves. Their actions only highlighted the fact that they had spent the day at the spa not the slopes. And, of course, there were the locals chatting up the bartender and grabbing the latest news on the hockey game.

This was the best part of my job, the people watching. Unfortunately, at times, it could be the worst part of my job. There were those days, and not all that few and far between, when it emphasized how alone I really was. As I puzzled over this fact, I quickly grabbed the next round of drinks from the bar and went to the corner table to deliver their long awaited goods. I was taking over the table from Karen who had to leave the pub rather quickly. It was unusual for her, and I hoped everything was ok. I made a mental note to give her a call when I got home.

I scooted between the wooden chairs that were now being shuffled around the tables to make room for everyone coming into the pub. The restaurant was getting packed early tonight. The sound of the chairs scraping and clunking on the well-worn wood floors gave me warning that tonight was going to be a busy night. Exactly what I needed to keep my mind occupied.

The antique snowshoes that were balancing so delicately on the wall snagged my ponytail as I tried to make my way through the tables, and thankfully, no one saw as I fought with the decorations. Once I became unsnarled from the thoughtfully placed décor, I made my way to the table waiting for me and more importantly, their drinks.

"Harmless," I whispered, as I approached the table Karen had left. I saw a man with dark golden hair gently nuzzling a woman's neck with his nose. She was thoroughly enjoying his affection. It was as if they were literally one unit. It made me chuckle. I'm not sure exactly why - maybe it was because it was a bit like my bulldog's reaction to me when I got home from work. Or maybe it was my standard reaction that would always appear when I longed for something I couldn't have, or more appropriately, never have had - except in my dreams.

Regardless, when I appeared with the drinks, they both looked up at me with the most staggering eyes. I was immediately jolted out of my doldrums. Their eyes were the most brilliant green that I'd ever seen, like an emerald. Their green eyes were filled with dark black centers, outlined with striking jets of yellow. It made my blood freeze. These two strangers were so familiar feeling. I almost gasped aloud but caught myself. My arms became weak, but I somehow managed to keep the tray steady. I stared in silence not sure what came over me as I tried to gain my composure. Instead, all that happened was that I couldn't concentrate. I felt faint. I looked at both of them again and realized they both had the same look in their eyes, almost the same eyes. The shape was different, hers more of an almond shape. His deeper set, but nonetheless, the expression and color were the same. My heart started beating too fast for its own good, and I suddenly was alive, a feeling I hadn't felt for a long time – if ever. I placed my hand over the rat's nest in my hair that the snowshoe fiasco created, trying to smooth it down. Attempting anything to try to look somewhat presentable around these unusually perfect creatures.

My fingertips were zinging with electricity as I grabbed the coasters and placed them in front of the couple. I tried to hide the smile that was coming across my face as I placed the napkins on the table. I caught at that moment that they, too, were taking me in. Strangely, they didn't seem the least bit unnerved by my reaction to them. Maybe, I was doing a better job of hiding my emotions than I thought. I doubted that though.

I was preparing to place the woman's mulled cider in front of her when I noticed I had three drinks for the table, but only two people anxiously awaiting them. I nervously looked at the woman as I tried so very hard to speak, but nothing would come out. I grabbed the mug of hot, steaming mulled cider and tried to place it in front of her as carefully as possible without spilling. My hands were shaking, and I couldn't fathom what was taking place. I looked at this woman who was the most ethereal, enchanting person I had ever seen; that is besides the person sitting next to her. She was otherworldly. That wasn't possible though. I was losing my mind. These nightmares finally caught up to me; lack of sleep now threatening my sanity. However, I couldn't shrug off their familiarity, knowing I had never seen them here in Whistler before only left one option that didn't seem plausible.

Wonderful feelings were drifting over me, wrapping every part of my body in an almost loving embrace. I didn't want to look away. I didn't want to lose these feelings. Their stares were too mesmerizing to look away. I had to control myself. I didn't want them to see my reaction any longer. This was way too bizarre. It had to be because of my lack of sleep.

An eternity seemed to go by as I was drinking everything in about this couple, but in actuality, it was only a mere second. My life stood still. After I glided the Blue Sapphire martini to the man without a drop spilt, I spun around and headed back to the safety of the bar register. Glancing quickly at them, I noticed they, too, were staring directly at me, smiling as if they knew something was about to take place. I couldn't look at them anymore. I had to come back to reality. I cursed my dull brown hair as it kept falling in my face, blocking my view of them. I shoved my hair behind my ear so I could get one last peek at them.

Once I came back to earth, I noticed that I had left the tray and the third drink on the table. Rather than go back to the table, I sprinted to the bathroom. Not knowing what was happening to me, I needed a moment to get myself back together. I swung open the bathroom door only to have the wooden sleigh crash against the door with a loud thud, yet another piece of décor out to get me. Everything in the Grizzly was placed with such great intention, which usually comforted me, but now it all seemed to get in my way. I needed to get to the sink and figure things out. I hoped I wasn't getting the flu. Maybe I had caught whatever it was that made Karen go home for the night. Any sort of bug compounded with the lack of sleep that I had been getting was a recipe for a disastrous event such as this one.

As I splashed water feverishly over my face, I couldn't stop thinking about the two people I encountered. What was it about them that made me feel this way and yearn for them? It was a euphoric sense that flooded over me. As I stood and looked in the mirror, I saw my reflection. I wished I hadn't splashed all my makeup off, especially since I would be serving them for the rest of the night, the golden gods. Compared to the woman sitting at the table, I looked like a disheveled rat to match my hair. My store bought brown hair looked especially lousy at a time like this. It made me wish I kept my natural auburn color.

I stared at my eyes reflecting in the mirror hoping to repair the mascara that dribbled down my cheek. Realizing there was no hope, I wiped it off completely. I looked at myself again, wondering if the dark brown eyes staring back at me would ever have light in them instead of the blank stare that usually surfaced. Not remembering much of my childhood, except for the memories that were told to me, always made me feel so alone, no siblings, no parents – only newspaper clippings. That is what I always blamed my lackluster expression on. Not feeling life became my comfort. When too much interaction began, that was my cue to exit the situation or leave the people behind, that's how I came to Whistler.

I heard laughing behind me and turned to see two bubbly ski bunnies bundled in cashmere coming through the door, obviously enjoying the evening. I tried not to roll my eyes and just flashed them a smile. I grabbed the paper towel dangling for me, did one last wipe of my cheeks and left the restroom.

The pub was really hustling now. I could hear the clanking of beer mugs and the chatter an octave higher. Buckets of beer, the nightly special, were parading from one table to the next like a revolving door. The lighting went down a shade, and the stone fireplace began roaring in the far corner right on time. I saw the newest group sitting in my section and quickly went over to take their drink order. As I heard the drink orders rattled off, I cautiously glanced at the couple I had left so feverishly and noticed Jen, another server on for the night, had graciously removed the tray and placed the third drink on a coaster in front of the empty chair. There was still no one sitting there. I was secretly relieved. I didn't need another perfect human adding to the complexity of the emotions running through me. I somehow knew I wasn't coming down with the flu. There was something about these people that lured me in.

"Miss," I heard pointedly, "can we add a starter of poutine to our order?"

"Of course! I'll put that right in." My smile returning to my face, I took a deep breath and continued on with my busy night. I was happy I had a full section tonight. I was certainly a creature of habit.

I was entering the poutine into the computer, when a wave of ice-cold, electrifying air penetrated me right through to my core. It was as if my bones would shatter with the slightest movement. I looked over at the front entrance expecting it to be open, but it wasn't. I quickly looked around to gauge anyone else's reaction, knowing I couldn't trust my own with my sleep deprivation. Then, right before me, I saw the third person sitting at my favorite table. He had arrived. It was from him that I was feeling the electricity. They were looking at me again, all except the newcomer. It was as if they were evaluating me, my reaction. Silly as it seemed,

11

that's what they had to be doing. But for what reason?

From behind, I could tell that he was really well-dressed. He was very firm, very upright, very oddly upright. He sat so still, almost like a statue. It struck me kind of funny, but in a good way. He, too, had golden brown hair. His looked a little less perfect, a little more disheveled, than his friends or relatives or whoever was with him at the table. I liked it. There was a bedraggled, rugged look about him - perfectly so. If he looked half as good as he did from the back, I couldn't wait to see him from the front. If only I could compose myself. Not that I had a shot, but at least, I could admire.

Promising myself that I wouldn't again lose my cool, I let the excitement ripple through me at the thought of getting to meet him. I knew what I was feeling was in my head. There was no way other people could make you feel this way.

I spun around and quickly marched to the bar. As I waited for the next order to come up, I excitedly embraced this new feeling of energy and exhilaration that was finally beginning to creep up on me.

"Hey, Ana," the bartender spoke, interrupting my thoughts, "Order's up."

"Thanks, Ben." I quickly grabbed the gravy and cheese covered fries, otherwise known as poutine, and trudged over to the table to drop it off so I could get over to the newcomer.

"Is there anything else you need or are you all set?" I asked, unable to hide my grin. They nodded their heads and off I went.

Finally, I was about to arrive at the table of life. The euphoria was beginning to set in as I saw a glow radiating from the table. Prismatic colors were dancing off the walls around them. Recognizing another side effect of my sleep deprivation, hallucinations, I just moved towards them. I had to meet the newcomer. It was like a magnet was pulling me over to him. I was certain that the others at his table noticed, but I didn't even care now. I went to the bar, grabbed some silverware as an excuse, and walked to the table of the night.

"Is there anything else I can get right now for you guys or are you doing ok?"

When the newcomer looked up at me for the first time, my heart began racing. He had the same hypnotizing eyes as the others. Only that was merely the beginning. His skin was an exquisite shade of ivory, showing slightly that he had missed a day of shaving. His features were so striking that they almost matched his startling eyes, which were outlined with such thick lashes that it made his green eyes stand out even more than the other two at the table. He was looking at me with such kindness and had a familiarity about him that I couldn't place. Secretly wondering if he could have been in one of my dreams, I did my best to keep the foolishness at bay that kept creeping in at such a preposterous notion. I wanted to clear the room and sit in front of him and do nothing but literally stare at the exquisite being in front of me.

I glanced at the couple to get my mind elsewhere only that didn't work out so well. I still felt the charge. However, this time I was certain it was coming directly from him. He continued to gaze at me when suddenly I realized that he was talking. His lips were moving, but I had no idea what he was saying. His voice was the most soothing and comforting sound, like a song. I had to get control of myself.

"I'm so sorry," I spoke from an unknown strength from within, "I need you to repeat what you said."

I could feel myself start to blush and went with it. I obviously couldn't be in control of myself around these people and gave up. It's not like I would see them again. Plus, I wasn't known for being the most eloquent anyway.

"Hey, no sweat. We were hoping for a pitcher of Whistler Ale and three glasses." He smiled at me as if he were half relieved, almost as if he were in on a secret I wasn't privy to. I did my best to try to place him from either one of my dreams or possibly around Whistler but fell flat. I was also mostly certain that I recognized a bit of excitement in his voice, but that didn't make any sense either. Beer wasn't that exciting, and I surely wasn't either. It must have to do with whatever they were speaking about before I arrived at their table, just an interrupted conversation I wandered into.

"Sounds good. I'll bring those right out." I spun around and went to the bar, excited by this new communication and secretly hoping that they would be at the restaurant all night.

CHAPTER 3

I got home later than usual, but decided I should still call Karen to make sure everything was okay with her. It was quite unusual for her to leave a shift like she did. When I got the familiar beep of her voicemail, I left a message.

"Hey, Karen, hope you're doing ok. I'm worried about you. Give me a call when you get this. Time doesn't matter. Talk to you soon."

I hung up and reluctantly went into my bathroom and turned on the shower. I was tempted to skip the shower and crawl into bed. I could hear the soft hum of Matilda, my English bulldog, snoring in the living room. If I had to place a bet, I was sure she was in her second favorite place right between the piano and the fireplace, also known as the chaise; her number one spot being on the bed with a freshly-fluffed goose down comforter.

I kept my portable phone near me in case Karen called while I was in the shower. Steam was rolling out of the bathroom pretty heavily as I was in my bedroom daydreaming about the family I met earlier in the evening. I was able to scrape together that the girl was the sister of the latecomer, and the other guy was her fiancé, but besides that, I didn't get any further. I hoped they would be back in the pub before they left to wherever it was they permanently lived. I took all of my perfectly placed red velvet pillows off my bed and piled them onto the chest.

I pulled my flannel pajamas out of the drawer and carried them into the bathroom and put them on the counter. As I grabbed a fresh, red towel to hang over the shower door, the phone rang. It completely startled me, even though I was expecting a call from Karen.

"Hi, Karen." I spoke into the phone louder than usual, since I could only hear the shower running.

"Uh, hey... This isn't Karen." A guy's voice started. It was vaguely familiar to me, and I couldn't figure out why. "I, um, I apologize for calling so late. I figured I would take the chance you were still up, since you barely got off work. Plus, I really couldn't wait until morning."

As the voice continued rattling off excuses, it dawned on me that it was the same wonderful melody that haunted me all night at the pub. The excitement was building into a full-blown explosion. "I hope I didn't assume wrong."

The tingling sensation in all of my extremities hit me again. How could a phone call do this to me too? I turned off the shower and walked back into my bedroom, completely stunned.

"No, not at all. I was about to hop in the shower." Wait a second, why was I telling a complete stranger this? My heart started to beat quickly again, but now I wasn't totally tongue-tied because I had the distance of the phone between us. I congratulated myself on this little feat, because I figured out that I might be able to actually handle myself. As long as I didn't have to look into his eyes I'd be fine.

"How did you get my number? I know I didn't give it to you."

"I had to bribe one of the bus boys, and it wasn't easy."

"Easy enough, I see, if you are calling me." I gave my best shot at sounding stern.

"Well, you can't exactly blame him. The price offered was pretty tempting."

I couldn't believe he went to this much trouble to reach me. On one hand I was concerned, on the other, completely flattered.

"Why didn't you ask me for my number when I was serving you?" I asked, trying to sound incensed but failing miserably.

"You weren't exactly what I would call coherent during our time together earlier, if you remember. I really didn't want to see what would happen if I did," he laughed, his voice as soothing as I could ever hope for. "I thought the distance of the phone might work in my favor."

It was like he was reading my mind. How very unnerved I must have appeared. A tiny bit of hope began swelling in the pit of my stomach, but it was quickly squashed knowing how out of my league he was. He truly was the most gorgeous guy I had ever laid my eyes on.

"You noticed?" I said jokingly. "Pretty astute of you."

I flipped the nightstand light on and bounced on my bed, feeling my goose down comforter invite me in for the night. His smile was coming through the phone - that same smile that stopped me dead in my tracks earlier.

"So, was there something I could help you with?" I was secretly hoping for something I knew wouldn't happen, not with him. I glanced at the clock, which read 11:15 pm, wondering why I hadn't heard from Karen.

"This is probably a stretch, and I know it's late, but I was wondering if maybe I could see you," his voice rang over the phone and then paused for a split second, "tonight."

My stomach flip-flopped. I couldn't understand what was going on. So many things were telling me not to. It was late at night, not much was open in the village, yet I was compelled to tell him yes. The thought of seeing him one more time almost made me lift off the ground. What if this would be the last time I saw him? I could literally feel my legs begin the Jell-O-like process again. It was dangerous, somehow, and so unlike anything that I would usually do. In fact, it was the exact opposite of anything I would do. Maybe that is why I was so intrigued.

I was about to tell him that it wouldn't be a good idea, when a light flashed into my bedroom. It was a radiant light, almost like a prism dancing on my walls. I was certain it was similar to the same lights I noticed at the pub. This time it was reflecting against my wall and looked as if it was coming from the direction of the window. It made no sense since it was completely dark outside. I was really getting tired of these sleep-deprived hallucinations. I was six-stories up, nothing should be reflecting. I shuffled to my window, looking down into the village where I saw him on his cell phone looking up at me with those almost glowing green eyes. Maybe it was a light from the cell phone to get my attention. Looking at him made my heart flop to my toes. I knew the only cure was to see him one more time.

"I'll be right down. I have to call my friend." I couldn't believe what was coming out of my mouth, and I hung up on him. This was meant to be.

I dialed Karen's number again, and this time she picked up. "Karen," I spoke quickly, "is everything ok?"

"Oh hey, Ana. I apologize that I haven't called. I just woke up. I'm so sorry to have left you guys in a lurch at the pub tonight. I couldn't continue. I needed to lay down. Something came over me. It was odd. It was like an immediate flu. I started serving that table with the couple..."

I interrupted, "The Gods of the village?"

"Yeah, that table. And it was almost like this weird spell came over me. It made me really sick. There is something wrong with those people. I couldn't put my finger on it, but the closer I got to them the worse it got. I had to leave. I'm so sorry. I'm feeling better now, and I'm sure it must have been the flu or something. I probably sound crazy."

"Don't worry about it at all, Karen," I spoke into the phone, trying to sound calm and nonchalant but secretly wanting to hang up on her. "Well, another one joined that table you are talking about, and he was even more impressive than the others."

"I can't imagine that, but I'll take your word for it. I don't want to run into them again. Like I said, something wasn't quite right. Sorry with leaving you with them. Did the evening go ok?"

"Yes, actually it went amazingly well. I... um, never mind, I should let you get some rest."

"Ana, what aren't you telling me?"

"OK, don't get mad or worried, but I'm about to go out with the guy who came to the table late. He asked me out."

There was a few seconds of silence before she began into me. I knew I wouldn't get off easily.

"Wait a second, Ana, I don't like this one bit. You don't even know these people. I don't feel good about them. What's his name? Where is he staying? This is so unlike you, Ana. What's going on? You of all people are going to go out with a guy who nobody knows and happens to be in town on vacation? Come on, they've never found those hikers from October. I know no one in the village wants to mention this, but I think we all know that having six people coming into a mishap at once is a little suspicious. They wouldn't all just walk off a cliff. It would kind of make sense it would take more than one person to harm the hikers, maybe a crazed family?"

"First of all, Karen, you shouldn't assume that the hikers are dead. You know from the papers that one of the theories is that they all faked their disappearance to avoid the financial issues back home." I found myself getting snotty with her, which was completely unlike me.

"I know it sounds over the top, Ana. I'm sorry. Like I said something didn't sit right with me, and I know it sounds crazy, but I just think you should be cautious. That's all I'm saying."

The more she spoke, the more I knew she was exactly right. This was careless and irresponsible. Nothing like I would ever do. Yet, I was going to do it tonight. I also, to my embarrassment, didn't even know his name.

"Karen, I'm glad you're feeling better, but you need to rest. I'll call you in the morning to check on you, and yes, I'm going out with him tonight. These guys aren't dangerous." I quickly hung up so she couldn't talk me out of it, grabbed my coat, and headed to my front door. I glanced at Matilda who was still snoring soundly by the fire. I was sure she wouldn't miss me for another hour or so. She had made one of her famous nests out of the chenille throw that fell off of the chair and obviously had no plans to move.

This was going to be a great night. I could feel it.

CHAPTER 4

I impatiently waited for the elevator and almost jumped out of my skin when the doors opened only to have *him* staring back at me with his sparkling green eyes.

"Ok, how did you know what floor I was on and which elevator to take? That is a bit creepy." I lied. Nothing he did could possibly be creepy.

"I figured by the time you pushed the button, I could be on the same elevator. I get bored easily." His eyes caught mine and did not let go. My cheeks began burning up again. I hoped he didn't notice. I couldn't bear to let go of his gaze.

"So, where are we off to in the village that sleeps by midnight? Unless we are clubbing it?" I giggled, stepping into the elevator, realizing that his presence was, once again, overwhelming. I wished I had the phone between us. There was no way he was going to find this endearing.

"I'm not actually into the whole clubbing thing. Hope you aren't disappointed," His words were music to my ears, "I thought we could go to the Mallard Lounge at the Fairmont. Do you know it?"

"Yeah, that's a great spot." I wanted to tell him I knew it well and almost bought a residence at the Fairmont, but that would probably open up too much conversation since I'm a waitress and shouldn't be able to afford such a place. My residence at the Westin was hard enough to explain.

As the elevator opened to the lobby level, he wrapped his arms around my shoulders and guided me out. Right before me stood his sister and her fiancé. I tried to stop myself from freezing in place. A family affair, that's better for safety. Things were looking up. The red flags started to diminish, unless Karen was right about the hikers needing to be taken down by a group. Looking at these people, I knew that was an absurd thought and followed his lead.

"Man, Athen! I can't believe you were able to find her. That really sucks." I looked up at the man I could now call Athen, and he saw the confusion in my eyes.

"Finding you doesn't suck, losing the bet he placed with me sucks. He owes me $100 cuz he said I wouldn't be able to jump on the right elevator to find you. Obviously, he was wrong," He hugged and kissed me on top of my head as if I had been declared his long ago, "You are my good luck charm already."

We walked towards the lobby exit, and I gazed at the many couples coming in to retreat up to their rooms, and for the first time ever, I wasn't looking at them with envy. Even if this was a fleeting moment, at least I was experiencing it for once, and I was going to eat it up as much as I could, every morsel of it. As the doors opened, the cold air blasted my face, and I reached for my hood, secretly hoping that my movement wouldn't make him drop his hold on me. Instead he squeezed even tighter. I was in heaven.

While walking next to Athen, I saw how happy his sister and her fiancé were. Holding each other tight, only letting go to grab the occasional fistful of snow and throw it at each other. I wondered what on earth had made me so jittery earlier. They all seem like such a sweet and fun loving unit - something that I had yearned for as long as I could remember. It made me feel a little silly for how I behaved earlier. As if Athen could sense my feelings, he wrapped his other arm around me.

"You look cold." He pulled me even closer. I looked up at him, noticing how much taller he was than I. The top of my head came only to his chin. My hood fell off, and I didn't care. I was secretly hoping for another kiss on the top of my head.

"So, I gathered that she is your sister, and he is her fiancé, but I don't know their names, and I only know yours because your future brother-in-law called you by it." I took a deep breath in and kept going, "I want to set the record straight and tell you that this is unlike anything I have ever done before. That being said, you better fill me in on a few facts before I start to listen to the red flags I see waving in my head right now and decide to go lock myself in my room." I started to slow my pace as the words left me, wishing a little that I could take them back.

We were almost to the middle of the village, about fifteen minutes away from the Fairmont. He stopped immediately as did his sister, turning to look at me.

He grabbed my face gently with both of his hands. I looked up at him, melting a little and wishing I hadn't attempted to lay down the law because I knew in my heart everything would be fine. For some reason, it already was. His eyes were piercing, full of concern, looking at me with an otherworldly sense, reminding me briefly of my dreams. He almost looked sheepish for a split second.

"Ana, you are so right. Someday my behavior will make complete sense. I keep jumping ahead of myself. I was so worried you wouldn't come out tonight, and I completely got caught up in everything. My sister's name is Aurelia, but we all call her Arie. Her fiancé is Cyril."

"Ok, that's a good start. So where are you guys from, and how long will you be here?"

Arie piped in next, "Well, our main residence is a tad outside of Seattle in Kingston. However, we recently purchased a residence at the Fairmont, which we are super excited about. So it's safe to say that we'll be here for a very long time. Now let's keep walking so we don't all become ice blocks." She looked at me with her calming, almond-shaped green eyes as Athen grabbed my hand. For now, that was all the explanation I needed. I belonged with this family for the evening, and I was going to enjoy it even if I had to let them go tomorrow and wake up from my wonderful dream.

We arrived at the Mallard Lounge, and I realized it was still pretty active. Apparently, because I went home to sleep every night, it didn't mean everyone else in the village did too. I followed the group to a table in the back corner that looked especially cozy. I hoped I wouldn't let anyone down with my lack of conversational skills. I always loved this place, with the wooden walls and dark lighting. The room was so inviting. As we were getting all settled, I noticed a look between Arie and Athen that sent shivers down my spine, not because I was scared, but because I almost could sense what they were thinking, and it was about me.

"Well, Ana, how long have you lived in Whistler?" Cyril began the questioning that I felt might last a very long time.

"I've lived here a couple of years. I moved here right out of high school, and I've been a server at the restaurant since. It's a pretty consistent job, and I can leave it once my shift is over. Carl, the owner, is very kind and has been very flexible."

"Have you lived in your condo long?" Arie asked.

"Guys, let's not interrogate her," Athen piped up, "I'm sure she has many questions, too, but is being polite." He looked at me and winked. All of a sudden, I didn't care if all I did tonight was answer questions. I didn't want this night to be over. I looked around the table and felt at home. Something I'd never experienced when hanging out with other people that I could remember. Even my friend Karen, who was as close to a friend as I could get, didn't give me this comfort level.

Our drinks came one after the other, and the words came spilling out. I couldn't tell if it was the two greyhounds I had, or if there was a real connection. I was leaning back watching these people. They seemed so out of my reach. They were so put together. I couldn't understand what I was doing here. I was definitely the black sheep.

They were intrigued with everything I had to say. It seemed truly genuine, unexplainable, but genuine. At times, though, there seemed to be a suggestion that they knew what my answers were going to be before I did. I also knew that was impossible, but that was the sense of it. We covered everything imaginable in conversation. I was filled in on Athen's college stint, Aries' favorite hobby, which is pottery. Actually, shopping was her favorite hobby, but pottery was a close second. They also covered their favorite places in Seattle to hang out. I tried to keep up with the pace adding in what I could about my life but certainly dancing around certain other aspects, like the lack of family and friends, or my ability to afford the condo I live in.

"I hate to mention this, but I should probably start to walk Ana home. It is pretty late, and I want her to be ready for our day tomorrow." Athen placed his hand on my knee, which sent a shot through my leg. I looked up at him thinking that maybe this was all a wonderful dream to replace all of the many nightmares until Arie interrupted my thoughts.

"That sounds like a good idea. I'm pretty tired from my day on the slopes anyway. Do you really want to walk her back? She could stay in our extra bedroom." Arie sounded so excited, but I then detected a slight edge of worry in her voice. I didn't want to offend her, but the thought completely terrified me - plus I had Matilda to get back to. Thankfully, Athen must have picked up on it.

"I don't mind walking her home. It will give us time to talk about things more privately." Once his words reached me, I was enthralled and invigorated for a whole new set of conversations. He smiled and grabbed my hand to help me up from our comfortable seats. As I sprung to my feet, I noticed Arie gazing at a guy two tables away who almost seemed to be glaring at me, though I knew that was ridiculous and brushed it off.

"Not to worry, man. We'll get the check." Cyrus ribbed Athen once more bringing me back to reality.

"Thanks. See ya in the morning. I'm sure you two will be sound asleep by the time I get in."

I could only hope, I thought to myself. I saw Athen nod his head at Cyril towards the direction of the glaring man, but I shrugged it off. I said my goodbyes to my new friends as Athen and I walked out of the lounge. My heart started beating a little faster again. The thought of being alone with him filled me with happiness. I looked over at him, and he was adjusting his grey knit cap. He looked sensational with his black wool coat, worn blue jeans, and the shiniest black shoes that seemed to work on him.

As we were headed to the door, I caught the evil stare of the man lurking a few feet away from me, and it hit me. He had made an appearance in one of my dreams. It wasn't a good one either. I was avoiding his eyes, afraid of what I might see. I could feel myself begin to get clammy and hoped that I wasn't starting down the slippery slope of paranoia, especially at a time like this. I tried to bring myself back to reality, turning my attention to Athen, hoping for something to pop into my head to start a conversation. As Athen's eyes caught mine, I saw a look of concern. I was sure it had to do with the stranger. I noticed him give the creep one last glance before he took hold of my hand, letting a calming sense of security wash through my body. I wasn't going to ruin tonight. I was going to stay in the moment, which when looking into Athen's eyes was not a hard thing to do. The butterflies returned, and I was eternally grateful. I was safe in his presence.

I couldn't believe that, for whatever reason, I was the lucky one to spend time with him tonight. He looked over at me with his dazzling, green eyes and half-smirk, shaking his head while opening the door that led out to the village. It really seemed like he was reading my mind when he did that. The blast of cold air reminded me to move as I floated through the door out to the village pathway. We walked at a nice pace. I tried to stop as many times as I could justify, adjusting my shoes or whatever else I could think of to make the night go on for that much longer. I was hoping he hadn't caught on. I'm sure he did, which would be one more reason why he would never call me again, too desperate. The snow had pretty much stopped by the time we got back to my condo. I hoped it would start again for the ski season's sake. We approached the automatic doors in the lobby leaving my heart to sink as I realized that this was the end to the night.

Athen grabbed my hand as I tried to dodge out of the sensors way that kept opening and closing the doors. He pulled me towards him swiftly making me fall right into his arms. A wave of embarrassment began to hit, realizing he probably never meant for that to happen. But as I tried to release myself, his arms wrapped around me tighter. It was such a firm embrace, and he didn't let go. I looked up at him, as he moved his lips closer to my ear, which sent shivers through me.

"Make sure you get a good amount of sleep," Athen murmured. "We'll meet in the center of the village at 9:00 am." His breath gently grazed my hair as he backed away and turned quietly towards his walk home. I stood staring at him for as long as I could justify. Taking a deep breath in and mustering the strength to head in, I spun on my heels and glided through the doors daydreaming about his fingers touching mine and his lips so near my own. This would be a hard night.

CHAPTER 5

I woke up from what seemed like the best dream ever. A wave of sadness crept over me at the thought of it being over. For once, in a very long time, I slept through the entire night with no nightmares gnawing at my every thought. As I rolled over to pet Matilda, my alarm clock went off. That's weird for a Saturday, I thought to myself. Then bolted upright as all the memories from the night before came flooding in. It wasn't a dream last night. I truly had gone out with Athen and his family and was expected to meet him in the center of the village this morning. I shot out of the bed and straightened out my goose-down comforter around Matilda and slapped the alarm clock off on my way to the bathroom to brush my teeth. As I got Matilda all set for the day, I did my best to remain calm and not get too excited for my meeting with Athen and his family. I was sure I was reading far too much into our encounter, but I couldn't wait to see him again. His image was blazed across everything I looked at. I saw his presence everywhere, and that feeling helped to calm my nerves.

"The thing a good night's sleep does for a person is incredible," I announced to Matilda.

Matilda gobbled down her kibbles, and I decided I had better call Karen as I had promised, even though she wouldn't be approving of my day's plans. I reached for the phone as it started to vibrate and began to flash Athen's number. A charge ran right through me, and I picked it up as fast as I could.

"Hey, Athen. Have the plans changed?" I asked, wishing I hadn't. It was as if any minute I expected this whole situation to implode.

"No, did you want them to?"

"No, not at all," I started to stammer, "I was only checking."

"Ana, I'm kidding. I wanted to see if you wanted to meet me for breakfast before we met up with my sister and Cyril?"

"Oh, sure. That sounds great. I need a few minutes to let Matilda out and finish getting dressed." My heart started beating a little faster, and as if on cue, he chuckled.

"What's so funny, Mister?"

"Well, if you want you can swing open your front door, and I'll take her downstairs."

"Of course, I should've known. I'll be right there."

I put the leash on Matilda, and she excitedly pulled me to the front door. When I opened the door, there he stood - jaw dropping as ever. Unfortunately, it only highlighted the fact that I hadn't even run a brush through my hair yet, let alone had a shower for the day.

"Wow, you look amazing." The kindness radiated in his voice, catching me off guard.

"Thanks, but I'm still in my flannels. It can't be that impressive." I smiled at him. His return smile melted me where I stood. Thankfully, Matilda had other things on her mind to distract me.

"I appreciate you taking her out, but you don't have to do this."

"I don't mind at all. We'll be back soon so you better be ready."

I closed the door as he waited for the elevator but not without noticing how well dressed he was in his dark jeans and green sweater. I took one more peek through the peephole, ran to the bathroom, and turned on the shower. I picked out a similar outfit to his and attempted to contain my building excitement. I was about ready to step in the shower when my phone rang. I instantly remembered that I had forgotten to call Karen after all. I decided to let it go to voicemail, hopping in to the shower.

We were at one of my favorite places in the village eating crepes when I saw Karen walk in with her boyfriend. What are the odds? I thought to myself. That is one thing about the village – everything and everyone is connected. The places are all so small; it's hard to be missed. Athen sensed something and immediately followed my eyes to the door.

"What's up?" he asked, rather confused sounding, "You look like you saw a ghost."

"No, it's my friend, who I forgot to call back this morning."

"Okay. Well, I doubt she'll be that upset. Why are you acting like it's that big of a deal?"

"Well, she wasn't thrilled that I was going out with you last night. It's so unlike me. Plus, we made a

33

pact not to date tourists because it never leads to anything good."

"Oh, is that all? Well, maybe we should flag her over and let her know the good news." He pretended to wave his hand in the air.

"What is that?"

"That I'm a resident, not a tourist." He smiled and laughed so loudly that Karen and her boyfriend looked over, and I gave her a sheepish smile as our eyes locked.

"Nice one, Athen," I said under my breath.

Karen started walking over, and I kicked Athen under the table to thank him. He looked at me with a smile wider than the Cheshire cat.

"Hey, Ana," Karen chided, "You didn't call me back. I was worried." She looked Athen up and down like he was an alien. "But I can see that you're alright."

"I think she's more than alright," Athen said beaming, and grabbed my hand across the table. I blushed and looked up at Karen, whose eyes were as big as saucers.

"It is not like that, Karen. I'm so sorry for not calling. I meant to. Then Athen picked me up early this morning, and I hurried out the door. I'm so sorry. I appreciate you worrying though. It looks like you're feeling better at least."

Karen's boyfriend came up behind her as I was rambling my apology when it hit me that I hadn't introduced anybody.

"Sorry for not introducing everyone. Athen, this is my friend Karen and her boyfriend Justin."

"Hey, man, nice to meet you." Athen stuck out his hand to Justin's, for the typical guy handshake. Karen looked over and mouthed something to me.

Like usual, I couldn't understand what she tried to say so I mouthed back, "What?"

At the same time, Athen turned back to me. I then caught what she was saying in the same moment as her boyfriend.

"Well, I guess you're hot, Athen," Justin laughed as he squeezed Karen. I couldn't help but smile, laughing as Karen's cheeks turned more scarlet than mine ever did.

The hostess came over to seat Karen and Justin at their table, and we said our goodbyes. I looked over at Athen. He was staring at me intently. I couldn't figure out why, so I looked down to make sure I didn't have crepe in my hair or syrup stuck to my sweater. It all looked clear.

"Do you know what I find most amazing about you, Ana?"

"No, can't say that I can figure that out."

"You are so stunning and have no idea. When people look at you to admire your beauty, you take it as if something must be wrong with you. You start to fidget, get uncomfortable, and stare back with the roundest eyes. I swear I can almost catch a glimpse of fear in them for what you might find out."

"Well, if you knew me better, you'd know that nine times out of ten I've spilled something down the front of me or stuck my hair in frosting or a latte, so there is usually something wrong with me so- HA."

"You are a bit feisty, aren't you?"

"Maybe a tad," I mumbled.

I looked at him fear starting to build, thinking that I could lose this feeling. I had never experienced this comfort level with someone before in all my life that I could remember. Even with my closest friend, Karen, I kept a distance. I had tried to knock it down, but I never could completely get that feeling to go away. Yet here within one day of meeting Athen and his family, I could be me. I hoped that feeling would last.

"Do you like your ham crepe? It's probably in my top two favorites," I said, trying to distract him from looking at me so intently. I didn't know how much longer I could stand having his enticing green eyes penetrate me that way.

"Yeah, it's pretty great. This was a good idea. Hopefully, it'll give us the stamina for today."

"Speaking of that, what do you have planned? You haven't told me one detail."

"It's a total surprise. I don't want to give you any chance to back out on me so no details."

"God, that is unfair!"

I noticed Athen briefly look behind me, and in that instant, his posture changed. I turned around and didn't see anything except a guy waiting for his meal to arrive.

"What are you doing? What's up?" I asked him.

He looked at me. His eyes showing a bit of disgust lodged behind them. He didn't express it. He shook his head and gathered more crepe on his fork.

I looked back at the guy again and thought he looked vaguely familiar. Then it occurred to me that he was the guy I saw in the lounge last night. He was, also, the same guy who I'd seen in a few of my nightmares. He had a real creepy vibe about him in the daylight too. That's a bit weird I thought to myself, dismissing the thought as quickly as it came. Must be a local who got caught up in my dream sequences. I couldn't let my imagination run anymore wild than it already had. Sure my subconscious had only seen him in the village, leaving my brain to enter him into one of my nightmares. There, now I'm sounding like a normal person again.

***

Arie and Cyril were waiting for us at the coffee shop in the middle of the village. It was bustling pretty mightily, but I managed to squeeze in, hoping I could slip in my favorite caramel flan latte before heading out for the day's unknown adventures.

Before I even got over to the table, Arie bounded towards me and gave me a great big hug. Usually, I would have been as stiff as a board and very uncomfortable, but for some reason, I hugged her right back, as if I had done it a million times before and then dashed into the coffee line that was getting incredibly long.

I felt Athen coming up behind me in line and wondered if I really could feel him, so I turned around and sure enough he was there.

"So are you going to tell me where we are headed?"

"Nope."

"Alrighty then. Sounds like a plan."

I got up to the counter to order my drink and noticed the girl paying more attention to Athen than myself. I'm sure I'd have to get used to that if, by any chance, this might actually last longer than forty-eight hours. I ordered my favorite latte, and Athen ordered the same. We wandered to the end of the counter to wait for our drinks. It was standing room only, and I was thankful that Arie and Cyril were already at a table.

My drink was called first so I grabbed it and started my way through the crowd in the tiny coffee shop. The last thing I needed was to spill my latte over someone or myself for that matter. As I got to the table, I remembered that I forgot a straw. As if on cue, Athen showed up with a straw in his hand giving me his usual half-lipped smirk that I loved so much.

"How did you know I used one in a hot drink?"

"Just a hunch."

"Huh, well, thank you. The thought of making it through the lines again was a little daunting."

"Well, not to rush you guys, but I think we better head on to our next destination," Arie piped up.

I longed for the table so that I wouldn't spill my drink on myself, but I decided I'd have to buck up and figure out how to drink a beverage like most normal people. On our way out of the coffee shop, I noticed the haunting images of the six hikers that were posted on the community bulletin board. It was a bleak reminder of the possible fate of the hikers, and my heart sank a bit. I quietly cursed Karen for placing the crazy thoughts in my head. Thankfully, all it took was a look at Athen to get myself out of the funk. There was no way this family was involved in anything like that.

"Are any of you guys going to let me in on the secret?" I asked, kind of not wanting the suspense to end. Nobody had ever put this much thought into anything that involved me, especially for me.

"Absolutely not. You're ours today. Plus, we can't give you any reason to ditch on us," Cyril said laughing and grabbing Arie's hand. At the same moment, I could feel Athen's hand wrap around mine and pull me through the crowd. Thank God for my lid.

We walked over to the center square where the activity groups often met. I was completely puzzled.

Athen's hand squeezed mine, leading me to an area that read Soo Valley.

"Can you figure it out? Do you know what it is yet?" Arie asked excitedly.

"I have honestly no idea. I thought I knew everything that was offered, but I have no idea what this could be."

"Good," Athen whispered in my ear, and chills ran up my spine.

If only his voice wasn't so amazingly haunting, I could concentrate better.

The guide came out to meet us and, as guides usually are, seemed very upbeat and excited to get us ready for the day's adventures, whatever they may be.

"Alright, who is Athen?" The guide asked.

Athen stepped forward and shook the guy's hand. "I am and this is my sister Arie and almost brother-in-law Cyril and the star of the show, Ana."

"Great. Good to meet you all. I'm Dave, and I'll be taking you to Soo Valley," he said, looking directly at me not lifting his gaze, "Are you ready to head to the van and start the day's event?"

"Uh, yeah. Whatever it is," I peeped up. Athen wrapped his arm around me, and we all shuffled to the parking lot where the van was kept.

"So, the guide must have thought you had syrup in your hair?" Athen whispered.

"What are you talking about, Athen?" I asked perplexed.

"Let me guess, you didn't notice how he was only talking to you?" Athen said laughing.

"I noticed, but I figured it was because I work in the village, or you told them ahead of time it was a surprise for me, the star of the show," I said sarcastically.

"Nada. You are so oblivious, Ana," he said, squeezing me.

"Oblivious to what?"

"How enchanting you are."

"Whatever. I'm sure there is a logical explanation for his stare."

As if on cue I slipped on the one piece of ice that hadn't melted from the heated walkway on the way to the lot. I grabbed Athen on the way down, and thankfully, that made it far less painful than it could have been. Of course, I still landed with a thud.

"Oh, my god. Are you ok?" Arie asked, not sure whether to laugh or be frightened.

"Oh yes. I'm totally fine. I thought I wasn't getting enough attention."

Athen grabbed me back up, and we piled into the van. The van had a rather musty smell, like most of the shuttles around the village from all of the melting snow that fell off of people day after day and all of the wet clothing that saturated the seats from the rides back from whatever fun place that they had ventured to that day.

As the van started up, I caught a glimpse of a conversation between Cyril and Arie. Embarrassment began to make an appearance as I was eavesdropping, but I was intrigued. I couldn't help myself from wanting to hear more. Athen must have sensed it because he immediately touched my chin, which sent a spark through me. It sounded a little serious, but I couldn't decipher the topic. The thought of the missing hikers entered my psyche in a flash, only to vanish as soon as he touched me.

"So, have you figured out where we are headed yet?"

"Soo Valley."

"And what is that?"

"I have no idea. You asked where, not what," I said, trying to give it back to him, instantly dismissing the uneasy feelings that Karen had so thoughtfully placed.

David, our guide, began the usual chitchat with all of us, asking us the typical questions like where were we from and if we liked the village. Thankfully, Athen and Cyril did most of the talking, and before I knew it, we were pulling down a long and winding road. It looked like a private road and was very narrow for the large van we were riding in, especially as we went over all of the bumps. The limbs brushed the side and top of the van creating a screeching sound, as we drove at a snail's pace. As I looked deeper into the woods, I could see a stately log cabin, which looked like it was in the direction we were heading. The snow was piled up pretty high on the sides of the road as if they had plowed recently.

"I still can't figure it out. The suspense is killing me! You've got to tell me."

"You'll find out soon enough," Arie piped up.

"Alright, alright," I complained.

The van circled around to the front of the log cabin and came to a stop. I peered out the window and saw an impressive stone porch with matching pillars leading up to where we were evidently supposed to meet.

"OK, guys, we are here," David said, as he climbed out of the van. He came over to our side of the van and helped us all out. I could hear dogs barking excitedly in the distance and wondered if they had anything to do with our adventure. I was hoping their idea of good time wasn't to dress in an assailant costume and be attacked by dogs.

As I was busy thinking these ridiculous thoughts, we climbed the stairs to enter the lobby of the log cabin. The warmth escaping hit my cheeks instantly. I looked around and saw a picture perfect seating area nestled near the fire that was throwing off all of the heat I was enjoying. The van was a bit colder than I expected. The couches that caught my attention were a homey, deep-brown leather, with red fleece blankets folded on the backs. The bright green shag rug that the coffee table sat on looked like a perfect bed for Matilda.

An older woman with pure white hair stepped out from behind the front counter, introducing herself as Marcy and asked if any of us would like coffee, tea, or hot chocolate before we were to set off for the afternoon. Since I still had no clue what was going on, I opted for the coffee in case we were going out snowshoeing for the day leaving behind all sense of warmth and security. I hoped they weren't counting on me being super athletic because I would most certainly disappoint. Although, it did look like athleticism ran in Athen's family.

As I reached for my coffee, I heard the back door open, and David, our guide, asked us to follow him. Everyone followed suit, and Athen grabbed my hand and had us linger in the lobby for a moment. I was hoping the older lady had gone back into her office, and in that moment, I heard the door click to the back office.

"Alright, Ana, I hope you like this," Athen said a little apprehensively, "We are going dog sledding and then stopping for a lunch before heading back to the lodge for drinks."

I looked up at Athen, realizing how hopeful he looked. He genuinely seemed to care about me and about pleasing me. I had no idea why. I couldn't explain for the life of me why he had chosen me, but I was the luckiest girl ever. I said a little prayer that I wouldn't disappoint him.

"Athen, you couldn't have done anything more perfect."

He looked down at me. His hands slowly rose up my back and cradled me as his lips touched down to mine. My senses were ignited in a way that I had never thought possible. The only way that I could help myself in this moment was to kiss him back. The warmth of his breath came over me as I held him tight, and the sensations ripped through my body. His lips stung mine like thistles. The electricity running between us was almost painful, but I couldn't stop being this close to him. It was as if a lifetime had passed between us in the last 24 hours of meeting, and I didn't want another second to go by without experiencing him throughout me.

"Yeah, love birds, let's get a move on it." I heard a loud thud and saw Arie smack Cyril with her bag. Then I heard her say," Let them be, Cy. It has been a long time."

The words made no sense to me. Athen must have caught it, too, because he instantly let go, and we walked down the stairs to the group with me tailing behind wondering what she meant.

I was quickly distracted by the sound of the excited dogs yipping away, and when I looked over to where they were harnessed, their wild beauty literally took my breath away. They were so happy and ready for their freedom on the trails. I knew immediately that I had better get my act together. David, our guide turned musher, was going over all of the features of the harnesses as we were getting situated in our sled.

"Hey, guys. This is Taylor. He is our other musher, not as good as me, but we take what we can get," David said laughing.

"Hi, hope you all enjoy our little adventure today, and David, no pay for you," Taylor said without missing a beat.

"Guess the owner doesn't have a sense of humor today," David said smiling, and Taylor smacked him on the back.

I couldn't wait for the dogs to take off. I was trying to get the hood of my very fluffy, goose-down jacket situated when I felt Athen pull up my collar without even looking, which made it much easier. I was so thankful to have worn such a warm outfit.

"All set," Cyril yelled, "I got my baby tied down before you did, huh, Athen?"

"Not a chance, Cy. I've been done for minutes. I was helping Ana get herself organized."

The quick lurch of the sled alerted me that the adventure was about to begin, as we bolted up the first snow and ice covered path.

"Oh my God, Athen, this is so awesome."

"Are you too cold?" He yelled back.

"No way! This is spectacular, wonderful... almost as wonderful as the kiss back in the lodge. Thank you so much for both experiences!" I said teasing him.

"Thank you, Ana."

I grabbed onto him tightly, nestling my head on his back as our sled ran over the trails. The snow dust picked up in the wind creating a beautiful swirl of light. I saw all the trees pass by us so quickly. The ground drizzled with downed logs in between creating a beautiful scene for me to lock in my memory forever. Everything was glistening and almost alive on the forest floor. I knew I was lucky to be able to take it all in, especially with him. There was nothing more peaceful than being in the mountains with the white, angelic hues dusting everything, casting a beautiful glow all around. I had a quick flash to the night before when Athen first called me on the phone and the beautiful glow that had entered my bedroom. I snapped out of my daydreaming and took a deep breath in, noticing the icicles that dangled from the bare tree limbs of the now naked maples that were peeking out from around the evergreens. They added something very special to the landscape and made the view stunning. With each bump, I grabbed onto Athen a little tighter. I was slowly becoming secure in this new world that had come my way very quickly, and I knew Karen was wrong about these people.

I could hear the barking begin as we rounded down the first corner deep into the forest. This was part of Whistler that I never would have seen if I hadn't met Athen. I wouldn't want to share this moment with anyone else. The forest was much more dense. The towering trees let very little light in, as we flew over the snow-packed trail, making the icicles now harder to spot.

Every once in a while, as we went over a large rut, I grabbed on more tightly to Athen's waist. I swear that I could feel him smile. I hoped I was right.

We rounded another bend, and the dogs began to pick up their pace. I wondered what could be up at the next hill. In between dog barks and laughing from Cyril, I thought I could hear something else, but I couldn't put my finger on it.

At that moment Athen's voice swirled back to me.

"There is a river over the hill. That is probably the noise you are hearing."

A pulse of exhilaration ran through me. How is it that he knows what I'm thinking or is this all in my head? Maybe, I spoke and didn't realize it. If he can hear my thoughts then he hears me now. Why do I do this? I'm sure I'm reading too much into this. Athen's body shook a little, and I couldn't tell if he was readjusting or trying to hide a laugh. I decided to bring up my suspicion.

"Do you know that you often answer my questions before I ask them?"

"How would I know what you are going to ask before you ask it? Don't you think we could just be in tune?"

I liked that thought and dropped it as we went gliding through the rest of the trail, resting my head on his back. Plus I didn't want to feel as silly for thinking such bizarre thoughts. I began to see what looked like a wooden structure up ahead and wondered if that was our resting spot for lunch.

"Is that where we are meeting for lunch? How long have we been on the sleds? It only seemed like a few minutes!" I yelled, hoping Athen would hear me.

I heard David's voice begin to answer my questions. Figuring out how loud I must have been. I hoped I didn't cause any hearing loss for Athen.

"We've been riding for about an hour, and that is our resting spot up ahead. We have sandwiches, salads, chips, hot chocolate, and coffee. But the best part is the triple fudge brownies that Marcy makes fresh daily. She is the gal you met at the front counter."

"Ooooh. I can't wait!" I heard Arie shout from behind us. She always added such excitement and happiness to wherever she landed.

We circled around the back of what looked like a pergola as he brought our dogs to a stop. We pulled in right next to Taylor's sled. The mushers unharnessed the dogs as we got out of the sled. We began walking up the steps to the picnic benches as our mushers went back to the sleds to grab the food, our boots crunching in the snow.

Arie came running over to me breathless and almost more excited than I think I was.

"What do you think, Ana? Athen thought this all up himself."

I blushed at the thought of someone going to so much trouble for me, and of all people, it was hard to imagine this particular set of beings giving me the time of day, let alone this much effort.

"Are you sure he thought this up all by himself?" Athen's arm wrapped itself around my waist as he jokingly acted as if he was going to take me down to the deck.

"Alright, alright. I believe you. I have to say that I have never had anyone go to this much trouble for me or put even half as much thought into something. It means a lot to me. Truly. I'll never forget this."

Arie bounded up to me and gave me a great big hug. "We are so happy to have you as part of our unit, Ana. You belong with us."

I thought this moment was getting kind of heavy, especially for as little time as I had known them, but deep inside I felt the stirrings too. I worried that I was over-exaggerating. Maybe, Arie was simply referring to all of our friendships and not specifically Athen's affections. Although, I secretly hoped not. I looked over at him as he was leaning up against the wooden post. He was truly gorgeous - without trying. His eyes had the familiar glow to them again. In fact, it was as if his entire being was throwing a cast off. I quickly attributed it to the cold air. It was hard to imagine that someone could be so breathtaking, especially since I should be used to looking at him by now. He started grinning pretty wide. His dark eyebrows went up as he looked over at me. Once again I was certain that he knew what I was thinking. I scolded myself for thinking such ridiculous thoughts.

Thankfully, the mushers interrupted my internal swooning by laying out all of the lunch preparations. They switched on the propane heater, which made me happy and excited to thaw out quickly. I walked over to the picnic table that held all of the food and scanned the many bowls and platters that were laid out. It was an incredible spread, especially for only us four.

"Wow, this is so gourmet," Arie squealed. I knew she was enjoying this as much as I was.

"I know. I could take a little bit of everything," I said, as I eyed the wonderful looking pesto salad and beefsteak tomato salad.

"That's what it's here for. If we go back to the lodge with anything left over, Marcy will take it personally so I suggest we all eat up," David told us all.

"Doesn't sound like a problem to me," Cyril said happily, as he piled his plate high.

We all found a seat at the picnic table and began eating as the mushers went over to feed the dogs. I was sitting across from Athen, and it was pretty hard to concentrate when sitting directly across from him again. I decided from now on I would always try to take a seat next to him, so I wouldn't be faced with having to look directly at him and not be able to concentrate or even be able to find my fork for that matter. He started laughing. I looked down at my plate sheepishly realizing, yet again, that it was like he was in my mind stealing my thoughts.

"Arie, do you ever get the feeling that Athen can read your mind?" I looked over to her. She gave a nervous glance towards Athen.

"No, not really. He tries but usually gets it wrong."

"Huh," I responded, "It seems like I can't have a private thought to save my life."

"You crack me up, Ana," Cyril piped in.

"Really?" I asked, ribbing him in the side as he forked in the next mouthful.

"Well, not to burst your bubble or change the subject, but you have to tell us if you have any vacation time that you can take from your job or what exactly might be going on with that because we would love for you to come home with us over the holidays to Seattle. I mean if you don't mind. Athen kind of mentioned that you weren't that fond of the holidays. I totally understand why and don't want to take anything away from you on that, but we would love to change your mind about them."

I looked over at Athen wondering if he had told her everything from last night. I didn't know if it was the couple of drinks I had downed or Athen's presence but talking to him was so effortless. I literally poured out my soul to him. I told him about losing my parents and having no family to bring me up or even a recollection of one. I also mentioned how I had received an inheritance but still worked to create sort of a social circle for myself. I told him how much I missed my parents or at least the idea of having parents since I didn't remember anything about them. I even told him how I felt so alone some nights when I had no one to go home to, except of course for Matilda, who more than made up for it. All I had of my existence was newspaper clippings. In hindsight, it was all probably things that should've scared him off, but instead he listened intently as if I was telling him something about his own past. It was a special night. I had hoped that level of trust and openness wouldn't go away.

"I told my sister how the holidays weren't your favorite because you didn't have family around. I hope I didn't overstep my bounds," Athen whispered truly concerned, looking up at me.

"Oh, of course not," I looked at both Arie and Athen recognizing nothing but kindness and concern radiating from them. I was so relieved.

"Well, I can certainly talk to my boss. I've never missed a day since I've been there, and I'm sure he wouldn't mind. He brought on a couple new girls for the winter so there should be plenty of coverage. It would be great to get another perspective on the holidays. I love the idea of them anyway."

Cyril went over the food table to replenish, and Athen was next when I looked down and noticed I had hardly touched my food. I looked over at Arie who was almost finished as well. I started to play catch up on my plate, and on my last bite, Arie hopped up and asked if there was anything else I wanted. I was super full, but because it all tasted so good, I decided to get a second round of my favorites and then, of course, dessert.

"Yeah, I think I'll join you in filling my plate for round two." I got up and grabbed my empty plate. I turned to go with Arie, and Athen's hand brushed my back as he was walking back to his seat, which sent an incredible sensation through me. I could do this forever. Once we got to the food table, Arie began to whisper something to me so quietly that I had to lean in to hear what she was saying.

"Ana, Athen likes you, and this is very unusual for him to be this struck. I'm getting the impression that it's the same for you. I'm not trying to interfere, but I want you to know that I think this could be the real thing if you let it. I have never seen my brother this way with anyone else, ever."

My heart started pounding as she whispered the magical words to me. The thought that I wasn't imagining the feelings I was experiencing with Athen was miraculous. I didn't understand the circumstances or the pairing in the least bit, but I prayed with every part of my being that this would turn into the real thing.

"I haven't ever gotten this close to anyone before, Arie, in two days or two years, so please don't think I'm taking it lightly. I almost feel like I'm in a dream and don't want to wake up. I've never felt this kind of ease before with people, and that includes you too. The last couple of days have been quite odd."

"I knew it," Arie sang on her way back to the table.

I grabbed the rest of my seconds and floated back to the table with such happiness zipping through my veins. I looked up at Athen as I got seated, realizing I had better get used to looking at him, but at that moment, he looked up and caught my eyes. The blush resurfaced. I gave him a faint smile and dropped my eyes back down to my plate determined to make the last of everything fit in my stomach. Being around him was going to be harder than I thought.

The mushers were getting the dogs all situated to take us back on our journey to the cabin, and my heart sank a little at thought of leaving Athen. My condo definitely needed some tender loving care, and that is what I planned to focus on once I returned this evening. At least that is what I was telling myself to get rid of the gnawing disappointment that was washing over me.

"Ok, guys. Anyone want any thirds? We did well on the salads and chicken, but it looks like we still have two brownies left."

"I got it," Athen and Cyril yelled in unison.

Arie and I walked over to the sleds to pet the beautiful huskies as the guys gobbled up the last tidbits of food. The mushers put the platters, bowls, and utensils back to where they came from and turned off the heater. I promised myself that I would treasure the ride back even more then the ride to the picnic. I glanced at Athen, noticing his hands running through his hair nervously. Then he turned towards me, staring intently at me, leaning effortlessly against the log post again. He was talking to Cyril, but it was painfully obvious that he wasn't paying much attention to anyone but me.

"One last check," Taylor announced. "Everyone got everything, gloves, hats? It is no fun to leave something out here, especially if you hope to get it back."

"Nope, we're all good. We've got everything," Arie assured him.

Athen walked over to me and grabbed my hand as we walked to enter our sled. When we got to the sled I could feel the dogs' newfound energy after their lunch and knew this was going to be an exciting ride back, and I'm sure far too fast. Athen got me fastened in before sliding into the sled himself, and before I knew it, we were off. This time, however, the mushers were going back around to enter a different trail than the one we came in on. Good, I thought. Anything to keep myself from getting sad at the thought of the day being over.

"Hey, Athen. Did you catch that?" I heard Cyril yell.

Athen held up his fist as if to acknowledge the sighting that Cyril was referring to. I had no idea what they saw, but whatever it was, it made Athen uncomfortable. His entire body tensed up.

"What did you see?" I asked Athen, "What did I miss?"

"It was only an animal we have been keeping our eye on for awhile up here. No big deal."

"Huh," I replied, thinking that was an incredibly unbelievable explanation. The gnawing feeling began to make its appearance again. I did my best to make it go away, but the feeling only went down to a low simmer. I decided I was going to press Arie and Cyril on it next time we had a chat. As we turned the last corner, I saw a glimpse of the lodge again and realized that route was much shorter than on the way to the picnic, which gave me a feeling of overall gloominess. Our dogs gave an extra charge in the home stretch as they saw the lodge. I took it as a personal insult as we slid in onto the patio. Once again, the mushers exuberantly jumped out of our sleds and turned to face us.

"So what did you think? Did you have fun with that?" Dave asked us.

"It was great!" Arie exclaimed. We all seconded Arie's exuberance as we climbed out of our sleds.

"Well, wonderful. I'm glad you enjoyed it. Our dogs are part of our family so they will be pleased to know you had fun, which translates into extra salmon for dinner for them and a few extra belly rubs for sure. There are drinks awaiting you in the front foyer. I wouldn't be surprised if there weren't more baked goods as well."

I was rearranging my jacket and hat when Athen lifted me up and carried me up over the steps. I looked behind me only to see Cyril doing the exact same thing to Arie.

"Holy crap, Athen. You scared me to death."

"Get used to it," I heard Arie proclaim, "It seems to be the only weight lifting they like to do."

"Oh, brother," I said laughing.

Athen and Cyril put us down so we could be somewhat presentable as we opened the lodge's doors leading into the foyer. Once they were opened, I saw the quaint room from earlier turned into a dreamy setting from another place. The lights had been dimmed. Candles had been placed everywhere, with the fireplace blazing, and Chopin playing softly in the background. It was a purely splendid setting.

"Geez, man. Could you get anymore over the top? There are more than just you two here you know." I could see Arie kick him gently in the shin, and he grimaced as we all walked in through the wooden doors.

"Wow, Athen. Did you do this for us? This is so touching."

"No, I did it for you," he whispered into my ear. Chills began to run through my entire body, creating energy between us both.

It was as if we were the only two in the universe. He led me to the table that was set up with wine glasses and a couple buckets of wine. The table had a luxurious silk tablecloth in an ivory that reflected the candles flickering an orange glow all over the room. The oversized log chairs, surrounding the table, were so comfortable, especially after the sleigh ride.

Everyone got situated around the table, and I thought it would be the perfect moment to ask about the animal that Athen and Cyril have been tracking. I wasn't sure whether to be serious about it or joke about it, so I tried my best at making light of it.

"Well, since tracking is kind of an off pastime, I'm kind of curious about what kind of animal you have been seeing and keeping tabs on up here? Is it the elusive Sasquatch or how about a werewolf?" As soon as the words left my lips, I felt the air get sucked out of the room. In that instant, I wished I hadn't said anything because the strain in the air definitely took away the relaxation that we experienced all afternoon. I saw Cyril look over at Athen and nod his head. I couldn't imagine that they were taking serious either of the creatures I threw out as possibilities, but something happened in the room. I just didn't know what.

"Um, there is an animal that looks like a bobcat that we have been noticing. The problem is that the coloring is off so we are trying to figure out what it is. Nothing more than that for a story.

Unfortunately, nothing as exciting as your Sasquatch or werewolf theory," Athen quibbled lightly. He gave me a squeeze, and Arie began talking nonstop to me about her favorite activities. I realized I had better drop it for now.

My heart knew that they had nothing to do with the missing hikers. Karen's silly paranoia was no longer mine. The good night's sleep did wonders too. The last thing I wanted to do was destroy this special time that Athen planned for me. I reached for my glass of wine and tasted the warmth run through my entire body as I sipped it slowly. I hoped that I could make this family mine.

***

We had gotten back to my condo around 8:00 pm that evening with Cyril and Athen, of course, dying of hunger; so Arie and I raided my pantry trying to put together something halfway decent. As I scanned my shelves and empty refrigerator doors, it dawned on me that I hadn't done my usual weekly grocery shopping and was now completely out of the staples. I was thankful my dog walker was in town this weekend so she could spend time with Matilda, but I made a mental note to give Matilda extra snuggles in the night. I definitely had to go to the pet store and grocery store the next day. Matilda only had enough food for the next morning.

Arie began defrosting the chicken as I gathered together the items to make a quick pasta dish. I still had cilantro and a lime rolling around in the fridge drawer. Hopefully that would do, I thought to myself. The television echoed in from the living room, and I heard the guys discussing something rather low. I couldn't decipher what they were saying, but my gut was telling me that it had to with the infamous bobcat that they were or were not looking for.

"So, have any special plans for tomorrow?" Arie asked me. She was squeezing the lime for me and had a hopeful look in her eyes.

"Well, I was going to play catch up and do some shopping and cleaning and stuff like that. Nothing that is too out of control. How about you?"

"Pretty much the same thing. I was going to try and squeeze in a facial though if you would be into a spa thing, my treat?"

"Sure. That sounds like fun before I hit the workweek again." I could hear Matilda snoring hard in the living room. My guess was that one of the guys let her on the couch with them.

"So, this alleged bobcat scenario... Are you by any chance going to let me on the secret? I highly doubt that Athen and Cyril are biologists," I teased Arie, and judging by the look on her face she was not expecting it at all.

"Ana, I swear it's true. They're trying to figure out if that is a bobcat they're seeing."

"You aren't very good at lying. But if you don't want to tell me either, I'll leave it alone...for now."

The microwave beeped at the perfect time for Arie to spin away from me and start on a new task. I grabbed the placemats to set the dining room table.

"So are you two in there scheming about the bobcat or what?"

"Boy, you are persistent," Athen said, as he started coming towards me as I finished setting the table.

"Oh yeah? Well, I'm pretty skeptical that you guys are so interested in an animal. I'm dying to know what got you two so riled up. Nothing personal but I don't take you two for biologists," I said grinning.

"Well, alright. You got us. But it won't make any sense right now. I promise we'll tell you when we figure out exactly what's up. Is that a deal?"

"Just as long as it doesn't have to do with the missing hikers, I think I can handle it," I told Athen, giggling. "You know, Karen will kill me for telling you... but that first night I went out with you she was rattling all sorts of reasons why I shouldn't go out, and that popped out."

"Wow, good to know. We won't mention any invites to her about camping then." Athen said grinning. I noticed concern swelling in his eyes. I couldn't place why that would be. Arie's laughter began ringing through the air, which broke my thought once more.

"That is pretty worrisome about those hikers though," Cyril piped up. "I wonder what did happen to them."

A shiver went through me. I shook my head in bewilderment. Being that I had never gotten this far before in obtaining an answer I took it. Besides, I knew I would keep digging until they told me the truth so I would eventually win.

Then the images began flooding in. I saw one of the female hikers completely disrobed, in a fetal position, staring bleakly onto what looked like a crimson puddle of liquid. Rainwater was rolling off of the cave walls that she was in, keeping a steady beat as it dripped to the floor to match her rocking back and forth. It was almost like I could smell the mustiness of the cave. I couldn't see any of the others. I sensed that there were more around her though. Not being able to see anyone else, I didn't know if it was the other hikers or her capturers in the cave.

A sigh escaped at the realization that my nightmares no longer had the need to wait until my eyes closed. I did my best to shake the despair that was rising in my chest. Being awake had been my one and only escape from these terrors. I guess that was no longer the case. I forced myself to come back to reality. I couldn't let these people in on my ever-growing stash of terrible secrets.

I looked up to catch Athen's eyes, which were lodged with worry.

"Is everything ok, Ana? You look ashen. Did I do something?"

"Oh, gosh no. I'm sorry. Just ignore me. I thought I left something on the trail earlier is all. I didn't though. Not to worry." Lying didn't come naturally, and I was pretty sure he knew that too.

Arie yelled from the kitchen for help from the guys as I sat down at the table while dinner was served. It was nice to have a table full of people in my dining room. I think Matilda appreciated it, too, as she waddled in from her resting spot in the living room to right under Cyril's feet. The guys dug into the pasta as if they hadn't eaten for days. It was a good thing I wasn't that hungry after the latest thoughts had invaded my mind as pile after pile went on their plates.

"So, Ana and I are going to do a spa thing tomorrow," Arie said.

Athen looked at me with a huge grin as a long noodle began its way down to the tablecloth, which he grabbed with his fingers in an instant. The poor noodle never had a chance. "You are going to go with Arie, huh? Well, that will be an experience."

I was baffled, and it must have shown because Arie jumped in to make sure I didn't back out on her.

"He is only kidding, Ana! I happen to enjoy the spa and can make it an entire day's process but not to worry! I know you have a lot of stuff to do tomorrow so it will be a quickie."

"Yeah, right," Cyril muttered under his breath.

"Well, whatever the case, I'll get up early and get everything done beforehand so I don't rain on Arie's parade."

"See, Athen, I told you she was a keeper," Arie said, as she pushed the bowl of pasta toward me.

"Sweet! Hopefully, all I have to do is keep spa dates penciled in to stay on everyone's good side."

"You already are!" Athen replied beaming, and laughter filled the air.

It got silent as everyone dug in, which gave me a chance to look around the dining room absorbing how wonderful things had become since I met these people. A void was slowly beginning to be filled. I might be okay after all. Matilda had given up on getting any scraps and was sound asleep under Cyril's chair. Minutes had gone by, and no one had said anything, yet it wasn't awkward at all, just peaceful.

"Well, I wanted to thank everyone for such a wonderful day today. It was pretty amazing. Totally unlike anything I have ever done before." I peeped up, noticing I was only staring at Athen, which made my cheeks begin their usual chameleon act.

"Are you kidding? It was a blast!" Arie exclaimed, and I became aware that if nothing else I could always count on her to lift the spirit of the conversation and lighten up my too serious overtones. If only she could be present in my dreams.

CHAPTER 6

Monday came so fast. I could finally relate to what everyone always talked about with the weekend flying by. I used to enjoy the thought of going into the pub and seeing everyone. But tonight, I wished I could stay at home and think of a reason to have my new friends over. I slowly got off the couch, repositioned Matilda on the cushion with her favorite fleece blanket and convinced myself to get dressed for the evening. The thought of my inheritance sitting in my brokerage account flashed into my head, and I flushed it right out. I have never once thought about touching it, except for buying the condo I was living in. I certainly wouldn't allow myself to go there off of meeting a guy. I was actually a little pissed at myself for letting a thought like that enter my head and pouted my way into my closet to choose my outfit for work. I was so thrilled to have had another wonderful night's sleep the night before and hoped my nightmares were possibly behind me.

I turned on the light in my closet, grabbing a black pair of leggings and a grey, oversized v-neck matching my bland mood since I was probably not going to see Athen tonight. I was doing my best to persuade myself that the time away from Athen was for the best so I could get my own things done and caught up, but I knew it was a lie. I wanted to be with him. As that last thought popped into my head, I had a sudden yearning to call in sick and go over to the Fairmont to say hi.

What was wrong with me? I thought to myself. I couldn't separate myself from these guys. I had only known them for a few days, yet I wanted to hang out with them constantly. I was normally so easily annoyed with people that it was hard to believe that it wasn't just Athen I was enamored with, but all of them were fun to be around. It was too fitting, too perfect. Because of that I think I was afraid to lose them, one in particular.

As I continued daydreaming about Athen, I managed to get the rest of my makeup applied and hair done. I was so thrilled to have two nights of sleep that I wasn't sure what to do with myself with this much energy. Work was probably the best answer. I shuffled in my house shoes into the kitchen to make sure that Matilda had plenty of food and water while I was at work, which she did. So I thought I'd better grab some water for myself. I filled up my glass with crushed ice and water and gulped it down fast telling myself once I got into work it would all be fine. I looked around my kitchen and was thankful I had cleaned it up for the week, even though I had thought twice about doing the dishes this morning.

I hadn't spoken with Karen since the crepe restaurant and was looking forward to chatting with her. I had a lot of explaining to do because I certainly hadn't been acting like my normal self, and out of anyone who would notice, it would be her. She was one of the first friends I had made in Whistler. She had always taken a bit of a protective role with me as if to shield me from all the male tourists and their motives. I never noticed the same things that she did when it came to guys, but I appreciated her efforts.

Matilda was softly snoring again as I went over to give her one last pat until my shift was over, and we could go on our usual midnight walk. I grabbed my coat and headed out the door to make it over to the Grizzly Pub, all the while trying to get thoughts of Athen out of my head. Knowing the images that can sometimes infiltrate my mind, I realized I had better take advantage of daydreaming about Athen and not flush his smiling face out so quickly. I felt instantly better.

By the time I reached the pub, I was taking in the twinkle lights that were already displayed throughout the village and saw that our manager must have set up ours over the weekend. It was very welcoming and was like a home away from home. I always loved how charming the village became in the fall, and the beauty lasted far into spring, for which I was grateful.

I entered through the side door and ran directly into Karen, who immediately grabbed me and pulled me into the women's lounge area where we all get ready for our shifts. This was not the reaction I was expecting from her. She seemed excited about something.

"So, you have got to tell me EVERYTHING!" Karen almost squealed.

I was so taken aback by her reaction that I started spurting out everything that came to mind and probably sounded crazy in the process.

"Well, Athen is positively, completely wonderful, possibly perfect. His sister is beyond fun and so is her fiancé. Athen has been the most thoughtful person that I have ever run into, apart from you of course." I had to give her some kudos, but truthfully Athen was winning in all categories. Plus, it was only the first weekend.

"He planned a wonderful Saturday with his family. Then on Sunday I did the spa with Arie, his sister. I have to be honest, Karen, it has been only a few days, and yet I'm wholly comfortable with them. I truthfully can't stop thinking about him. If I read a magazine, I drift off thinking about Athen, watching television makes me think about him and hearing music has me daydreaming. I feel like I have turned into the girl I always said I wouldn't."

"Oh my God, Ana! You are so into him. I have never seen you like this. I have to admit I wasn't too keen on this idea when you first told me you were going out at midnight to see him, but I guess maybe I was wrong... Have you guys?"

"God, Karen." I rolled my eyes.

"Oh, well let's hope that's not the killer with the relationship, since he sounds perfect in every other way."

"Wow, thanks for spoiling it, you nerd," I said smiling. I knew she was only kidding but was kind of hoping she didn't jinx it. Then I thought back to him and knew there was no way. He was precisely perfect in every way. "Well, I hope that this isn't a dream. I still can't quite figure out what he sees in me, but I'm trying to let that part go."

"Yes, I know self-conscious Sally, but you really do need to trust us when we tell you that you are one fine chick." Karen was cracking herself up as she punched her id into the computer and then punched in mine.

"Come on now. Let's see if we can get you back to reality," she said, pulling me into the dining room. "You've got section three tonight. It ought to keep your mind off of the mystical family."

"Very funny," I mouthed to her.

The pub was still pretty slow since it was so early in the evening. The snow conditions weren't at their best, but it was early in the season, and days like this did happen. I went over to the couple who had been seated and asked for their drink order, thankfully pretty simple – a Bailey's coffee and a hard cider. I trudged off to the bar to relay the drink order when I had a flashback to Friday when I first saw Arie and Cyril. The overwhelming feelings washed over me with a warmth that I never wanted to lose. Never did I dream so much could happen over the weekend with complete strangers.

While I waited for Tim, the bartender, to make their drinks, the pit of my stomach began to get an overly anxious feeling. I couldn't figure out why. It was like the memory of these people almost made me ache because I wanted to be near them so badly. Now this I couldn't relay to Karen because it sounded obsessive, and I certainly didn't want that to come across. In fact, the more I thought about it, the more I began to worry whether or not I was possibly becoming a little obsessive with them.

"Oh, Lord," I said aloud.

"What, Ana?" Tim asked.

"Nothing, sorry... I'm talking to myself."

I grabbed the drinks and carted them over to the table and asked if they were ready to order their meals, which they weren't. So off I went to the next table that had filled up.

The pub continued to fill up, but regrettably I had to admit that every time the door opened, I secretly hoped that Athen and everyone would trickle in, but that didn't happen, which then led to me wondering if he got tired of me. I had no idea how self-conscious I became at the thought of losing him. Being around him makes me feel like I can do anything, but the moment he is not around I worry that I'm not enough. It doesn't make sense that it is me that he would want to hang out with.

"Miss?" Reality came knocking, "I think something is wrong with our order."

I spun around and noticed they had nothing on the table. Shoot! I forgot to get their drink order. Strike one, I thought to myself. Things were becoming painfully obvious that I was not on my game tonight.

"I'm so sorry. I'll bring that right to you, and this round is on me," I said, hoping to make what amends I could. In that instant, I knew I had to pull myself out of la-la land. I had to get my act together regardless of what I wanted to daydream about.

I went up to the bar, and their drinks were on the counter. I grabbed them quickly and marched them over to the table. They were a nice couple, dressed in sweaters and jeans. Her hair was dyed a perfect, pale shade of yellow, looking a little too polished for this pub. Nonetheless, they were very nice and forgiving. I'm sure they were from the states arriving for the upcoming Thanksgiving week. I apologized again as I dropped off the drinks. They seemed happy they got two free drinks for the evening.

A new table was seated, and I quickly darted over to make sure I didn't make any more mistakes. On my approach, I got an unpleasant feeling. I couldn't put my finger on it. My skin began to crawl and having experienced all kinds of senses in the universe over the weekend, I was sure that this wasn't a good one. I noticed that the guy sitting at the table had a strange look about him. I wasn't sure exactly what struck me peculiar about him, because on the surface he seemed pretty much like anyone else sitting in the pub. He wore a blue flannel shirt with the sleeves rolled up and a grey t-shirt under. He sat relaxed in his chair, but as I approached, I saw his eyes look me up and down in a manner that definitely did not have good intent. I saw a menu laid out in the chair across from him. I hoped whomever he was with would show up soon to distract him.

"Hi, I'm Ana, and I'll be your server tonight. Is there anything I can start you with?" I asked, trying to push all of my uneasy feelings aside.

"Yeah, give me a Jack and Pepsi." He replied as his gaze lifted to meet mine, and a flood of uncertainty ran through me. His eyes were the coldest, darkest eyes I had ever encountered. There was no sense of light in them whatsoever. I tried my absolute best to hide my fear but worried he would see through it. I figured I had better spin around and get his order in.

"Certainly." I was pretty positive with all of the different types of characters that I had seen come in throughout the years that he didn't fit the mold for any of them. Maybe, he was a sociopath. All I knew was that I wanted to steer clear of him on my way out tonight. Hopefully, he would be long gone. Running into someone like that really brought to light the glorious feelings I got from Athen and his family only a few nights prior. Things really can change quickly. It reminded me to pay attention to instincts, especially with the missing hikers and all.

I went up to the bar and placed the guy's order.

"Hey, is everything ok, Ana?" Tim asked genuinely concerned.

"I think so. Actually, it's that guy at table six. He is a bit creepy. I'm sure it's fine, but there is something off with him."

"Alright. I'll let the other girls know too."

"Thanks." That, I thought to myself, was one of the many reasons I enjoy working here. It was a very protective place to work. I felt very cared for, as much as workers can anyway.

I scurried from table to table as the evening picked up, and nothing too eventful happened at the table with the man, but the feeling did not go away. Every time I approached the table, the feeling got worse than the last time. His guest finally showed up, and it was a woman, who seemed pretty harmless, but it didn't lessen my fears any. I made a mental note to check everywhere before I left for home. Maybe I would even call Athen to meet me. No, that would be overkill and would probably completely scare him off.

I went to the back to take a quick five-minute break when Karen came back.

"Hey, what's up with the guy at table six?" she asked.

"You noticed?"

"Heck yeah, I noticed. He's been following you with his stare all night."

Hearing her say that sent shivers up my spine. I thought I noticed that but talked myself out of it.

"Well, the scary part is his eyes, Karen. It is like they are dead – entirely black. There is no light reflecting from them."

"Wow. I haven't been close enough to see that, but I think we should walk home together for sure."

"Thanks, Karen. I appreciate it. I guess it's back to the grind, huh?"

I went over to the kitchen and grabbed the couple of plates that had come up while I'd been in the back and delivered them to their respective homes, all the while trying to sneak a peek at the creepy guy. To my disappointment, he was looking right back at me. At that very moment, a blast of icy cold air entered the room, which sent electricity right through me – exactly like Friday night. I began to get almost giddy with hope that it might possibly be Athen. I turned quickly to look at the front door, my body filling up with great disappointment as I saw he was nowhere to be found. Curse my imagination.

"Hey." I heard the most lyrical melody in the world enter my space and became exhilarated at the thought of Athen being somewhere around. I didn't look in the right place. I didn't imagine it. Thank God! I quickly scanned to see where his voice was coming from and saw him at the far end of the bar by the flatscreen. How he got there without me seeing, I had no idea, but nothing with these people surprised me. He waved with his typical ease, which made me want to run over and jump in his arms, but I knew I had to compose myself. It was far too early in the relationship to do that. Plus, I was at work.

I knew I couldn't hide my grin, so I waved back at him and found myself jumping up a little bit, which caught the attention of Karen, of course. She rushed over and whispered to me.

"Awesome. Did you call Athen? This is a much better idea. I was kind of worried about the two of us walking alone. I know I could kick butt and all, but Athen is pretty buff."

"Yes he is, and no, I didn't. This was a surprise - a really good one. I haven't filled him in on the creepy dude yet, but I will. Hopefully, he'll stay till closing."

I looked up at Athen, following his gaze to the man sitting at the table. Something bigger was going on. It looked like he already figured it out. I knew instantly that there was no way that he happened to come into the bar tonight. It also dawned on me that he had to be able to read my mind. This was no coincidence. Athen was searing the man with his eyes. How would he know to be wary or suspicious of that guy? One thing that was certain was that the longer I was around Athen, the more unanswered questions became present. If I were to voice any of them aloud, I would sound like I needed to be committed. Athen turned his attention away from the man and looked back at me. His green eyes changed instantly back to kindness, which made my world melt. I saw his lips move and was so enamored with the shape of his lips as he spoke, I wasn't paying attention to what he was saying so I looked harder and mouthed back to him, "What?"

"You're not crazy," he mouthed back, smiling at me, but then returning his gaze back to the man at the table.

I knew it. I knew something was going on. Some of the pieces to the puzzle were finally starting to take shape. My world was spinning. I needed to sit, but I had to keep going, not call any attention to myself. Whatever was taking place was larger than I was, and I reasoned that all I could do was be open to the possibilities that may shape the rest of my life by chance. I was so thankful that Athen was beginning to let me in on this secret that seemed to involve me so deeply. Then it hit me like a ton of bricks. He knew what I was thinking for sure, no question about it. I'm not crazy.

I looked at the clock behind the counter, and it was already 10:30pm. I hoped the last 30 minutes would speed by so that I could go hang out with Athen and find out what was going on. This night with all of its mystery was taking its toll. At least, now I knew one thing for sure. I had, without a doubt, fallen for Athen. I had to stop holding back because I didn't get the feeling he was.

As I cleared the last few cups from the remaining table, Athen was looking at me, and I began to blush. The thought of him watching me clean tables made me feel a little silly and sheepish. Karen was already in the back getting ready to come with us so we could all leave together. The guy from earlier still had her a little on edge too, but somehow Athen in our presence made it a lot better. I looked back at Athen, smiling and mouthing for him to knock it off. I almost ran to the back to take off my apron and grab my coat, but of course, he was still admiring me with his eyes.

"I still can't get over that Athen appeared tonight. That was pretty lucky, huh, Ana? I think he really likes you. I didn't think it was a booty call thing, and I'm sorry for suggesting that earlier. It's all happening kind of fast, is all."

"I know, Karen. Believe me, it's not in my nature either. I feel like I'd be cheating myself if I fought it though, and I can't do that. All right, enough of that stuff. Let's go." I grabbed my coat off the hook and immediately tripped over the box of onions that the chef had put out for the morning hash.

"Nice one."

"I know, I know."

We walked out together and met up with Athen who was sitting on the bar stool looking as wonderful as ever. His hair was a little more disheveled than usual. I think it was a nervous thing he did. I noticed him holding his head quite a bit throughout the evening as he was eyeing that guy. Nonetheless, he looked great.

"Hey, beautiful," he said, grabbing me and spinning me around.

"I could get used to this," I laughed, and Karen rolled her eyes.

We began walking outside, and as the doors opened, Cyril met us.

"Geez, Cyril. You scared the crap out of me. I wasn't expecting anyone out here."

I saw Cyril and Athen exchange the same glance as in the woods when we were dog sledding. I knew beyond certainty that there was something definitely going on, which had nothing to do with an animal. I also knew now was not the time or the place to bring it up. Athen grabbed my hand, and we began walking back to my condo. Karen lived in the condos behind mine, and she called her fiancé on the way to have him meet her in our lobby. Whistler was a very safe place so when something odd like this took place, everyone took it pretty seriously.

"So, Karen, have you lived here long?" Cyril asked her.

"Almost my entire life. I lived in the town below here growing up, but I spent most of my time up here in the village in the winter. I love it here."

"Yeah, it's pretty special." Cyril nodded.

We got to my lobby without an issue. Karen's boyfriend had already made it there and was waiting for us with a worried expression on his face.

"Hey, man. Thanks for this," he said, looking at Athen.

"No problem. I'm sure it was nothing but better to be safe, ey?" They did the typical guy grab and handshake, and Karen and Justin took off back to their place.

"Thanks, Athen. I'm not sure how you knew to show up, but I appreciate it," I said looking at Cyril, "You too."

"It was coincidence. I can assure you," Cyril piped up.

"Can you?" I said slyly. I knew I would get my answer soon enough. I also knew it wouldn't be tonight.

I stood on my tippy toes, giving Athen a kiss good night.

"Thanks for walking me home, guys. Have a good night."

"Oh, actually Arie is up in your condo. She took Matilda for a walk. With the creep hanging around the pub tonight, we thought maybe we would make it a movie night or something?"

I looked at both of them, knowing that the decision had already been made, and honestly, I didn't mind the company so I nodded, and we piled into the elevator. The answers would come. I was completely sure of that.

"So, when are you guys going to start to give me a little bit to go on here?"

"I know there is no bobcat, obviously. I'm sharp like that," I said, giggling a bit, hoping to lighten the intent of my question, "but I would like some sort of clue here. The guy you saw tonight, was that the same person you saw while we were dog sledding?"

Cyril glanced over at Athen as if to tell him he would follow Athen's lead.

"Kind of. It's a long story, and it's pretty crazy, but maybe tonight we can relax and not worry about it? I promise I'll tell you what's going on. It's that we don't know yet... completely."

"Should we get the authorities involved?" I asked, testing the waters. Maybe they were into something illegal, which is why they had so much money and free time, I thought to myself.

"No need. It's nothing like that. I can assure you," Athen said, and he held my hand as we left the elevator

"Well, just as long as you don't tell me you are a part of the underworld like the elusive vampire or werewolf or something crazy like that," I laughed, as I smacked Athen on his rear; only my joke fell flat. My heart skipped a beat as my mind wandered to the sudden disappearances Whistler just encountered. I sure hoped my instincts were right about these people.

CHAPTER 7

The next morning I awoke to Matilda already alert and waiting for me. It brought me back to the reality that everyone was probably still here. Unfortunately, my streak of good luck had ended the night before with a restless sleep. I had woken up twice frightened by what my nightmares had left me with. Of course, the black creatures, mouths wide open, were attacking again, but this time it was not me who was attacked. Athen was their target. My stomach was nauseous at the thought of the few gruesome images that I could remember. I just wanted these thoughts to vanish as quickly as they came. I couldn't really remember what the sequence was about this time, but the feelings that were left behind were more than enough to make me frightened. The most terrorizing image that I couldn't shake, was seeing Athen facedown in a pasture of some sort with the evil creatures taunting him, pulling and tearing at him from every direction, while he lay lifeless.   Barely able only to allow a guttural sound to escape, I saw him look at me before his eyes closed.   I knew what I saw was impossible, had to be. I tried valiantly to shake the images but seeing the blood drip, drop by drop, from the evil creature's shark-like teeth made me search Athen's flesh for any sign of entrance wounds, which I didn't come across. I don't think he made it, but I forced myself to wake up before I found out the answer, nightmare or not. I certainly couldn't share anything like this with them either.   I had grown accustomed to not sharing my misery with others. This was no different. Hoping that since I still had guests, I would be able to shake the memories of the night before.

Cyril and Arie slept in the guest bedroom. Athen crashed on the couch. That was a hard one to take. Why such a gentleman? I tried not to read too much into it, but needless to say, I was a tad disappointed. I hopped into the shower, letting the hot droplets bring my senses back one at a time - optimism replacing fear.

The thought of Athen in the next room as I was in the shower was almost unbearable. I tried to hurry as fast as I could on the off chance they would take off before I got out. The very idea made me hurry a little more.

Once I got dried off and was as presentable as I could get compared to this family, I smelled the wonderful aroma of coffee drifting down the hall. The thought of getting my caffeine drip going got me down the hall even faster with Matilda right on my heels.

"Hey, sweetie," Athen whispered, as he swooped me up from around the corner, "I got the coffee going for you."

"I know! I could smell it in my bedroom. That's so sweet of you. Where's Arie and Cyril?" I asked, kind of hoping it might be just us two.

"Oh, they took off to run a few errands."

My heart started beating a little faster as he spoke those magical words. I was hoping I could keep a handle on things alone with him. He let go of me and handed me a mug full of coffee with a splash of non-fat milk. Exactly how I liked it. Before I knew it, he grabbed Matilda's leash, which got her completely excited for the day's adventures.

"You don't have to do that!"

"Well, come with me then." He led the way so I followed right behind him with Matilda wagging her stubby little tail and tagging along. I didn't want to let him out of my sight for the day. I wasn't ready for that yet. We waited for the elevator, and Matilda paced a little so she must have had something on her mind for sure. When the elevator arrived we stepped in, and the people who were already on the elevator made room for us and Matilda, who, of course, stole the show.

"What's her name?" The older woman asked.

Athen replied very smoothly, "Tabby."

I looked at him quickly out of the corner of my eye, baffled beyond all belief why he would have given them the wrong name. I was certain he knew her name was Matilda. It had to have been on purpose.

"What a perfect name for such a perfect little girl," the woman exclaimed.

"Yeah, she's a sweetheart." I gave my two cents hoping Athen would appreciate my feeble efforts in this most confusing of facades.

The elevator opened up sprinkling us out into the lobby, followed by the couple charging out right behind us. They looked as if they were in an awful hurry all of a sudden, when it hit me - the man in the elevator was the same man who was at the pub the night before. How could I have missed it? Something this important, I let slip. I have got to get a handle on myself around Athen. My ability to be observant around him seemed to go out the window. We kept walking toward the side entrance where we could take Matilda for a walk as Athen grabbed my hand. We didn't say anything the rest of the time in the lobby. That changed the moment we got outside, however. The words came flooding.

"Wow, Athen. I'm so sorry. I didn't even recognize that guy until we were in the lobby. Is that why you said what you did? I can't believe I missed that."

"Yeah, that was him. I guess it will be sooner rather than later to have our chat. I was hoping to hold off a little longer, but by the looks of things, we need to get everyone involved. Since he now knows what floor you're on."

"What are you talking about? Are you saying that he is after me for some reason? I don't have anything he could possibly want. And he is not the guy from my nightmares." I couldn't believe it slipped out.

"What do you mean from your nightmares? How long have those been going on? What have they been about?" His voice was full of worry, and I thought it was odd for someone to react to someone else's nightmares like this.

"Uh, well, I have been having them almost nightly for several months. Before that they were far more sporadic. Truthfully, once you guys showed up they seem to have subsided a bit - until last night. It's nothing at all. I don't know why I said anything."

"Have you recognized people from them?" he asked blankly.

"Well, yeah, actually... The guy from the lounge and then the next morning at the crepe place when he appeared again. He has appeared a few times. It hasn't been pleasant with any of his appearances."

"Have you recognized anyone else?"

I detected a hint of hopefulness, but for what in particular, I wasn't certain.

"No, not that I can remember." Hoping my ability to lie had gotten better than normal.

"Oh, ok." His voice was full of disappointment. There was a quiet pause.

"Well, I don't know how to bring this up, but the authorities found the gear from all six hikers, including their clothes. It doesn't look good, whatever it was."

"Are you telling me those people on the elevator are involved?" I was getting nauseous and lightheaded again. I had no idea what he was getting at. Why it would involve me or the hikers in the same thought didn't make sense. The image of the female hiker suddenly appeared. I squashed it instantly to avoid the slippery slope of insanity.

Matilda continued walking on to her favorite patch of grass that was now covered by snow, but I was so entranced with what Athen was talking about I wasn't even sure how I got to where Matilda was sniffing around.

"This is pretty big isn't it, Athen? Is this why you are here, because of him?" I was almost worried to hear the answer. What if Athen wasn't interested in me, but was only here to protect me for some odd reason. Not that I could think of any reason why anyone would want anything to do with me. I shuddered at the thought of having all of these feelings being introduced only to have them ripped away making me more ill by the second.

Athen held me close to his chest. His fingers pushed aside some the strands of hair that were stuck to my face from the mist in the air. He sensed my disappointment, and with that alone, a glimpse of hope began to emerge that maybe he was here for me too. I looked up at him as he began speaking in the softest voice that had ever left his lips.

"Ana, I'm here because I love you. I have been in love with you for a very long time. There is much you wouldn't understand and would only make me sound crazy. We'll work hard to get you up to speed because it is far too dangerous to keep you in the dark. You are going to have to fill us in on these nightmares too." His eyes were searching me for something.

"I honestly don't understand."

"Yeah, I know. I don't expect you to, which is why we have to start the process sooner rather than later. I had no idea you were having dreams. This isn't exactly going as we had planned. Promise me one thing. You'll try to keep a watchful eye and not go out alone at night, especially."

"You are worrying me."

"Things are beginning to unravel in this perfect little village of yours, and I want you to understand the big picture so you can protect yourself. We just can't explain everything right now. You are going to have to give in a little, learn to trust."

"How do you know what happened to the hikers, Athen? What are you getting at? I haven't seen anything in the papers. You are really scaring me."

"I don't mean to, Ana. This has been coming for a long time. I don't want anything to come between us again. I promise it will all make sense soon. You'll have to trust me a little bit, and by the way, it's in this morning's paper."

"Oh my word... Those poor people. I wonder what happened?"

"You might actually hold the key to that one, sweetie."

I looked up at him, knowing instantly that I trusted him beyond anything or anyone in this world. I even wondered if somehow he saw some of the gruesome images that had flashed through me of one of the missing female hikers. I had no idea how he could but was certain he did. I was so lost in their world. I didn't think that I could even begin to figure out what he was talking about, what world he belonged in or possibly what world I belonged in. I had to let it go until the time was right. I had to trust him.

He looked at me with such intensity. The feeling of electricity was running between our two bodies allowing me to dismiss the images that much easier and begin to trust him. Matilda finished up her business and began to get antsy so we took her cue and headed back up to my condo.

As we waited for the elevator, it seemed like an eternity was going by. I couldn't wait to get into my condo with the security of all four walls and my own personal space. I had no idea what was going on, but for the first time, I realized that I could be in danger. I wasn't sure if it was because of the new arrivals, or if they were actually here to help me. I hoped I would find my answers soon.

I heard Athen's sigh from the guest room, and it made my heart fall a little bit, and then his words met me down the hallway, "So this morning hasn't gone exactly as planned."

"Really? There was a plan?" I asked, a little more relaxed than when I was outside minutes earlier, thinking the world was out to get me.

"Well, for starters, I was going to make you breakfast. Then I thought we could chill like a normal couple. Take it slow, maybe watch a movie, or talk about plans for the weekend. I don't know. I wasn't expecting this. I can't shake that you have been having nightmares haunting you." Athen's voice had a hint of worry to it still, which began to make me feel uncomfortable yet again.

"I still don't know what this is, and I'm trusting you to fill me in, so why don't we go with your first plan and try to start the morning over?" I walked over to him. His eyes were full of worry and very distracted. I didn't have the strength to go over my nightmares on a generic level and certainly not a blow by blow. I attempted to switch gears as best I could.

I noticed that he had already changed the sheets from his sister's stay the night before. "Wow, you didn't have to do that. You never cease to amaze me," I said laughing, and before I knew it he had latched onto me and taken me down to the bed with him. My heart began fluttering as I was filled with excitement for what the morning might have in store for me after all.

Athen's firm hands were gently running up my arm as he brought his lips close to mine. I put everything out of my mind, focusing only on Athen's gentle touch and his soft lips as they met mine. Nothing mattered except to be here in Athen's arms. All I wanted was to experience him as close to me as possible. I looked deep into his normally calm, green eyes, seeing a ravaging brilliance look back at me as he was taking me in.

He began gently kissing my neck, yet all I could feel was the heaviness of the moment. Thoughts began flooding my mind. I hoped beyond anything that this was the real thing - that Athen was meant to be mine and that we would live together forever. His breath slipped over my cheek as I began kissing him as intensely as humanly possible. His eyes were filled with desire to rival mine – the worry gone. I certainly did not want to disappoint. The feelings that were building inside me seemed to lead the way in this unchartered territory. I was enjoying every minute of it. I never wanted his lips to leave mine. I was devouring every inch of him but still wasn't getting enough. I began unbuttoning his shirt as his hand gently maneuvered me away from the buttons. I tried again, which made him roll over me and place my hands over my head.

"Not now, not yet," he whispered, as he continued to gently sting me with the nettle feeling from his lips.

"Why not?" I whined. I couldn't believe I was so at his mercy.

"You'll see, soon. Be in the moment, enjoy now," he began kissing me again, and I didn't think I could handle anymore. Then the phone rang.

"See, timing is everything," he said laughing.

I rolled over and saw the caller id, which read AAC.

"AAC. I don't know who or what that is."

"Oh!" Athen exclaimed, and jumped up, "Go ahead and pick up. It's our home number. We don't really use it much."

I grabbed the phone before it started its last ring before voicemail.

"Hello?" I tried to catch my breath as I answered.

"Hey, Ana, I'm so sorry to bother you. I tried your cell and Athen's first, but didn't get any answer. Is Athen still there?" Arie's voice had a sense of urgency. I knew, once again, it must have to do with the strangers who seemed to be lurking and possibly tied to my nightmares, tied to me.

"Sure, he's right here." I handed him the phone and begrudgingly rolled off the bed to go visit Matilda. This was starting to get very wearing, especially not knowing what the heck was going on around me or possibly about me. I knew by staying in the bedroom and listening I wouldn't be able to decipher what was going on anyhow. Athen and Arie were far too cryptic in their messages when they didn't want to give anything away. Somehow, they still managed to communicate the necessities to each other. I hoped I got to that point sometime soon.

After giving Matilda the well-deserved scratching, I began tidying up the coffee table and hoped that Athen would return off the phone soon. Like clockwork, he appeared within seconds. He seemed pretty relaxed, especially compared to earlier this morning.

"So, I have a little surprise planned for you. Arie was confirming the details for me. She figured I might be a little too busy to finish up the details this morning." His laugh echoing through the air.

"Pretty perceptive of her. Did you fill her in on the mystery man this morning as well?" I asked innocently, hoping I could latch onto something more than the boogeyman.

"Yeah, I mentioned it," he replied coolly.

"And?" I began to get a little impatient.

"Well, not much. It's already been taken care of," he said, trying not to make any waves.

"Earlier you were rattling off how I would be told what was going on. Now, it's like none of that ever happened." I could feel my temper begin to rise, and I didn't care. I wanted answers.

"Fair enough." Athen sat down on the couch, and I followed his lead.

"Tell me what you think is going on," he asked flatly.

"I honestly don't know. Maybe you guys are into something bad, and I'm an innocent bystander, or maybe somebody is after me, and you work for the government, and this is all a ruse. I honestly don't know. Maybe, I've read too many spy novels. I know I had a very boring existence before I met you, not that I would trade for it back, but I'm less in control than I ever felt in my life, and I don't enjoy being in the dark."

"Alright, what I'll tell you is not going to make much sense, but this is the first piece, and the other pieces will come out in time. But for now you are, in part, correct. There is someone after you. No, we don't work for the government or anyone for that matter. We kind of belong to this subset of society.

Because of that, there are certain situations that come to us that don't usually involve most people."

"Are you criminals? Is that the subset? Is that why you don't work?" I asked, my heart pounding fast, knowing deep in my heart that these people could do no wrong.

"No, you can rest assured, it's nothing mundane like that," Athen said laughing a little, trying to lighten the mood. He began to get that overly confident, almost cocky air about him. In all honesty, that was one of the qualities that seemed too hard for me to resist, and it was starting again.

"Well, I'm at a loss, and you aren't explaining it very well," I told him, once again beginning to get a little impatient.

"I know. It is going to take showing you more so than telling you. We have gifts that aren't typical. It tends to bring a little more baggage. You do too, believe it or not." He grabbed my hand, and I pulled away from him for the first time ever. I didn't like where this was going. Either I was crazy for believing this, or he was crazy for telling me this. Either way, it wasn't a good outcome.

"The dreams, for instance... " He paused, "Listen, Ana, imagine if there was a possibility that life as you know it was only one part of the world. That there was more than the human world, maybe more of a good and evil underlying that was directing life from behind the scenes. God, I'm not making sense!"

Athen was truly upset. The angst was building in him over how bizarre he was sounding, which made me realize how hard this was for him. In my heart, I knew whatever I was going to find out was something big. The feelings that would come over me by merely being in his presence seemed very abnormal. I was sure of that but accepting that didn't mean I could pin my reaction on anything tangible though. Rather than making this more difficult on both of us, I decided to end the discussion for the moment. Much to my amazement, I was pretty sure that I could only handle little snippets at this point.

"Ok, I'll wait to be shown as you put it. Until then, please assure me that this is the real thing." I closed my eyes, inhaling and feeling his lips on mine. This time I could feel myself falling into the possibility of a world that I had never imagined. I was okay with the unknown as long as it involved Athen and his family. He loosened his embrace. I opened my eyes to see him looking back at me, eyes glistening with dampness.

"About that surprise?" I asked, trying to break the seriousness of the moment.

"Have you ever ziplined before?" Athen laughed.

"Oh God," I sighed, "I do hope I actually live to hear about everything with all the surprises you seem to have set up for me."

"Well, it isn't for a few days out, so you should have plenty of time to get your nerve up. Think of it as learning something about us with a set of training wheels." His eyes twinkled mischievously, which made me wish the phone hadn't interrupted us earlier.

CHAPTER 8

I looked over at Athen who gave me a wink. I went for it. I closed my eyes, took one step off the perch, letting my body fall as if I have done it a million times before. The sound of the metal harness racing down the wire became amplified as I picked up speed. With my eyes shut, I began to hear the sound of trickling water down below. I glided down the mountain as if I was floating. The fear overtook me. My eyes still remained tightly closed, and I tried to scream, but nothing came out. I took deep breaths as the wind rushed past me. My face turning as cold as stone. I heard Athen hollering and forced myself to quit missing everything this almost out-of-body experience had to offer. I slowly opened one eye and peered down below as my hands were squeezing the rope to an almost liquid state. I saw the most stunning sight; a rushing river heading down the snowy mountain as swiftly and smoothly as I was. Could this be? Am I really flying? I had a few more seconds of bliss before it came painfully obvious that I was indeed still human and was about to crash into the man standing on the platform waiting to catch me. The scream from within finally appeared as the man put on the brake.

"Oh my God! That was so incredible," I told the guide, as my heart was still pounding a million miles a minute. "Are they all like that?" I asked, as I began smoothing down my ponytail that had erupted into a frizzy mess.

"I'm glad you liked it because that is the only way off the mountain. You have several more lines to go. They get longer as we head down the mountain. Hey, here comes your boyfriend."

I was so happy hearing the word boyfriend ring through the air. As I was thinking about how lucky I was to find someone so perfect for me, I spun around to see Athen gliding in hanging upside down from the line, looking as graceful as ever. The snow covered limbs almost brushing him as he landed on the platform right side up. As the guide unhooked his harness, Athen grabbed me and spun me around. I didn't want to let go, but I knew the next person on our trip would be landing in a few seconds, so I held on tight, and Athen hopped down to the next level.

"Thank you, Athen. Thank you so much. I never thought I could do something like this. It was incredibly amazing."

"Of course, angel, I knew you could do it. Wait until you do it without the harness," his voice whispered in my hair, just soft enough to leave me wondering if that's what I really heard. He squeezed my waist sending chills through me. I squeezed him back as hard as I could.

"Yeah, right," I laughed, but partly wondering if he was kidding or not. I had never seen any of them fly or have any abilities for that matter. Although, I did wonder about their speed; they seemed to get everywhere quickly and without any obstacles. Still not knowing what they were, I laughed at myself for even indulging in the insanity of it all. I was sure there was a logical explanation for that. I do tend to take the long way everywhere. The fact that I would even let my mind wander like that was so embarrassing. It's not like these people can have supernatural powers – they're just people. Things like that don't exist. The more I tried to talk myself out of the things I imagined, the more my stomach began feeling like it was tied in knots. Maybe that is what he meant by subset. I could drive myself insane trying to figure things out that were impossible.

I found myself deep in thought, bouncing around all of the crazy ideas, but his laughter alerted me back to reality, as our group walked to the next zip line. This one seemed far higher than the last one and much longer. I couldn't even see the end of the line. My blood was pumping extra hard. I wasn't sure I wanted to continue. Nonetheless, I put a brave face on and climbed the stairs to the next platform.

My positive memory of the last line was quickly fading as I approached the platform. I looked down from the Douglas fir respecting every inch of how truly high we were. All I could hear was the blood pounding in my ears. Suddenly everyone's voices began to fade into a soft rumble, and a light ringing began in my ears. I turned to look at Athen, and that last swirl of my head was all it took. My knees gave out. I was headed face first towards the wood platform when the strength of Athen's arm swiftly surrounded me before I hit the ground. I heard our group give a gasp as he moved me to the bench that was built so graciously on the platform as if its sole function was to wait for people like me, which totally embarrassed me enough to become alert.

"Ana, are you ok?" Of course, hearing Athen's voice made me feel better instantly.

"Yeah, I'm a hundred percent fine. I'm a bit flustered, but I'm fine - really. I probably didn't eat enough this morning or something." I saw the guide making his way through the group of people, and my embarrassment level grew tenfold.

"Hey, miss. How are you doing? You seemed to be holding your own. What happened?"

I shook my head not knowing what did happen. I certainly didn't want to admit it could be the height factor.

"Well, we are going to have to double harness you to someone to get down the next line or two for a safety measure." I grabbed Athen's hand immediately.

"I can take her down, if you don't mind," Athen offered, as he squeezed my hand. "I've done doubles before." Hearing him say that made me wonder who with. A twinge of jealousy entered my veins.

The other guide had already started harnessing the waiting customers and began sending them one by one down to the next perch. Slowly clearing out the crowd of onlookers.

"That sounds good, man. We'll get you all hooked up."

I looked up at Athen somewhat embarrassed. He touched my cheek gently and gave me a wink.

"Don't feel bad, Ana. It's no big deal. It's kind of funny. I can't wait to add it to the list."

I managed to kick him right in the ankle, which only made him laugh harder.

"Ok, are you feeling up to this or would you like to rest a little? We don't have to keep up with the group."

"No, no, I'm good. I'm so sorry about this. I don't know what came over me." I shot straight up like I was a contestant in a spelling bee trying to prove to everyone I belonged on this adventure. Thankfully, I didn't feel woozy any longer. I'd gotten my bearings back. I walked with our guide and Athen over to the equipment and couldn't figure out what led to my demise because now I was feeling as energized as before. Maybe, it was the thought of being fastened directly to Athen for the rest of the way down the mountain that made me feel so alert. The guide fastened two extra clips and a belt around my waist, with a strap that went around Athen, and then we both stepped into our connected harness.

"Alright, the only tricky part is walking to the line now."

I followed Athen's moves, and we got there as if we were one in a fluid motion. Another sign we were meant to be together. Athen tried to stifle a laugh.

"What's so funny?" I demanded.

"Nothing really. I kind of think it's cute how you can find so many things to reassure yourself of our relationship."

"What do you mean?" I asked incredulously. I never said anything like that. At times, it still occurred to me that he was meddling in my thoughts. I knew that was impossible... Or was it? I honestly had no idea anymore. As always with his perfect timing, he took a step off the platform, and we were flying. I held onto him with all my might, hoping I wouldn't crush him. Being with him made me feel so safe. Instead of being terrified, I could actually look around and see the wonderful scenery. I didn't even have any screams welling up inside.

"My God, Athen. This is breathtaking. I like it better this way – with you."

"I knew you would." I heard the wind whipping by my ears, seeing the majestic rock formation rising from the snow capped mountain, and the baby trees trying to poke out from under the snow and still sheltered behind the larger more grandiose trees. All things I would normally overlook, but being with Athen always made me appreciate the little things.

With the added weight to the harness, we sped up swiftly as we sailed down the mountain. The snow became patchier near the river, and the firs got a little thinner in the forest. For a split second, I thought I saw something large in one of the trees- almost like a human, but I knew that wasn't possible. It turned into a black streak and darted through the trees. Great, I can never get away from my dreams.

"Is that a bear in the tree?" I yelled at the top of my lungs, hoping for a sense of normalcy to be yelled back at me. We had long since whipped by my sighting by the time my words reached Athen's ear, and before I knew it we were landing on the platform.

"Did you see that thing in the tree?" I asked Athen again. He told me to be vigilant and aware of my surroundings, and I was doing my best.

"No, I didn't see anything," he replied, "What did it look like?"

"It was so fast it looked like a streak, but that isn't possible so I would say a bear because it was so high up." Then it hit me. It truly was one of those black things I had seen in my nightmares. My body tensed up, and I began to become sick. My night creatures were now haunting me in the day.

Athen's eyes changed instantly, a gathering swell of angst building quickly through him.

"It wasn't a bear. They are hibernating."

"Sure. What do you think it is? I thought that other situation was taken care of..." I trailed off hoping he would give me something to latch on to.

He grabbed my hand as we walked to the next platform. He was detached a bit, on alert now. For what, I didn't know. It wasn't like my dreams could be a reality.

"Nothing. Just promise to keep your eyes open."

I whispered softly to him as we stepped off the platform, "I have seen them in my nightmares."

Athen wrapped his arm behind him so he could touch me as best he could to comfort me, as we sailed down the rest of the mountain. Once we got to the base, we unharnessed in silence and wandered over to the benches waiting for us all. Because of my little mishap earlier on the mountain, we were behind everyone so the place was pretty cleared out.

"How many times have they appeared in your dreams?"

"Well, first of all I would say nightmares and several. The last one, before I met you, was one of the worst. There were a lot of them. They were swirling all around me." Athen reached for my hand and squeezed it.

"And?" he asked gently.

"I didn't make it. All I was left with was loneliness and desperation. I..." That's when it hit me. It was Athen who tried to protect me from these creatures. It was Athen standing there with tears running down his face. Cyril and Arie were the other two people with him in my nightmare. How did I not see this before? That's why they seemed so familiar.

All of the color drained from my face. My hands were cold and numb. I couldn't move my arms. I wanted to reach for him, but I couldn't. I looked in his eyes, an understanding beginning to spread.

"You were there. You were there, Athen! That's why you have felt so familiar. Your family - everyone. I don't understand." My entire body was numb now. It barely registered that his arms wrapped around me. I didn't understand what was taking place. He kissed my cheek gently.

"You are almost home, sweetie. The time is almost here. I have missed you so much, my darling. You are my everything. You always have been."

As I was trying to make sense of even a morsel of what was taking place, I heard footsteps coming up behind me.

"You seem to be doing a lot better."

"Yeah, thanks. Not sure what happened. I'm so sorry about that."

"Oh heck, not a problem. We are all going down to the Dublin Gate to grab some beers. Feel free to meet us there if you want. I'm sure we'll be there for a long stretch."

"Sounds good, man. I'll call my sister and see if they want to meet us there. Thanks again for all of your help up on the mountain. Seems like my angel is a bit scared of heights." He kissed the top of my head like the night of our first meeting, and I immediately warmed.

"Kind of ironic. An angel afraid of heights." The guide winked at us and walked back to his friends.

"Yeah, it is," Athen said, as he tied up his boots and looked at me with an honest curiosity.

"Well," I said, "I guess it would be even more ironic if I actually were an angel."

"Whatever," Athen whispered in my ear, and grabbed me only to give me a peck on my cheek.

"So are we going to meet up with our newfound friends tonight?" I asked, wanting to continue the night with Athen. " I was kind of hoping for a more detailed explanation about what is going on."

"Well, the time is not exactly right. I think this would be a fun outing to lighten the mood. We are almost there, Ana. We can't rush it. In fact, I never expected things to go this fast in the first place. The fact that you have been having these dreams is beyond anything I could have imagined."

"I'm counting on an explanation and will go tonight on the condition that you'll tell me everything in the next 24 hours. That being said, I would like to go back to my house to get changed and see Matilda for a little while."

"Would you mind company?" Athen asked so innocently, as if I could possibly mind.

"Have I ever?" The excitement began building, replacing the fear with every second that passed. I loved being alone with him. I stood up and grabbed my backpack, and Athen grabbed it away from me to carry the rest of the way to my condo. God, he's so considerate in every possible facet, such a gentleman. I looked over at him. He was beaming as we headed down the hill. Sometimes I wished I knew what he was thinking when he had expressions like that.

We made our way through the side of the village, with the streets starting to empty out a little as people began heading back to their hotel rooms to change for the evening too. The Westin looked pretty inviting with all of the room windows glowing from the lights inside. We walked by the fudge shop, and I made a mental note to replenish my sweets stock in the pantry. As we were making our way closer to my condo, I was getting thrilled at the thought of showering and warming up before heading back out to meet up with everyone in the village. I didn't realize how cold I must have gotten flying down the mountain, goose-down or not. I thought about how so many things had changed in such a short time. I never wanted this to end, but I desperately wanted answers. I knew I couldn't tell him of the dream he was in. I knew he was searching for something, but I couldn't tell him. Not yet, if ever.

CHAPTER 9

We met Cyril and Arie at the Dublin Gate, and as promised, our new friends had saved a few seats for us and a few others at a table near the stage. The evening was already in full swing by the time we got there. I found myself taking extra time back at the house to hang out with Athen alone before heading out, so it was well worth missing some of the beginning festivities, translating -a few pitchers of beer. I sat next to Arie, and Athen sat next to me. We were able to turn our chairs toward the stage to get a glimpse of the local Irish band who was performing. They were entertaining and wonderfully haunting.

The band played an incredible mix of Irish music and current songs to keep the night rolling. I saw people beginning to get up and dance, and at first, Athen and I did nothing but laugh amongst ourselves as we noticed most of them were drunk out of their minds. Definitely not a feeling I wanted to have.

There was no way I wanted to miss soaking up time with Athen and his family for a second because of having too much to drink. Life was my high right now. I hoped it never ended. Before I knew it, Athen pulled me to the small dance floor that was now starting to lose some of its drunken crowd because the song had turned to a slow song.

"One of my favorites," I whispered in Athen's ear. "*I Will Follow You Into the Dark*. How fitting."

He held me as we swayed back and forth to the seraphic melody, my arms wrapped around his neck. His breath brushed the top of my head, as he held me tightly. My body was so close to his. It was hard to stay focused on dancing.

"You know, it truly is forever and all eternity, my angel," he whispered in my ear, as he began kissing my cheek ever so lightly. I pulled back a little to see his green eyes staring back at me, searching intently for something. I wasn't sure what he was looking for. I could feel Cyril and Arie behind me dancing to the song as well. I wondered how it was that I was beginning to feel the presence of Athen, Cyril, and Arie without ever seeing them. I rested my head back on Athen's chest and breathed in this moment, hoping to retain it for as long as I lived. The music began to slow, which signaled to us to exit the dance floor because there were very few slow songs that would be coming off the stage tonight. We didn't want to be trampled by way of overzealous Guinness drinkers.

"Well, glad we got that out of the way," Cyril boomed, trying to save some face around the strangers.

"Whatever, Cy," Arie said, smacking his shoulder. "So, Athen mentioned that you were thinking about giving your notice at the pub?"

"Yeah, I was thinking about it, you know, since I might be taking so much time off for the holidays." I looked at Athen for some sort of confirmation. "I don't want to put the owner in a lurch. It is better for him to find someone now right before the busy season hits, and I'm sure I could always get my job back if I left on a good note."

Athen squeezed my hand under the table, feeling his excitement building only made me feel more confident in my decision to leave work behind. All my life, I had an emptiness inside me. I was always in a constant misstep, yet with the arrival of Athen, Arie, and Cyril my life became filled with joy – instantly. Even though there have been a few oddities, I was certain of my life and Athen. By far the good seemed to outweigh any slight misgivings that might creep in now and then. If, somehow, they also held the key to ending my nightmares, I would finally be able to be at peace again.

"Wow, that would be awesome, Ana! I know I would enjoy having a partner in crime. I can't tell you how much more wonderful my life could get having Athen actually be with you versus talking to us all the time about you. It would take the heat off. He just never shuts up."

I looked up at Athen only to see him nodding in agreement, "It's true. I have gotten a little narrow-minded on my selection of topics to speak about."

"Thank, God," Cyril nodded in agreement. "The less I have to hear Athen's musings about you the better. No offense, Ana."

"None taken. I'm sure Karen at work feels the same way," I said grinning.

Our guide looked like he had been slapping them back in double digits before we got to the pub, so when he excused himself none of us were that surprised. He was having some issues making his way through the chairs. I hoped he would make it through the village. At least, it was a walking village. I was sure I would see him around in the village but for now wouldn't hold him up for small talk. He looked like he was in serious need of a flat surface. It made me nurse my hard cider that much slower. I had this habit now of making sure I was on high alert for anything. I didn't even know for what. Athen was always so vague, I figured it was better to be coherent at all times. It was hard enough to be around Athen and be even somewhat alert. However, seeing a black streak dodging through the forest trees earlier made it very evident that something was amiss, and I had to take it for what it's worth. Having the details of my nightmares now beginning to align with my reality was almost more than I could handle.

"Athen, what happened to that guy who was following me?" I'm not sure what made me ask him. I couldn't believe it came out of my mouth. Since it did, I looked him directly in his green eyes praying I would not be detoured. Arie spoke up first.

"He intended to harm you, Ana. We had to offer him something that he couldn't refuse to leave you alone."

"How do you know he wanted to hurt me?"

Cyril and Athen quickly exchanged concerned glances, which I didn't even have to see. I sensed it. I was getting way better at that talent I must say.

"We knew he wasn't fully human, Ana. He wasn't one of us either. The only reason for following someone like you is to cause you harm. He had to be stopped."

"Wow, you're as vague as Athen. But, I feel like we are getting a little closer. Does that mean I don't have to be so vigilant in staring down strange people now, because I can't tell who is who? What about the black streak I saw earlier?"

Athen got up abruptly and grabbed his jacket and helped me up from the table. I must have upset him. I knew I shouldn't have pushed it. I wanted to know, and I'm now kicking myself for possibly ruining the night and my search for answers.

"Ana, you didn't ruin anything. It's time. Let's get out of here. I'll start to fill you in as best I can. Arie, Cyril get some rest. You'll know when the moment arrives."

My heart started pounding so fast it was almost hard to distinguish individual beats. Fear began to wash through my veins. This was the first time I was hesitant to find out what was waiting for me. I could finally say, without a doubt, that Athen could hear my thoughts. In addition to being scared beyond belief, this revelation began to produce a wave of embarrassment, as I began remembering some of the things I have thought to myself since meeting him.

"How did you know I was worried I ruined the night?" My skin turned cold with anticipation waiting to hear the answer that never came.

CHAPTER 10

I held Athen's hand as we went out into the village. We began walking slowly as I let him formulate his thoughts. I wasn't sure what the night held for me. A sense of relief began to grip me since I would finally begin to get the answers I have been waiting for. The snow began to gently fall again. How fitting I thought to myself. I stopped walking and took Athen in one more time, in case what he was about to tell me changed my perception of him. I didn't want to lose what I once had.

"It's gonna be ok, sweetheart. I promise." He looked at me, a piercing sensation right behind my eyes incapacitated me. I didn't understand where it was coming from. I had never had a migraine. Too much was going on to be slowed down right now, but once he looked away the pain was gone.

"Athen, was that you giving me that?"

He wrapped his arms around me, which solidified that it was Athen who caused it.

"I'm sorry. I didn't mean to hurt you, but I was seeing if you were receptive yet. It looks like you are. The process can finally begin."

"Ok, still not telling me much. Please, don't do that again."

"You are one of us, Ana. You always have been. You were phased and taken away from us. We had to wait until the timing was right to get you back."

"What do you mean phased? Are you trying to tell me that you are from another dimension or something? I have no idea what you are talking about."

"It's as close as we come to death, but instead we start over. For some, like the nomads, it makes no difference if they're phased. No one notices or cares. They start over again and move on. For us, the families, it makes life almost unbearable for those of us who have to wait."

"Wait for what?"

"We may have to wait anywhere from a few days to a century to track our loved ones down. Then we wait for the timing to be right for the reintroduction process. Ana, I have been waiting for you for fifty-seven years to begin the reintroduction process. This isn't the first time we have fallen in love. We are destined to be together. We are beyond anything that your mind can imagine as soul mates."

"I don't understand what you are talking about or how I fit in? There is no way you have been waiting fifty-seven years for anything. You aren't that old and neither am I. I don't understand, and a reintroduction process?"

"Yes, where we introduce you to your eternal life, not the one that was created artificially for you. The life that you most recently remember is not your true life. It's not your reality, Ana. You are not human. If you had a human age it would probably be about twenty years old, but with the wisdom that only our fate can bring us, there is no comparison. We do have an id for you that says twenty-one, though." He tried to laugh, but only coarseness came through.

My blood curdled. These people were crazy, even evil quite possibly. Karen was right. I was in danger. There was no way to get help at this moment. I tried to play it cool.

"I'm not following. I grew up with my family, and there was an accident, and I was the only survivor." I began again.

"Yes, Ana. I know what you think you know but have you ever wondered why you can't remember anything from before the accident? I have been waiting for so long for this moment, Ana. My family, your family, all have been too. From the moment we began the Awakening on you decades ago, we have followed you through every incomplete phase until finally we were able to tell that you were ready for the reintroduction process this time. You were receptive to us. You noticed us, our eyes - our glow in the pub. You saw the flash of light in your condo that first night. I know you did. I know you knew it was coming from me. The moment that you could feel us in the pub was the sign that your senses had started to come back. We have been in front of you time after time, and you never noticed us. This time, at long last, you did. My sister and Cyril were at the pub testing the environment out. They called me as soon as they figured out that you were able to sense them. I had been disappointed and let down so many times before, hopeful that you would recognize us, only to start the grieving process over and over when it was a false alarm. We have always been in the wings, Ana, waiting for you and watching over you. When I heard your thoughts, I realized that you saw my prism in your condo. I knew that this time was different. This was our best shot so far to get you back. Nobody else can see or feel those things, Ana. No one else would have seen the light in your condo that night. Only you, my angel. Never mind the dreams you've been apparently having. Those only add to the readiness."

Athen's words were spreading through me like a virus. My body started to uncontrollably crumble. I was faint, as if my world was spinning. I reached for the bench, but before I could sit down, my legs gave out. Athen grabbed me before I hit the ice. He held me so tight. This time I knew why everything was so familiar- his smell, his eyes, his breath, everything that I had been longing for. It was something I had already had. The emptiness had finally fallen away. I knew it wasn't a dream any longer. Athen was my soul mate. Even the test of time couldn't tear us apart. I held onto his neck as hard as I could as he sat on the bench placing me on his lap. The tears started streaming down my face. They weren't tears of sadness- only great joy and relief.

All of the years of solitude and loneliness in life began drifting away from my mind. Athen's hand lightly caressed my back. It brought me back to the first night I met him. How secure I felt in his embrace, so sure of his comforting gestures as if I had experienced them before. He was so self-assured, now I knew why. I didn't understand what he was saying, yet I knew it was true. It had to be. I knew in time I would fully understand. For the moment, I was purely content holding him and not letting this moment disappear.

I looked out under the eaves and saw the snowflakes falling and quietly melting on the heated path, wondering if that is what my life had done. I hoped with every part of my being that I would be able to recover all of the past that I couldn't remember now. I hoped my memories would come back. I didn't ever want to think that I couldn't recover any second with Athen.

"Athen, what are you telling me?"

"What do you say we get back to Matilda? I'm sure she is missing us," Athen spoke softly in my ear.

I nodded and slid off his lap as he grabbed my hand, and we walked back to my condo. I looked around the village seeing things that I had overlooked the last while of living here. It was as if the rocks had become alive. The beautiful curvatures melded with a harshness that always existed in nature. The streetlights welcomed me to my life once again. I didn't know what the future or the past held for me, but I was truly invigorated. I knew it could only get better from here, and this was pretty perfect already.

"Athen, if I'm not human, then what am I? Will the nightmares go away?"

"I'll let Arie and Cyril know to meet us at your place. It's going to be a long night. We won't be able to cover everything tonight, but we do have eternity for that," he laughed and squeezed my hand, realizing it wasn't that funny to someone who had no idea what he was talking about.

I looked at Athen and knew instantly that he wasn't kidding. Life as I knew it was gone. I couldn't wait to find out why. There was no sadness, only expectation filled with hope.

As we got into the elevator, I pressed my floor. Athen grabbed my waist and pulled me towards him. He held me with all his might. I could feel the restrained strength in his arms. I had never felt this level of intensity come from him before. As he was holding me, he whispered in my ear that he would never lose me again. His warm and gentle lips skimming my forehead bringing me back to the first night I met him. I was yearning for him, thankful he sensed it as he slowly brought his lips down closer to mine. There was so little that I understood, but one thing I knew with all my heart was that we were meant to be together for all eternity, whatever that might mean. I was hoping the elevator would take longer than usual as Athen's hands ran up the back of my spine, his breath lingering on my lips, before his lips parted on mine at first softly, but intensifying with every floor that we went up. I wrapped my arms around his neck as he lifted me gently onto the elevator railing. I continued to feel the nettle-like stinging that intensified with every kiss.

As if on cue, when I was sure I couldn't handle anymore, the doors to the elevator opened. He brought me down to the floor so that we could exit the elevator. We walked to my door, which I noticed wasn't closed all of the way. Athen must have noticed my body stiffen because he got in front of me and turned around.

"It's only Arie and Cyril. They got here already but good job on trusting your senses."

"How did... Never mind -I guess their speed will be explained tonight too?" I asked, smiling up at him, attempting a laugh. He shook his head as he pushed my front door open, and my eyes instantly became blinded by the light that was pouring out of my living room. I closed my eyes as fast as I could, but the light was penetrating through my closed lids as if I was staring directly into a spotlight. It took his idea of a prism to a whole new level.

"Whoa, what is it, I can't see. Can you stop doing that?"

"Ana, we aren't doing anything. This is how we look to you in your initial reintroduction process. Your eyes are adjusting to seeing us in our true form. It won't last long, I promise. Athen is leading you to the couch, and you'll be ok." Hearing Arie's voice was calming, but I was still worried about what I was about to encounter.

Athen placed his hand around my waist, as he led me into my living room. Approaching the couch, the light was almost unbearable. Matilda's snoring was coming through the wall softly from my bedroom, which was a source of great comfort. It was the only sense of normalcy that I had.

"Tonight will overload your senses beyond anything you have experienced. At times it may seem intolerable, but we'll be here and everything will be ok. You will get through it." Athen squeezed my hand. I tried to return the favor but couldn't. My fingers were detached from my body.

"Can I get a glass of water?" I asked, hoping my voice was somewhat recognizable, since nothing much was coming out. "My mouth feels like cotton."

"Sure, Ana. I'll go grab one for you."

I could feel Cyril bounding off of the couch in front of me. I had the familiar sense of feeling movements rather than seeing movements, especially in this moment with the blinding light.

"Thanks. Can someone please start to explain what is going on here?"

I could hear Arie take a deep breath in and knew she would be the one beginning the story of our lives, my life, and giving me my future. Too many things had happened to me in the short time since

Athen and his family, my family, had come into my life not to believe what they were telling me.

"Ana, we have been waiting a very long time for you. We have followed you for decades eagerly waiting for the right time for you to come back to us. I'm sure what we are going to share with you will seem unbelievable, but we need to share with you the truth, our history, and that is how I will begin."

I sat back against the couch leaning into Athen, gratefully swallowing down the water as fast as I could hoping to rid myself of the terrible thirst I couldn't make go away. My mouth continued to feel as though it was full of cotton, and the water only seemed to make it worse.

"I'm sorry, honey. That is part of the process." I heard Arie telling me. It sounded a bit muffled because all I could do was concentrate on how thirsty I was. In order to not go crazy, I knew I had to relinquish myself. The thought of not quenching my thirst or being able to open my eyes was more than I could handle on a human level. I had to let go. I had to trust the process since I seemed unable to control any of my senses or natural human tendencies. I heard Arie begin to speak and knew I had better pay attention.

"OK, sweetie." Athen kissed the top of my head, but instead of the normal warmth and comfort I normally felt, there was a sharp pain, kind of like what I had experienced earlier this evening. It made me pull away, which he recognized, " I'm sorry. I guess all of your senses are beginning to adjust."

I could feel Arie move back to her chair and begin to suck all of the air out of the room as she began a speech that I'm sure she practiced many times before. Her voice was very soft, and she sounded a bit nervous.

"The most common folklore that the human race has been able to come up with surrounding our existence is all pretty entertaining. It does manage to grab bits and pieces of what we are about. It's amazing how astute humans are when they want to be. However, they only seem to dwell on the unexplained - the darker side of our existence. That being said, they certainly are missing out on the more positive side of our existence. It's not all evil. There are two sides. Some terms that we've heard about ourselves in the human language range from a subclass of death, to angels who were demoted, or floating spirits, and of course, demons. The truth of it is, though, those are all based on human forms to begin with when in actuality it's something quite different and much more spectacular."

"Please, that can't be. You are scaring me. That stuff doesn't even exist." I ventured to get out, but my words were only falling to a slight mumble.

"I'm sorry, Ana. I practiced this speech for decades, and I still can't get it out. Here goes again, in the Bible it's written, 'the sons of God saw the daughters of men that they were beautiful; and they took wives for themselves of all whom they chose. And the Lord said, "My Spirit shall not strive with man forever, for he is indeed flesh; yet his days shall be one hundred and twenty years." There were giants on the earth in those days, and also afterward, when the sons of God came in to the daughters of men they bore children to them.'"

I interrupted Arie.

"Why are you quoting me Bible verses from Genesis, Arie? I don't understand what that would have to do with anything, and in all honesty, I don't even understand what you're getting at."

"Well, Ana, that is the beginning of our existence."

"You mean mankind?   Why would that explain everything that is going on if we are supposedly something different?"   My body began to quiver, and I could do nothing to control it.   Whatever these people were talking about was a horror and not one that I was part of.

"Because that verse does not just describe the beginning of mankind.   It details our first existence too.   There is a whole world that exists within the human world that goes unnoticed.   All of the legends and myths that you have grown to know are generally true or have some form of truth to them. There is this inner working between good and evil in the world.   It isn't being controlled by humans, as much as they would like to think it is.   There is an underworld. God didn't ever intend for humans to fall to the demons that exist, but unfortunately, the demons found a way to get around that.   The dark side figured out early on what kind of race could be made between humans and angels."

"Could you fast forward a little and tell me where this is going or what I am?   Maybe give the history lesson after?"   I was surprised at my shortness, but they didn't seem bothered by it.   Thankfully, they must have expected it.

"Sure.   Plainly, we are the children of fallen angels. Our fathers fell in love with human women.   We were the result.   However, that wasn't how it was for all families.   Some of the fallen angels had ill intent when mating with the women, and an evil was created that was most unimaginable.   Since there were many couplings and children created between the mystic

113

world and human world, God felt it needed to be stopped before it became out of control. He wanted to teach the fallen angels a lesson."

Cyril began next, "Many of the children were killed in the flood, but there were some who survived. In the meantime, the fathers, our fathers, were condemned to a life most unimaginable, even though they had no impure intentions. God thought that the act of mating between angels and human women would cease after examples were made, but indeed, it was more difficult to control, if not impossible, and more children like us were born, even after the flood. Even our fathers who had pure hearts were condemned and labeled as fallen angels. It didn't matter what the intent was between the angels and the humans, God treated any angel who overstepped the immortal boundaries the same. This has created new races wherein good and evil was literally created and a line drawn. There are children who chose to take the wrong path, and those of us who have chosen to take the more righteous path, but with that, we are often forced to fight for the good of humanity. We are The Watchers of mankind, Ana. There is a network of us, and we try to intercede when possible and guide humans to make the right choices when they're tempted to fall. We are not evil."

I don't know what I was expecting to hear from Arie, Cyril, and Athen, but this was not it. I imagined common ideas, like vampires or werewolves, but nothing like this. My stomach was in knots, and there was a dull aching pain at the base of my neck. My hands were clammy. The room was spinning.

"We made a choice in the beginning to be good, do good and not follow the ways of some of our cousins, if you want to call them that. You, along with us, made the choice to be a white demon. Unfortunately, in some cases the mating that occurred between certain fallen angels and women created children who became known as..."

"Nephilim. I know what those are. You don't need to explain that to me." I was unable to move by this point. I looked around and noticed that the light started to dissipate. I could see the figures of Cyril and Arie, not in any detail, but that was something at least. I wanted to leave. I wanted them to leave. For the first time since meeting these people, I didn't want to be around them. I'm not related to demons. I cannot believe I got myself wrapped up with people who believe they're descendants of such creatures. The one time I let myself fall in love and gravitate toward a family, this is what I come up with. Anger started building inside of me. I heard Athen's voice but wasn't listening to what he was saying. All I could hear was my heart's rapid pace. Tears welled up in my eyes. There was nothing I could do to control my emotions. How could these ineffable people be descendants of something so wrong and evil, and how could they be trying to include me in that? I heard Cyril's voice and looked over at him and could see him clearly now. The light had diminished. His eyes were as green as always, but there was sadness in them, mixed with great kindness. He came over to me and knelt down, grabbing my hand.

"Ana, we are not descendants of evil. Our fathers were not banished for those reasons. Our fathers fell in love. They couldn't help who they fell in love with. Ana, we, you included- have worked our entire lives to make things right. I'm not saying there are not demons out there who are doing bad things, but we are trying to stop them. We are not part of that, Ana. We are not evil. You are not evil. You are a Watcher, like us, Ana. We are here to help the world, not destroy it."

I knew deep in my heart what Cyril was saying was true. I also knew I might not be able to accept it. I wasn't sure of my fate any longer and didn't care. I didn't know if I could ever consider myself such a being of the underworld, good or not. Maybe I should just try to end it now. I was looking into Cyril's eyes and saw nothing but love and kindness, and I was completely torn. I found the strength to speak. Only a few words ventured out.

"Athen, is this true? Are we truly descendants of fallen angels? Are we demons?"

"Ana, it's true. But our fathers were not considered fallen angels until after their relationship with a mortal. That is a key difference. One not to ever forget. Our fathers were good angels and acted with love. They were in love with the mortal women. That can't be said for some. We are white demons, fallen angels, not what you are thinking. There are a lot of us on earth, and we're all trying our hardest to defeat evil."

"I can't believe this. It doesn't make any sense. Why can't I remember this?"

"Once the reintroduction process is complete, you'll be able to remember everything. It takes time."

"How did I get to this point where I don't remember anything?"

"We have been in a battle since the beginning of time, our time. We have been in a constant struggle on this earth to protect humans from the evil that was born by the angels mating with the women. It created evil beings that were set on controlling earth, the humans that resided on it, their intentions. The only thing that can stop them is our kind. That is what we are here to do. However, sometimes they do inflict injury, and in those instances, this is what can happen. They can't kill us, but it can feel like a death for the families, like us, who are left behind waiting for the right time to begin the phasing of their loved one. Getting the Awakening started as soon as possible is crucial. As soon as one of us is taken, we start the Awakening to begin the process to get our loved one back. It's the very first step in a very long process. If the Awakening isn't done properly, it can take centuries to reunite." He paused.

"We've been waiting for you for a very long time. It has been so painful not being able to communicate with you or hold you but to still see your existence on this earth, roaming from stage to stage. My time has been filled with watching you, waiting for you. Every few years, your process would begin again. A new city, a new identity, and we were just waiting. It's not over. We still have a long process, but the fact that we have gotten this far is a great sign. We've never been able to get here before."

I could see Arie's eyes fill with tears as she stood up from where she was sitting. She came over and knelt before us, placing her hand on my knee, and Cyril went back to sit in the chair. As Arie's hand touched me, a searing pain went through my head, directly behind my eyes, and images started flashing into my head as if memories were being placed. They were so fast, there was no way I could make any sort of semblance out of it. The pain was getting more intense, and I wasn't sure that I could endure it much longer. When Athen held me as tight as he could without crushing me, I made myself hold on.

"I'm so sorry, Ana. She's almost finished."

The images continued pouring through me. I saw Athen dressed in clothes from all different eras flashing through my mind; some I didn't even recognize. I would then see Arie and Cyril, and every so often, a picture of myself flash in. More memories continued to flood through my mind and penetrate different emotional areas. I would feel great happiness but not before crashing down to great sadness, and with every emotion came great pain. I saw us all briefly at what looked like a university during the turn of the century, and then before I could focus on that memory, a new one flashed in with us all surrounding a Christmas tree, but this time it looked like it was set in the thirties. I couldn't believe all of the pictures that were resurfacing, but with each new memory, an excruciating pain whipped through my veins. Athen moved me to the couch, sitting next to me on the floor caressing my head. I couldn't do anything other than wince from the next flash of life that would appear in my mind. I heard Cyril tell Arie that it was going to be a long night. Upon those words my body exploded into needles, and I fell into darkness.

CHAPTER 11

I awoke but had no idea where I was or what day it was. I felt Matilda snuggling on my feet. I was so relieved that I had something somewhat familiar to me. This latest nightmare was a rough one. Shivers were running through me as I relived the nebulous talk of demons and fallen angels. This was one of the most realistic nightmares to date. My head was groggy. My entire body ached. I couldn't remember what I was doing right before I fell asleep, but I vaguely remembered what was happening that evening. It was like a distant and foggy dream or maybe another nightmare. I'm not sure yet how I would classify it. I saw the curtains closed tightly and secured to each other to not allow any light in, and I recognized my room immediately. Then I remembered last night was not a nightmare. It was real.

I heard Athen tell the others I had awoke, but I wasn't sure how he knew that. Several sets of feet began walking down the hallway. I wasn't sure what may have changed since I last saw them. They were truly my family. I didn't want to go any longer without seeing them, especially Athen. There was no disputing that this was where I belonged. My heart began to fall a little at the terms that popped back into my head - fallen angels, demons – nothing I wanted to recognize as being in existence. It wasn't a dream last night. It was my destiny.

My door began to slowly open. I saw Athen. It was so good to see Athen. I needed him so badly. His eyes were piercing as ever but full of great concern. He looked tired, circles were showing slightly under his eyes, and I had never seen him with the level of stress that I saw outlining his face. Arie was peering from behind him, but I couldn't see Cyril. I only felt him there.

"Hey, sunshine. How are you feeling?" Athen's calm voice made me feel better instantly.

"I feel like I'm recovering from some horrible flu or something but other than that, great," I said, trying to be funny, instead sounding completely worn out.

"We have water going for some tea. It might help you feel a little better. Really, sleep is probably the best answer."

"How long have I been sleeping?"

Athen came over to sit on my bed, as I tried to scoot over. I had no strength and became frustrated. Athen must have sensed it because he scooped me up and nestled me over a little bit so he could sit next to me. Arie and Cyril left to go back to the kitchen and retrieve the tea.

"You've been out for about twenty-six hours. I was expecting you to be out for a few more hours. You never cease to amaze me. Karen stopped by."

"Oh no, she did? What did you tell her?"

"Well, Arie opened the door and told her you had the flu. She counted on the fact that you would be so out if Karen wanted to see you that you wouldn't wake up anyway, which of course is what happened. Karen certainly is protective of you."

"She saw me?"

"Yeah, she did. She thanked us for taking such good care of you. If we hadn't let her see you, she probably would've thought we'd done something with you, like with the hikers," he said, half smirking, trying to lighten up the severity of everything I had just experienced.

I was able to muster up enough strength to laugh because I knew that he wasn't kidding. I could feel my body begin to respond again to my surroundings. I was beginning to realize what was making my body so tired. I could feel everything. I could feel emotion- mine and others. I could feel the air. I could feel love. I could feel the presence of thoughts. This was going to take some getting used to.

"Is this normal? To be this tired and worn out?"

"It is, sweetie. You have been through so much. Your body is still adjusting. There are things that you are experiencing, in this moment, that will come naturally. Right now, I'm sure it feels as if the weight of the world is on you. That feeling will go away. You'll be able to categorize the thoughts and emotions that you're feeling from others and only pull them out when you need them. Right now, however, your brain processing is on overload. I promise it will get better."

I could feel Arie getting my tea ready, so I tried to prepare myself for the possible discussion that she might have in store for me. To my surprise when she brought in the tea she was quiet. She placed the cup of tea on a coaster, patted my leg, and closed the door on her way out.

"Wow. That is the first time ever that she didn't have something to say."

"Well, in addition to you being able to read our minds eventually, we are able to read your thoughts more clearly too. She sensed that now wouldn't be the best time. She probably figured that out once you knew she was coming in with the tea."

"This is going to take some getting used to. So, you've been able to read my thoughts this entire time?" I asked nervously.

"Yes, partially. It will definitely take some getting used to. You'll be amazed at how fast it all comes together, Ana. I promise."

"I can't believe some of the things you must have heard me think! How absolutely mortifying. Since we are on embarrassing topics, I should probably go get washed up."

"I have to admit, it was kind of nice hearing some of those things you thought, though." His smile kind, as he was moving the hair that was stuck to my face.

I began to move but quickly realized I needed help, which he gently provided.

"By the way, Ana, everything I heard you contemplating made me even more committed to getting you back this round. I missed you too much to let it fail again."

I took a couple sips of the tea as the anger began to swell about what I was told I was the last time I spoke to Athen, still not believing it.

After I finished up trying to be presentable again, he helped me back into bed, where I definitely needed to be.

"Am I really a white demon or was it another nightmare?" My eyelids became burdened with a heaviness, and I fell fast asleep not hearing his answer.

CHAPTER 12

I was told that days had gone by - how many I didn't even care about it. I only faintly remember being carried from one room to another, right before passing out again. What I was concerned with was how I was going to continue on with this newfound information. The entire time I was out of consciousness, I struggled with the images that were flooding back into my memory. I never seemed to actually sleep. It was more like a movie that was on fast forward. I never got to that next level of sleep. Every time I awoke, I was as exhausted as the time before. My family, thankfully, was at my side the entire time. The few times I was alert enough to notice, I saw that Athen looked as if he hadn't slept for days either, but before I could talk to him, I would drift back to the foggy state.

This last time that I awoke, I had a feeling of strength and certainty, a feeling that I hadn't grasped for a very long time. My days of sleeping, if that is what they could be called, were behind me. I could begin living again. I knew questions would come up, but unlike before, this time they would be answered.

I looked up at Athen who was already by my side with a cup of tea, smiling. I was the happiest girl in the world. My life had been given back to me, the greatest gift of all. I had to fight the uncertainties that kept creeping into my mind about what I was told, but I didn't have the strength to fight anything.

"Hey, how are you feeling? You were out for quite awhile," Athen said to me as he helped me up in my bed.

"I'm feeling like the weight of the world has been lifted, like anything is possible. That being said, though, I'm exhausted, but I can't stand the thought of sleeping anymore."

"I'm sure. The good news is the next time you go to sleep, it will be for real, no more memory overload. The worst is over." Athen's eyes were sparkling. It must have been even harder on him than I knew. At least for me, I was completely out of it. He had to be alert the entire time.

"Do you think the nightmares will be over now?" I asked, hopeful beyond belief.

"Not necessarily." Athen ruffled my hair. "It's a bit complicated."

"Isn't it always?" I murmured rolling my eyes.

"How are you, sleepyhead?" I heard Cyril's voice ringing down the hall.

"Very funny," I said, and threw a pillow at him before he managed to catch it around the corner.

"Not bad." He chucked it back. "Did you tell her the good news?"

"No, can't say that I had the chance yet," Athen said, shaking his head.

"What good news?" I asked, thinking that things were beginning to be pretty wonderful already.

"Well, we, uh, put your notice in at the pub since so much time had gone by. I was pretty sure you wouldn't need to go back there for a job. Always best to not call attention to our existence and follow the proper etiquette." He seemed kind of hesitant as he looked at me waiting for a reaction.

"Oh, thank goodness. I didn't even think about that! I appreciate that so much. I was starting to worry about doing it before finding everything out and being talked into staying and all. How did you do it?"

"We sent Karen in with a letter explaining about your flu and the holidays. I don't know. They seemed kind of relieved, almost."

"Huh, well, I was kind of screwing up a bit at the end. It seemed I could only focus on one thing," I said laughing.

"Oh God, that's my cue to exit. I'm glad you are up, Ana. It's been painful hanging around with Athen so much." He waved and trudged back down the hallway. I could hear him talking to Arie on the phone letting her know that I was up for good this time.

"So do you think you are up to maybe walking around the village a little bit?" Athen's eyes were sparkling with hope.

"I don't want to be in this bed a minute longer."

Athen helped me get ready for my first evening out since the long process began introducing me to my new life. He turned on the shower, got jeans and a sweater laid out for me, and let me know when the water temp was perfect. Even though I was hopelessly exhausted, there was a part of me that hoped he would help me into the shower, but being the gentleman that he was, he backed out of the bathroom when that time came. Truthfully, it was probably for the better. I doubt I was up for much more than holding onto him, let alone feeling his lips on mine. The water pelted me endlessly in the same nonstop way that the images kept flooding through me, giving me no reprieve as I saw Athen's body crumpled on the ground once more. I frantically massaged the suds in my hair hoping to rinse away the overwhelming feelings of despair.

"How's it going in there? Are you doing ok?" Athen must have gotten Arie to come and check on me. How she got here so fast from across the village, I definitely couldn't figure out.

"I'm doing quite well. This shower feels so wonderful, but I'll be out in a second. Tell Athen that I appreciate him checking up on me." I couldn't tell her the truth.

"Will do." Arie's voice sang out.

I turned off the shower and wrapped my hair in the towel that Athen had thrown over the shower door. I put my clothes on that Athen had laid out for me and quickly grabbed the hair dryer. The last thing I wanted to do was catch a cold from wet hair. I flipped the towel off my hair feeling the slap of wet strands against my neck, looking in the mirror, my knees began to give out. Grabbing the sink vanity to stabilize myself, I looked closer in the mirror. My eyes had changed color. They were green now. Almost as green as Athen's, and my hair was no longer the store bought color. It shined its glorious deep auburn brown and with the green eyes, it certainly changed the complexion of things quite a bit. I couldn't understand how that could be. I couldn't stop looking in the mirror. I didn't even care if I put any makeup on. This newfound confidence was nice. I grabbed a brush, ran the blow dryer and decided that was it. I left the bathroom, turned off the light, and Matilda followed me out to meet the others. I couldn't believe I now had green eyes.

CHAPTER 13

The holidays were in full swing in the village. It wasn't even Thanksgiving yet, and lights were hung on patios, and wreaths were placed on the entrances of all the buildings to ensure that the holiday spirit wasn't lost on anybody. Every tree and shrub was covered in a smattering of twinkling white lights. I was anticipating this holiday season with a joy I hadn't had before in my most recent existence, especially during this time of year. I was looking forward to all of the unknowns and new traditions that I hoped I would get to take part in for years to come. I couldn't wait for more memories to come of this time together in years past with my family. I noticed quite a lot of snow had fallen since I was out for those few days. Athen grabbed my hand, as we walked in the direction of the grocery store.

"Incredible isn't it?"

"That's an understatement," I said to Athen, as I absorbed everything as if it was the first time I had seen the village.

The scents of all the little shops were almost overpowering. There was the bath shop with all of the wonderful perfumery notes, and then the smell of cinnamon wafting out of the bakery hit, followed quickly by the coffee shop. I had walked this path many times before. Never did I have this explosion of the senses. It was incredible.

"Is it always like this?" I asked quietly.

"Yep, you learn to block some of them out with time, though, and focus on only certain senses."

"Wow, it's incredible. Where is this scent coming from?" I felt like Matilda all of a sudden, sniffing the air with each breath like it held a mystery for me to unravel.

"That's the florist shop," Athen said laughing.

"Oh, huh," I said feeling a little sheepish.

"You know, I had no idea how much fun it would be experiencing everything through your eyes," Athen said, squeezing my hand. He must have sensed my embarrassment.

"Thanks." I returned my attention to the wonderful things awaiting me in this new form, all the while trying to ignore what I might actually be, a fallen angel. "Please make sure I don't start behaving like Matilda, endlessly sniffing the air. I need to save face around the village a little bit."

"You've got my word," Athen said, still holding my hand as we ventured into the grocery store.

Athen grabbed a cart and I followed along.

"I'm sure you must be starving."

I was, and I didn't realize it until he mentioned it.

"Wow, you aren't kidding."

"I figured you may want to spend the evening at the house, in case you needed to rest unexpectedly or something."

"Yeah, that may not be the only reason," I suggested.

"Nice." Athen retorted, and threw a loaf of bread in the cart.

"I'm craving citrus." I pushed the cart over to the fruit section.

"Like oranges?" Athen asked laughing.

"Exactly!" I started putting one after another into the small plastic bag.

"Geez, you weren't kidding. I think you missed one."

"You know what sounds good?" I asked Athen in all seriousness.

"Besides oranges? I haven't a clue!" He replied as amused as I had seen him in a long time.

"Cinnamon rolls! Let's go to the bakery on our way out."

"Sounds good, but what about for dinner? Spaghetti sound tasty?"

"Of course! Now let's go pay and grab the cinnamon rolls at the bakery before they go away."

On our way out of the grocery store, I noticed a missing person flyer on the bulletin board. It showed a young local. I faintly recognized him. He was twenty - the same supposed age as myself. I was sure he had come into the Pub. He looked so familiar.

"Athen, what's this?" I stopped to look at the picture more closely. "When did this happen?"

Athen came over and looked at the flyer with me.

"He went missing the first day you were out. He was snowboarding in the backcountry and never showed up in the evening. His roommates notified the authorities. They have been looking for him since. The police think he fell into a tree well or something."

I looked at Athen searching for something more, some sort of definitive answer. I knew the answers were there. I just had to get them out.

"Well, did he? You think otherwise?"

"We aren't sure what happened, but it wasn't accidental. Come on, sweetie. Let's get back to the condo," he said, gently kissing my forehead, holding me as we walked down the stairs.

We walked down the stone path through the main village to our condo. The weight of my new existence beginning to creep up on me, I tried my best to keep distracted. I wasn't sure I was ready to begin solving the world's problems.

We got back to the condo and began prepping for dinner. I had greedily munched down two oranges and a cinnamon roll on the way back and was more than ready for the spaghetti. Cyril and Arie were still at my house, for which I was thankful. It seemed like the family I had longed for magically appeared, and in a way, that's exactly what happened. I loved having a house full of people. I know Matilda enjoyed it too. She was far more exuberant than normal, even for a bulldog. I only hoped that I could handle the baggage that this new existence apparently brought with it. The title of Fallen Angel or white demon wasn't exactly sitting well.

"I thought Ana was going to eat the town out. It's a good thing dinner won't take long." Athen grabbed the loaf of bread out of the bakery bag, and Arie began mixing together the garlic butter for the bread, snapping me back to reality and out of my gloomy thoughts.

"Is it that bad?" I asked innocently.

"It's pretty impressive. Not that you have ever held back on food, but I'm surprised you can keep it going. It's a good thing though. It's only normal," Athen added.

"Huh." I looked around my kitchen and loved what I saw. Cyril was helping Arie with the marinara sauce, and they were so into one another. I could feel the love they held for each other across the room. I was thankful that I, too, now had that blessing. No one with that kind of consummate love could be evil. I had to try my hardest to accept the realities that were before me. I looked at Athen who seemed to be smiling nonstop since I had awoken. At the moment, he was smearing the garlic spread on the French bread. He was such a calming, stabilizing force. I was thankful for that since I had a tendency to be a little high-strung. It was a good balance. This was all going to work out, regardless of what I might actually be. Besides, what options did I have? Runaway? Doubtful.

"So, did you guys talk about heading to Seattle yet for the holidays?" Arie asked me, surely knowing the answer. We had no time to talk about what just happened let alone plans for the future.

"Boy, you don't let the grass grow, do you?" Athen said pointedly. "Give her a moment."

Were they thinking Thanksgiving or Christmas? I wondered.

"We were thinking of going down for Thanksgiving and then maybe come back up here for a little while before Christmas to get our fix of snow."

"That sounds good to me," I said laughing.

"What's so funny?" Cyril asked, grabbing Arie's waist and holding her from behind.

"Well, I didn't ask that aloud. I only thought it. This is going to take some getting used to."

"There are definitely tricks, Ana! I promise," Arie said laughing as well. "I definitely know when not to pick your brain. Let's leave it that," she said grinning.

"That's gross, Arie." Athen coughed up, making a gagging sound while throwing a kitchen towel at her.

"Cyril, Athen, and I are going to take a quick trip down there to make sure the house is all set up. We're going to fly down and back in a day if that works for you?" Arie asked a little hesitantly.

"No, that's cool. I have some stuff I should get done around here anyway before heading south."

The oven dinged, alerting us that it was ready to take in the garlic bread. I went into the dining room, grabbed my placemats and began setting the table. So much had changed since our last time in here. A memory ran through me that I knew must have been recently placed. It was Athen and I hiking. We reached an area with boulders where he held me tight as we looked over the valley. It was a truly peaceful setting, but I couldn't place the time. His clothing definitely looked of another era. He was in suspenders. I was in some sort of brown wool pant that was rolled up. I honestly didn't know when it would have been.

"Hey, sweetie, how are you doing with everything?" Athen came into the dining room as if sensing my confusion over the latest memory to enter my mind.

"Oh pretty good, I would say... A little puzzled possibly, but other than that I'm incredibly happy to be with my family and you. I'm trying to comprehend what it all means. The Fallen Angel, demon thing really isn't transitioning well for me. The thoughts make me queasy actually." I looked up at him knowing that he knew what I was going through.

"Well, the memory you just had appear was right before you were taken away from us." He tried to change the subject. "We had hiked up one of the areas near Mount St. Helens. You and I had spent a few hours at Spirit Lake, which was one of your favorite places. It was unusual for women to be hiking like you did with me. You never seemed to care though. We were never apart. You loved that Indian legend that went with it. I was reciting it to you in that memory. Do you remember it?"

"I have been trying. It's not coming to me yet." I was a bit upset with how slow some memories seemed to take to come back in their entirety. Sometimes, I would only see images with no sound but could see that we were talking.

"It was believed that the three mountain peaks, Mount St. Helen's, Mount Hood, and Mount Adams were all created because of a love triangle. There were two men who were sons of an Indian Chief. They were fighting over a beautiful woman, and she couldn't decide between them. Because of that the sons were bringing great destruction to villages and the surrounding deep green forests as they were demonstrating their love for her, fighting for her attention. The Chief turned them all into each of the mountain peaks to stop the destruction. The maiden was Mount St. Helens."

Athen wrapped his arms around me, and I suddenly remembered more. He was telling me the story when we were overlooking that valley. We had finished a picnic that Arie had prepared for us. It was a lovely day.

"I do remember that. It was delightful and so calm. Arie had prepared us a picnic. It was an awesome sight. Can we go there this summer?" I asked Athen.

He pulled back from me a little bit and spun me around so he could look at me, his eyes intense.

"Mount St. Helens blew up."

"Are you serious? What happened? When did it happen?" I was shocked.

"It was back in 1980. She had given signs and she finally blew. Ash spread throughout the Northwest. It was pretty intense. There is a visitor station there now, though. It brings home what mother earth and natural forces are capable of. We'll put that on the to-do list, for sure. Like we need reminding of that."

"Wow." I hugged him extra hard, feeling his chest against my skin. I breathed in a deep breath treasuring every second I had him back in my life. I saw the black iron sconce on the wall turn on and knew Arie and Cyril must be on their way with the spaghetti and bread.

"Thanks for the warning light, sis!" Athen sighed.

Everyone was quietly passing around the garlic bread and pasta when I realized that there was something that wasn't being said. Somehow, I was being left out of the loop again. As I got handed the basket of garlic bread from Arie, I took my piece and held it hostage from Athen.

"What aren't you guys telling me now?" I said, looking directly at Athen.

Arie piped in immediately, "We were going to tell you right after dinner. We didn't want to spoil your first meal after everything you've been through."

I saw Athen give Arie a warning look, which I took to mean she was to stop speaking as to not give anything away. Having never had this kind of tension before with the group, I wanted whatever it was to be out in the open.

"I think I can handle about anything right now, guys, so you might as well say what you've got to say. I'll be fine. It isn't like it could get much more unbelievable, right?" I said, shaking my head.

"Well, there have been some developments," Athen began softly, "and we need to get some things figured out."

"That's pretty vague," I said, holding the bread still, trying to lighten the air a little bit. "Is that why you are going down to the house in Kingston?"

"Yes, that's part of it," Athen replied, looking very uncomfortable. "There's been a lot of activity, and we're trying to determine if it's related to our family reuniting."

"Activity with what?" I asked, not sure I wanted to know the answer, finally relinquishing the bread to Athen.

"The black demons," he said point-blank, looking for my reaction.

"Whoa! What does that mean?" I asked, looking at Cyril.

"Generally black demons leave the white demons alone because there isn't much they can do to us, except disrupt families, but the families eventually always reunite so it doesn't provide them with any long-term pleasure. Their prey is usually human centered. Their goal is to persuade as many humans as possible to do wrong. They enjoy the hunt of the human, toying with their decisions and waiting to see the outcomes, so generally we aren't that interesting to them. They like to feel like they have more control over the fate of mankind versus dabbling with distant cousins." He stopped and Athen continued.

"We are usually pretty in tune with their motives so we can try to intervene when possible. However, recently we haven't been able to track all of the usual players. Some have gone missing, in a sense, possibly planning something underground. New ones have come to the area in their place. We really aren't sure what to make of it. Other than to assume, it has to do with your reintroduction process. Plus, the missing hikers and snowboarder just complicates everything."

"Not to sound selfish, but should I be left alone, and what would merit an actual fight with a demon?" I asked, my heart pounding faster with every breath I took in. The thought of demons after me was beyond frightening. Not remembering what I went through the first time I got separated from my family and not wanting to be separated again sent chills through me. I saw all three look at each other before Athen began the answer. I knew they were hiding something. I, also, knew I wouldn't find out what it was.

"You'll be taken care of. You won't be in danger. I can assure you of that. I won't lose you again," Athen said, reaching for my hand.

"We'll be taking a quick shuttle down and back up. They won't try anything while we're away." Arie offered as best she could a response to make me calmer. I knew she was lying and didn't know why. I had to trust – something I had never been very good at.

"So when do you think you guys will be taking the trip?" I asked, trying to make sure my voice did not indicate the actual amount of fear that was welling up inside.

"In a couple of days," Athen mumbled.

"Eat your pasta," Arie commanded, "This is why we didn't want to tell you until after dinner."

"Guys, I'm fine. Really. It's kind of a shock to hear that someone or something might be after me. Not to mention that I'm still trying to digest what I supposedly am." I paused not sure I wanted to ask my next question, but figured that I already messed with the tone of the meal so I might as well round it out. "How did it happen? I mean last time? How did I end up like I did? Do my nightmares have anything to do with it?" Nothing was said for several seconds. All I could hear was Matilda working on a piece of bread someone must have slipped her under the table.

"I was only curious because earlier you had said that the black demons don't tend to come after us, but they obviously did. It kind of sounds like they could do it again." This time I was determined to wait for an answer.

"It was out of revenge. Pure and simple." Cyril looked over at me as if that answer would calm me. "We disrupted a very heinous crime from taking place. It was something Azazel was working on for a very long time. The short version is the human chose different because of our interference. Azazel saw fit to tear our lives apart. He took you away from us. That's the short version. It sums it up though. He intended to punish us, and in a sense it worked, but we still managed to do good while we were waiting for you. "

I sat back in disbelief. The underworld that was slowly being exposed to me held so many answers but left so many questions.

"You were the one who did the final act that detoured the human from making the wrong choice he was about to make. We think that is why they went after you specifically," Athen replied quietly. I could tell rehashing this story was as hard for him as it was for me. The pain was running through each syllable he uttered.

"They didn't strike right away. In fact years had gone by, which is why we were off our guard. We learned the hard way, to say the least, but we had figured that the demons had decided to let it slide. We guessed wrong. They waited for our defenses to be down."

"You said the demon was Azazel, but then you said they. So was there more than one?" I asked, trying to get as much clarity as I possibly could, considering how foreign the stories were to begin with.

"Well, as we had mentioned before, the black demons tend to work alone. They certainly don't have the same family structures that we have created over the centuries. However, they will group up on tasks and side with one another when they run into interference of any kind. They have a network, and they will use it if they think it will better their chances to screw with mankind or connect with us, apparently. Our biggest concern is always the possible formation of legions with them. Thankfully, it's been centuries since they have attempted that."

"Who is Azazel? How does he have so much power or ability?"

"He was the principal angel, before he fell, who really led the whole movement of angels cohabitating with mortal women. He's also known as the demon of the desert. Supposedly, that is where you would find him, where he rounds up his minions to do his dirty work so to speak. He is all things evil."

I looked around the table and understood the outpouring of love and concern from Cyril, Arie, and Athen trying to comfort me in all of the confusion. I was so thankful that they chose to tell me rather than keep me in the dark. It had made things much more clear. It put into perspective what kind of creatures I was possibly dealing with. I hoped I didn't ever experience the evil of these creatures again. I, also, secretly prayed I had none of the evil inside of me.

"If it makes you feel any better, my appetite has come back. I'm ready to plow through my plate of pasta." I spurted out my feeble attempt to lift the mood.

"Under the circumstances, I didn't expect it to take too long," Cyril said laughing, and I was relieved that I hadn't spoiled the mood for the rest of the evening, especially in light of knowing they would be leaving in a couple days.

CHAPTER 14

The morning light came through my bedroom and woke me up from a wonderful dream that I was in the middle of. I rolled over trying to get back to that state of sleep where I could recover my dream and begin it again. I didn't want to lose any time with Athen, even if it was in my dreams. I was still in the process of relearning memories, and sometimes, they came in the form of dreams, which I certainly didn't want to miss out on. Anything to take the place of the nightmares was wonderful. I tossed and turned trying to get back to sleep, but it was hopeless. The light continued to blaze through the windows and was far too intense. I vowed going forward I would keep the curtains closed, even if it meant missing out on waking up to falling snow. I looked over at my alarm clock and saw that it read 6:30am - curse it. There was no way I would be able to get Matilda up this early, let alone go outside to do her business. I wondered if Athen was still asleep. My guess was that he was. Everyone left pretty late the night before. My heart ached a little at the thought of him at his condo and me across the village. I was so relieved to experience a night's worth of sleep filled with happiness instead of the horrific images usually invading my mind.

I begrudgingly lifted the comforter up and climbed out of bed. I knew I was too amped up to get back to sleep, which made me think I didn't remember my dream as well as I thought I did. I pattered into the bathroom to brush my teeth and hoped that I still had enough beans left to make a pot of coffee.

I was still on information overload from the night before but knew that those missing pieces were so very important in helping me understand the dangers that were still out there as well as what happened so many decades before. I knew the journey to fully regain my memories would be a long one. I was thankful that I had my family around to help with them. The mere thought of Cyril, Athen, and Arie made my heart automatically begin to warm. I was truly blessed. I only hoped that I would get over the uneasy feelings of my heritage. I kept trying to spin it in a positive manner, to no avail. I opened the cabinet, relieved to find enough beans to make that pot of coffee. I also made a mental note to stop by Karen's later today to avoid losing the one quasi friend that I could call my own.

I sat at the breakfast bar waiting for the coffee to brew while I decided to start a to-do list. Since spending so much time with Athen and his family, a lot of my personal duties seemed to slip through the cracks. First on the list was a grocery trip, followed by pre-paying some of my bills through the holidays so I didn't have to come back to a dark house because, at this rate, I would forget to pay the electric bill. I could feel myself begin to daydream about Athen again and wondered if that is how it always would be.

The day before I was so thrilled to have another memory resurface of us all at a lake, enjoying some sort of summer party with games, and many people, who I did not recognize, wandering around. I knew I wanted to ask Arie about that memory because so far the only people that have appeared were Cyril, Athen, and Arie – not strangers. I knew I was safer asking about the happy dreams rather than the scary ones. I hoped the nightmares were just that – nightmares. I didn't want to ask though.

The morning had gone by fast, and it was a smidge before 11:00 am. I managed to get all of my grocery shopping done as well as put everything away tidily in the pantry cupboards and even got many of my bills paid online early. My next hope was that I would be able to get a hold of Karen for an afternoon visit. I decided I had better call her and head over before she had to start her shift at the Pub.

I reached for the phone, feeling a burning pain run through my fingertips, almost as if I was being poked with hot needles. I couldn't quite fathom that so I took my hand away and readjusted how I was sitting; maybe I scuffled around the floor too much, I thought to myself. I picked up the phone quickly this time hoping to avoid that same level of pain and dialed Karen's number. My technique worked, no pain. The phone rang and rang, but the machine didn't pick up so I held on a little longer about to give up when I heard the receiver click.

"Hello?" I heard Karen's familiar voice and was thrilled.

"Hey, Karen!" I exclaimed, not able to hold back my excitement.

"Ana! I'm so glad you called. I was planning on stopping by to say hi. How are you feeling? That was some horrible flu you got. Are you back to normal yet?"

Always like Karen to be concerned. I pushed away the guilt for not being honest, but I knew the truth would get me locked up in some sort of facility that I would never get out of.

"I'm doing so much better. Still not a hundred percent but getting close – worn out mostly."

"Well, we really miss you at the pub."

As soon as Karen spoke the words a little pang of guilt came over me because I knew deep down that I was having so much fun with my family that I didn't think about working at the pub at all.

"I miss you all too. It certainly is odd not worrying about my shift, or what kind of crowd might be coming in," I told her, trying as hard as possible to sound convincing.

"Yeah, I'm sure that is what you are thinking about," she said teasing. Obviously, my attempt failed.

"Very funny! So I called to see if you are free this afternoon to catch up. I know it's short notice, but..."

"No problem at all. I finished cleaning everything up so come on over whenever you want. I don't go in until 7:00 pm tonight, and I work until closing. We've got plenty of time to chat." I could tell that she was getting excited. I was relieved that my lack of communication, over the last while, didn't rub her the wrong way.

"Great. See you in a bit," I said and hung up the phone quickly. This would work out great, since I wasn't meeting Athen for dinner until 8 pm tonight. I decided to get ready for the dinner with Athen now, in case I was running late coming back from Karen's.

I was standing at Karen's door waiting for her to appear, while I delicately balanced the fresh baked pretzels I'd picked up. One of our favorite things we used to munch on during a movie night.

She flung open the door and came pouncing to hug me before she noticed that my hands were full. I managed to grab everything before it hit the ground, and I couldn't stop laughing.

"Well, some things don't change," I said, barely able to move through the door because I was laughing so hard.

"Oh yum! Pretzels!" Karen was as excited as always to see the baked goods. I delicately maneuvered through her entry hall as she carefully tried to grab items to make it easier. I made it to the dining room, happy I didn't drop anything.

"Wow, did you get a new rug?" I asked her, not remembering an off white rug in her dining room before.

"Yep. Got it on sale down in Squamish. I was tired of always having cold feet at the dining room table."

"Well, I love it."

We were getting all situated when Karen got a text. The needle sensation ran through my fingers again. It had to be the rug. I quickly sat down and raised my feet up, but this time it didn't go away. An image flashed in my head of a guy, I didn't recognize, texting to Karen's number. I looked over at Karen who looked very uncomfortable and was beginning to blush.

"So did you get something from your boyfriend? Do I need to leave the room?" I said laughing.

She looked a little relieved and smiled.

"Yeah, that's who it was."

I wanted to believe her, but somehow something wasn't adding up. I had a very uncomfortable feeling building up, and the feeling in my fingers was not going away. It dulled a little but was still very much present. I smiled quickly to hopefully make her at ease and decided I would bring it up a little later to give us enough time to bond again.

"Something seems different about you. I can't put my finger on it though," Karen said, looking at me puzzled.

"Hmmm," I said aloud, "Oh geez. I know what it is. I have green contacts in."

"Wow, well not sure what would have possessed you to do that, but it looks good. Usually those things look so fake."

"Yeah, thanks. I think."

She relaxed a bit as we both dove into the pretzels I brought as we covered every topic imaginable. I told her all about Athen and his family, leaving out the obvious parts. She was quite agreeable as to how caring he seemed to be. I could tell we were back to normal so I decided to pounce. I looked at the clock and back at Karen.

"I should probably get going. Give you time to get ready for the night and text you know who back. Hey, I'm gonna text him a hello and tell him he made my girl blush." I said laughing. As I feared, her reaction wasn't what I hoped.

"No, don't do that. He's at an appointment."

"Oh, is that so?" I asked, eyeing her suspiciously. "What kind of appointment? It's kind of late for one. Wouldn't he have his phone turned off? I want to reach out," I told her, looking her in her eyes knowing, unfortunately, that wasn't her boyfriend who texted her earlier.

"Why are you looking at me that way, Ana? Why would I be lying about where he is this afternoon?"

"You are right," I told her. "I guess I've been away a wee bit too long and didn't read you right. You haven't acted that way before over me texting him, that's all." I hoped my softening voice would win her over a little to come clean. Instead, she sat silently staring at the table runner. I hopped up and grabbed my purse.

"Sorry, Karen. I didn't mean to overstep my bounds." I went over and hugged her. "I can let myself out."

"No, don't be silly. I'm fine. You're fine. You did nothing."

We walked together through the living room. Once we got to the front door, I turned to her and gave her a hug.

"Thanks for always being there, Karen. I'm thankful. You should come to dinner with us all and, of course, bring Justin. It has been too long since the crepe house, I think." I could feel her squeezing harder than when I first arrived to her house earlier. I knew my suspicions were right. She let go and stood back and looked at me.

"You look amazingly great, Ana – more confident or something."

"Thanks." I gave her a quick hug as I left and quietly whispered, "Don't do it, Karen. It's not you. Be the kind soul you are."

I could hear the door shut silently behind me. I knew she was about to make a choice that could alter her future forever. I wondered why on earth I knew any of that off of a text.

I was relieved. I got back to my place in time to let Matilda out for a quick walk. I was still fiddling with my key in the door when Athen appeared opening the door in front of me. He was already at my place. I could feel the excitement level swell instantly, and I almost let out a little squeal of delight. He picked me up and spun me around as I shut the door with my leg. He put me down and began kissing me when I began smelling something over the top delicious. I backed away slowly and looked around the living room, which was completely dark except for the fire and a few candles that he had placed along the coffee table with rose petals surrounding them. My eyes started to fill with tears as I took in what he had planned for me. I couldn't believe that he had snuck in and done this for me.

"Looks like we are staying in tonight?" I said smiling from ear to ear.

"Well, we don't have to," he said, toying with my hair that had fallen from my ponytail.

"This is so incredible, Athen. Thank you. I'm dying to know what I'm smelling? It's making me delirious."

"A rib roast with rosemary and garlic."

"Oh, my gosh, my favorite!" I exclaimed, and before I knew it, Athen had grabbed me and wrestled me to the couch.

"Whoa, fine sir. What do you have planned?" I mischievously asked and hoped for something that had eluded me thus far with him.

He began placing pillows behind my head and grabbed my red throw to cover me up with. I couldn't believe my good fortune.

"Well, I want you to do nothing and be comfortable while doing that." He leaned next to me, gently kissing my neck. My heart started beating faster as his breath was crawling on my skin. I reached around and grabbed his shoulder bringing him closer to me. His fingers grazed my breast, leaving me to want so much more. I looked up at him, hoping for the next step, when the oven bell went off. For the first time in my life, I would have been willing to pass up my favorite meal. I knew that was not on the agenda tonight, no matter how much I begged for it.

**

The night flew by way too fast, my heart was heavy with the thought of Athen, Cyril, and Arie all leaving for Seattle. It was hard telling Athen goodnight. I knew they said everything would be fine but knowing what was out in the world now certainly changed my perspective on what was considered fine. I got the knock on the door at 4:00 am, because I made Athen promise that he would stop by before they all hopped on the highway to the airport. I opened the door expecting Athen but, instead, was greeted by the entire crew and a bag of pastries.

"Wow, where did you get pastries this early? The village is never open at this hour." They were still warm even.

"I know the gal at the hotel, and she made some for us," Arie said, very proud of herself.

"Geez, thanks."

Everyone came in and piled through to the kitchen. I was secretly relieved that they all showed up. I could now spend a little longer with them before they took off. I knew I was taking this a bit hard. I seemed to be filled with fear more than I knew. My worry that dreams and reality would someday collide seemed to be at the forefront of most thoughts. We were all quietly munching on our pastries when Cyril began speaking.

"We know you'll be fine, Ana. We're all very connected to you and will be able to sense anything that may occur or may be in the works. Believe me, we're all on high alert." I looked at him wanting to fully believe him, trying to ignore the fear still sitting heavy in my belly. Athen grabbed my hand and began his turn at trying to convince me.

"We wouldn't let anything happen to you. I promise. Remember, you are my everything, my angel. You are what makes my life complete. Without you I barely exist. I mean it. You'll be fine. Promise to stay in the village."

"Actually, I was thinking of staying in my house except to take Matilda out."

"Well, that's fine too," Arie piped up. "But really, Ana, it's okay to go outside. We maybe shouldn't have told you all that. We didn't mean to spook you so badly."

"Oh, please, I would much rather know the truth," I said emphatically. "Really."

Seeing Athen crumpled on the ground in my thoughts began to paralyze me. Forcing myself to rid those images from my memory, I would not let myself look at Athen. The lump in my throat began to make it hard to swallow, hard to believe the two sets of realities could be parallel.

CHAPTER 15

I was so happy that Athen and everyone was coming back in the evening. They had been gone not even a day, and I missed them greatly. On a positive note, I was able to get everything done that I had planned in my condo, but I certainly felt like I was missing a piece of me. I think Matilda was even sad.

I had managed to sneak in a lunch with Karen who filled me in on the entire goings on back at the pub, for which I was certainly grateful. We never did get to that at her apartment. It was nice to hear how everyone was doing, and although at the time, I thought I would miss it if I left, I guiltily knew I missed it not at all. I did get an earful, because apparently there were a couple of new hires that did not work out, partied more than they worked, but that was a pretty common occurrence in Whistler, which is why I was treated so well. I was and am still dependable.

She also thanked me for bringing her back to reality. I knew exactly what she was referring to. I was relieved to hear those words. As I left, she told me nothing had happened, yet. I made a mental note to ask Arie if those sensations that came over me with Karen were the warnings for me. It seemed like I was learning everything in bits and pieces and by trial and error. I hadn't told them the details surrounding my visions yet either. I didn't want to send them all on a wild goose chase because I couldn't separate fact from fiction.

I was tidying up the last of the living room when I heard the familiar knock on my front door. My heart started beating a little faster, and the excitement was building. I wasn't expecting them for another couple hours, but maybe, they caught an earlier shuttle flight. I ran to the door, swinging it open to see Athen staring right back at me with shades on as he was leaning against the doorframe, smooth as ever. He picked me up before I saw it coming and spun me around. I was so happy he was here. I looked quickly behind him and saw that he was alone. The excitement was bubbling over. Maybe with his exuberance, we could finally get some long awaited alone time. I slithered down from Athen's embrace, pulling him to the bedroom, hopeful as usual.

Before I had time to blink, Athen grabbed me, shoving me up the bedroom wall as he lifted my sweater. His hands roughly swiping at my skin as I wrapped my legs around him and heard the sound of my suede skirt splitting. My hands made their way through Athen's hair, and he pulled away, which startled me. In this quick encounter, Athen hadn't even tried to kiss me, and that was unheard of. Maybe, he was experimenting. We'd never gotten to this next level before anyway. His strength was beginning to overpower my every move. He removed his glasses, not letting me look into his eyes. I could feel his hand gravitating towards my thigh. I didn't know what was going on. Things were suddenly not feeling right. None of the electricity was present that I usually had by being near Athen - let alone during this type of encounter.

Athen must have felt my body turn a little bit limp under his forcefulness, because I felt a repositioning. His eyes looking over my body as if he had never seen it before. I latched onto his hair this time, pulling his face towards me, when I suddenly realized that this was not Athen. The eyes staring back at me were lifeless, hollow. It was as if death was radiating from this imposter. I was looking into a creature from beyond, but how could this be? Where was my real Athen? Was he alive? All of these thoughts started running through me like a faucet that couldn't be turned off. I scrambled to get away from this imposter, but with every kick and scrape, his grip became firmer. His nails were digging deeper and deeper into my skin. I looked down to see his repulsively long, pointy brown fingernails sliding up my arm. How could I not have caught these signs earlier?

Matilda was starting to move around in the living room, and I was hoping she would stay out of the bedroom. I couldn't bear to have anything happen to her. She was too innocent and loyal for her to see what was about to take place. I knew there was nothing I could do against this creature. I had to keep reminding myself that this was not Athen. This creature was very possibly the demon who everyone had been trying to protect me from during this whole process.

I was looking for anything around my bedroom that might help me get away from this imposter, and as he was gazing around the room with me, it hit me that he might be able to read my mind, like Athen. To what degree, I didn't know.

I tried to rack my brain about what my family said about the other worldlies, and how this creature could fit into that scenario. It couldn't be a vampire or werewolf because they can't morph into others. My entire body shuddered as the realization washed over me that what was standing before me was truly a demon, the very demon who had been stalking me since I began this process.

This had to be one of the demons that my family spoke about whose sole mission was to create havoc throughout humanity. His fingers kept crawling up and down my body, and I was attempting to reach into my newfound powers to try to feel what his motive was. I was trying to concentrate so hard that I didn't even hear the front door open. The demon's gaze turned towards the door, and my heart fell to the floor knowing that someone must have entered my condo.

"Please don't," I whispered into the Demon's ear. "Just take me. Don't hurt them. Do what you came to do but please, spare my family."

"Your family?" The demon seethed in an almost snake-like pitch. "We don't have families."

"Some of us do. I'm begging you to leave mine alone."

"Alright, my white demon. I'll do as you say."

So he was what I thought- a demon, and he knew what I was as well. I was terrified. He came here with a mission. The thought of this creature hurting my family gave me strength from within that I knew I could use to my benefit. Every part of my body strengthened with a stiffness ready for protection. I was ready for any attack he may have planned for me. I would do anything as long as it would save my family.

I didn't know who had come in the front door, or where they were, or what the demon had planned to do to me, but all I could do was think about where Athen was, and if he was ok. I hoped with all of my heart that he was still on the plane with his sister. The demon pulled me away from the wall and threw me across the room with such speed that my skin stung with pain as the flesh was exposed to the comforter turned sandpaper as my body skidded across it.

A light that I recognized flashed from outside my window flashed. The prismatic colors told me that I was no longer alone. It was Athen's prism. My family was here. I fought with everything to keep the thoughts out of my head so the demon wouldn't pick them out. I didn't understand why the demon was no longer interested in whoever it was that came into my house.

"Ana?" I heard Arie's voice coming down the hall. "Are you down here?"

I looked up at the demon for guidance, and he shook his head.

"Um, hey, Arie. I'm in the bedroom."

Arie rounded the corner and looked up at the demon and immediately started backtracking.

"Oh, my word, Ana! Why didn't you say you and Athen were in here? This is utterly not right. Gross actually. I'm going to wait in the living room until you guys come out."

My soul fell with a heavy realization that even Athen's own sister didn't recognize the imposter. I closed my eyes as tightly as I could, hoping that I could wish this entire encounter away, knowing this could only turn out horribly. The black mist creatures appeared in my thoughts. Could this be where I meet my demise, so soon? I did my best to shove those thoughts aside, but the images of the black creatures plowing through me and ripping me apart were getting harder to ignore.

I braced myself for whatever was going to happen next, hoping my soul could survive if nothing else did. I heard a guttural sound rumbling from the being standing over me. His hand anchoring my hair to the bed, I took in a deep breath feeling my lungs burn. Then my skirt began to be torn from my body. I fought with every ounce of strength to keep any thoughts from entering my head. I didn't want to jeopardize my family anymore than I already had. I wasn't sure what would happen if we were all destroyed at the same time.

The wretched breath of the beast slowly surfaced up my thigh as he started pressing up against me. The tears in my eyes finally broke free, and each tear was like a blade penetrating my cheek. Those stinging tears would be nothing compared to the pain I was about to endure, but I did my best to focus. It finally sunk in that what this creature wanted from me was a child, a creation from his underworld.

I started thrashing with all of the strength I had. My nails became the sharpest claws imaginable. I tried with all of my power to defend myself from the impersonator. Matilda began barking, and within in a flash, my bedroom became full of light. A deafening crack came through the air almost paralyzing me.

I opened my eyes and saw both Athens standing in my room crouched as low as humanly possible, hovering as if the air between them was creating a wall between good and evil. The imposter was no longer holding me down. I stared intently at them both, attempting to raise myself from the bed. Arie grabbed my shoulders and lifted me quickly off of the bed as I caught a glimpse of Athen's green eyes staring intently at the demon before him.

"Let me help him, Arie," I screamed at her with all my might.

"No, Ana, he's got this. It will be all right. You are a complete distraction right now. Come on, honey. I promise."

Arie half dragged my kicking and screaming body as she firmly held onto me moving out of my bedroom. The cheery color in the hallway did nothing to help my mood. The despair was multiplying within me. All I could hear was the sound of light buzzing. I strained to get out of Arie's grasp so I could see one more glimpse of Athen. I somehow managed to free myself and turned around in time to see Athen lunge toward the demon with such speed that it was a blur of color turning into a ball. A piercing noise jarred me as Arie grabbed me again. A black streak was darting around, and I didn't understand what I was seeing. I was certain that the image before me was the same kind as in my nightmares.

"No, Arie, I'm far enough away. Please let me stay. I need to make sure Athen is ok."

"Oh, that's right your eyes haven't completely developed yet."

"What do you mean?" I asked, but not being able to take my eyes off the speeding mass that was literally destroying everything in my bedroom. I didn't care if all the walls came down. I wanted this to be over and to embrace the real Athen, my Athen.

"Ana, sweetie, if your eyesight was completely developed you'd be able to see that your hero, Athen, is winning. He could end him now if he wanted, but because of what he did to you, he's prolonging the torment for your sake. They feel pain like we do, if we are the ones to inflict it."

My heart started to untwist a little bit as every syllable hit me. I still couldn't believe it and wouldn't until Athen flashed his smile at me. The force of the demon that I experienced didn't seem like he would be as easily thrown down as Arie described, but I so desperately wanted to believe her. I still was in complete shock and horror over mistaking my boyfriend the way I did and what that creature was capable of. Cyril came bounding through the front door.

"What did I miss? Did Athen have his fun yet or can I still join in?"

In that instant, I recognized the same look that I had seen several times before since I had met Cyril. The first time being when we were all dog sledding, and they were tracking the so-called animal. The second time was at the bar when he met up with Athen, Karen, and myself when the weirdo was casing me. All of those times led to this creature. They were tracking this evil thing.

"Arie, you've got to tell me what's going on! Is that one of the creatures who's been following me? Is that the same one from the dog sledding and pub, or is it a different one? Has it been following me this whole time? Why are there so many? It's turning into one of those beings from my nightmares. I don't understand."

Cyril leaped from the hallway and joined the chaos with Athen. I suddenly knew that everything was going to be fine for now. Arie grabbed my hand and squeezed it.

"It will be over soon. Keep watching."

The images started to slow down to an almost normal human speed that I could recognize. I could finally distinguish between the two Athens and Cyril and saw that the imposter Athen was badly wounded. He looked like a shell of a human. Depleted in every sense of the word, his face sunken in. His skin was a light ashy grey, and there were scratch marks all over his body that revealed burned flesh underneath. As I got a good look, I saw the real Athen's hand grab the imposter's neck with one fluid motion. He squeezed the creature with one graceful gesture as Cyril stood back. In a mere second, the imposter went limp, and a black mist began swirling up to the ceiling. The imposter's shell vanished. I thought I was doing fine, but as soon as Athen looked over at me, I slumped to the floor and began sobbing. Instantly, he was at my side holding me, gently brushing my hair from my face. He cradled me so quickly. A level of protection surrounded me that I never knew I craved. He truly was my hero in the greatest sense of the word.

"It's ok, my love. He won't hurt you. I'm here. I'll always be here. You'll be protected. We never went to Seattle."

Hearing those words made me realize it was true. As long as he was with me, I would make it. I only hoped that I could offer him the same sense of protection someday. I couldn't imagine ever living my life again without him. My sobbing turned to a softer whimper, trying hard to control myself. Looking up at Athen and his radiant green eyes, I ventured my first words.

It was hard to fathom that they never left town, and this was a setup. They were here this entire time waiting for this creature.

"I saw you finish him. I couldn't see anything up until that point except a big blob of colors swirling around."

"You saw that? I'm so sorry. I never wanted you to see that. I figured you couldn't yet."

"Well, I'm kind of glad I did. It makes me realize you weren't kidding about being a bad ass. I only saw it at the end. It was a big blur right up until you grabbed him."

Cyril, never one to miss a beat, yelled from the bedroom, "It wasn't all him, kid."

Athen helped me up, and we walked down the hallway to my living room. I was so happy to see everything in its place. I realized how tired I was from the attack and the fear of possibly losing Athen. My brown leather chair was calling me, I beelined for it sinking in to the cushion.

"Your room is pretty destroyed. How about if you hang out at our place for a few days while we get it taken care of?" Arie looked hopeful. I wondered what she had up her sleeve. With everything that had gone on over the last few weeks, I figured I would give in. It was probably for the best anyway.

"I think that sounds like a plan, but at the moment, I'm going to snuggle in my chair with Matilda."

I was beginning to feel like a real wimp. The moment anything unusual occurred, I needed to sleep, hopefully trying to wake up to a sense of normalcy that may not longer exist.

"Great! I'm going to get you all packed up." Arie darted down the hallway as I curled up with Matilda and fell fast asleep.

Unfortunately, once again, my mind was no longer my own. I was in for a long night of torment. I just didn't know it yet.

CHAPTER 16

Her serpentine eyes were taking me in. If I didn't know better, I would think she could literally swallow me whole. The only thing missing was her devil horns. I was sure that she had them. She had to be one of them, one of the evil ones. Her deathly eyes scanned the room as her laughter rolled off the walls of the Starbucks I was in. I was pretty sure I was the target of the joke, whatever it was. The door swung open, and her raven hair blew gracefully in the wind, landing strand by strand, creating a web to disguise the person who just came in through the door. My world began to swirl around me. Nothing seemed right about what I was seeing. It was Athen, and he was heading straight over to greet her, not even glancing my direction.

Why would he know her? He spent his life fighting creatures like her. I spent my life fighting creatures like her, her evil. We all have. Emptiness was filling every part of my body. I caught his eyes for a brief moment only to realize there was absolutely no recognition. It's like I never existed. I was just another patron waiting for a latte. I tried screaming as loud as I could. Nothing came out of my lips. This nightmare had to end. I had to wake up. I tried to force myself out of my deepest level of sleep yet. It wasn't working. He was enamored with her, with her beauty. There she was, staring back at me, grinning with her perfectly polished teeth. And then, her hand slipped through his as they exited, throwing me one last smile for the road. I immediately crumpled to the floor, feeling like a hollow shell of a person.

I awoke not in the leather chair that I fell asleep in, but in Athen's bedroom. Matilda was sound asleep next to me, and Athen must have slept somewhere else. Sadness crept in very quietly, especially in light of my latest nightmare. I refused to call it a vision. I tried to force myself back to reality as if I could make these images less credible by ignoring them. I let the last shudder run through before I let myself enjoy where I was.

I secretly imagined what sleeping next to him must feel like. I had seen Athen's room before a couple of times but seeing it from this vantage point was nice. I had the comforter pulled up all the way to my shoulders, and I embraced the warmth from his flannel sheets surrounding me. I noticed for the first time that he had a few pictures of me scattered in frames on his dresser. There was one of me at the dog sledding tour and one when I was dangling from the zipline, but there was one that I knew didn't occur in Whistler. I wasn't even sure what decade it was, but there I was in full glory standing by a Christmas tree with Athen, his sister Arie and Cyril.

It was so weird to be looking at a piece of history, my history, but with no recollection. I looked so happy. I hoped I would be able to remember all of those times. As I was daydreaming about the picture, I noticed a dog that looked an awful lot like

Matilda stretched out under the Christmas tree. I shot up and ran over to the photo and looked at it closely. Sure enough, it was Matilda. I was barely able to wrap my brain around our situation, but now I really couldn't begin to fathom how Matilda would continually be in our presence. I made a mental note to ask Athen about that one. I looked at her on the bed still snuggled up as tight as a bulldog could be and decided to climb back in bed. Everything in Athen's house was so meticulous and in its place, but his bedroom showed his character. It was attractive, bold, and very soothing. The décor was all in earth tones and very modern. There were dashes of red in the pillows and drapes – my favorite color. He had the softest grey throw on the bed. I couldn't help but pull it up as I snuggled back in.

I kept trying to purge the images from the night before. I didn't know if my nightmares were back because of the attack or if they were actually visions. I prayed with all of my heart that what I was seeing were not visions of the future. The darkest nightmares always ended with someone I loved being destroyed or vanishing. Last night losing Athen's love was almost worse than any of the other dreams so far. Maybe that is how Athen has felt for all of the years unable to connect with me. I didn't know. I knew I could bring him back from a lot of things, even these creatures supposedly - but another's love, deceitful or not? I had no idea. I hoped to never find out. A few weeks ago, being woken up in terror by beasts tearing me apart seemed like the worst case scenario, but after being reunited with my family, I knew the visions that were most devastating were when any of them were in danger.

I would be lying to myself if I didn't recognize that more times than not, they were staring danger straight on, and the outcome was not always as I hoped. I shivered as the image of Athen being defeated flew into my mind in an instant with his glow being diminished and floating gracefully up to the sky. I immediately flushed it out as fast as it came as if the mere acknowledgment would make it real. It was almost too much for me to handle between thinking that Athen could be taken away from me by these horrid creatures, whisked to the sky with nothing left or, possibly worse yet, stolen by a woman claiming to love him and possibly getting to him before me. This had to be my mind trying to reconcile the stories I was told of my demise mixed with the worry that I could lose my love again. There was no way any of this could happen. His love was too strong for me. I was certain of it, but the serpentine eyes piercing through me wouldn't leave my thoughts.

Matilda readjusted herself as I found my spot when I heard rustling come from down the hall. It sounded like the others were getting up. I hesitantly got up from the comfort of Athen's bed and decided to go shower. I trudged into the bathroom, seeing all of my things organized perfectly on Athen's bathroom counter. Excitement began to build, but self-doubt started infiltrating my happiness. I didn't want to get my hopes up in case I woke up from this dream life that suddenly started presenting itself to me as complex and unbelievable as it may be.

The previous night's dream didn't help either. Their hands interlocking; I pushed the image out of my mind instantly. The shower was running hot as chills came over me. I began shaking and had to sit down before I fell down. Between the nightmares while I was sleeping and the battle that took place before falling asleep, I felt like I was burdened with more than I could handle. How did I even know what was what anymore? What was real; what was fantasy? I was safe for now, and I knew that I was protected with everyone by my side, but the fear that ran through me the night before wouldn't go away. I was sitting on the floor holding my head trying to make the imposter stop attacking me when I heard footsteps coming. I knew at once who it was going to be so I tried to sit up before he caught me looking so miserable. It didn't work. I was a wreck.

Athen knelt down, gently reaching for my chin. I grabbed him as the tears began flowing down my face, unable to control the emotions that I prided myself in hiding. I couldn't stop and wasn't even sure what made me start. Not even being able to decipher fact from fiction any longer, I didn't know if it was the actual events that took place or my dream with the serpentine eyes, but being in his arms began to make me feel halfway human again – even though I never really was.

"I'm so sorry." I began sobbing over and over again into his shirt, which was quickly becoming saturated.

"Ana, you have nothing to apologize for. If anything I put you in danger. I didn't tell you the gravity of the situation because I always counted on being there when the demon arrived. I knew I could finish him, but I didn't expect him to get to you before I was there. I'm the one who should be apologizing."

"I never understood the seriousness of the situation before. I'm so sorry. I know you had told me that the demons tried to procreate with humans and us, the white demons, but I never imagined it would happen to me. If only I had paid attention. I knew it wasn't you, but it looked so much like you that I let everything override my senses. You could have been killed, and it would have been my fault."

"Ana, first, I was never in any danger. It was a young demon. It probably thought it had a chance. As you saw, it didn't. Second, the demon's ability to morph is what gives them and us the advantage. We can morph as well. That is something that you'll relearn in time. It can work to our advantage. I should've told you the full implications of a demon's actions, and I didn't. I was too cocky. I have been so happy to have you back in my life. It's like I'm showing off all over again. This did teach me to be more cognizant of our surroundings, like when we were searching for you. I let my guard down. What you witnessed is what happens to us. The only difference, if it matters, is that the black demons turn to the black mist that you probably saw or they shatter to pieces. Whereas the white demons or fallen angels, like us, turn to white, sometimes with a green cast, as they're phased out. We almost look like a fog that is rolling to the sky. If it didn't signify what it did, it would probably be quite breathtaking. Hence the term white demons."

I crumbled in his arms, and his warmth came through to my bones. The image of him being taken away from me in my dream made the tears resurface. I couldn't lose him. I made myself switch thoughts immediately. I couldn't jeopardize Athen possibly reading my mind. I saw Matilda wagging her tail as best she could, which reminded me of the pictures I saw in his room and figured now was as good of a time as any to ask. Good way to switch gears.

"Athen, I saw some of our pictures in your bedroom. I was wondering how Matilda could be in the pictures that aren't current?"

"That's a funny one to explain."

"Really? I think, at this point, it's all about the same," I said laughing to myself, more than to him.

"So she is kind of like our little homing beacon. She is the only link we have when or if we get separated. She is our family's spirit in a sense. That is the one benefit that the white fallen angels have over the demons. That is why if we choose, we can stay together as a family. It's the one gift that was given to us when this entire thing started. It just so happens that we chose in recent decades to have our spirit masquerade as a bulldog."

"Huh, I've heard more bizarre."

Athen squeezed me one last time. I was so relieved I could confront him and get honest answers. I think he sensed that I was feeling better and wouldn't be breaking down into tears again soon. He helped me up into the shower as I prepared for my day. I could tell this was going to be a long shower. I definitely needed it after everything the last twenty-four hours presented, both real and imagined. The thought of almost losing Athen, even though I have repeatedly been told that wasn't going to happen, and finding out my little Matilda is a homing beacon, made for a headache bigger than my meager shell could handle.

CHAPTER 17

It was mid morning on the Monday before Thanksgiving, and I was trying to get the last of my things together for our trip down to Seattle and then to Kingston for the holiday. I was confident that had I grabbed everything but went through my bag one last time. Besides I could always buy something I forgot, I told myself. It was lightly snowing outside, and I was hoping by the time we got back up here that snow would be covering the entire mountain.

"Are you packed? What all did you bring?" I heard Arie blasting down the hall towards my direction, with Matilda following swiftly behind her. Her energy was undeniable.

"I packed everything you told me to. I swear!" I exclaimed.

I was so thrilled to be going to Seattle and then on to their home, my home. It was so exciting. I was hopeful it could even be a way to escape the horrible nightmares that kept trailing me.

"Awesome! As long as you bring layers, we should be good," Arie said, bouncing on my bed. "It's a bit more wet down there."

"Where's Athen?" I asked, trying to seem nonchalant.

"He's with Cyril getting snacks for the road trip. You'd think we were driving to Florida with as much as they were talking about getting."

"Great minds think alike."

I tried to think of anything else I might need. We were only going to be in Seattle for a couple days and then head on to the Kingston home for Thanksgiving. I gathered Matilda's bed, food, and a couple toys and couldn't think of anything else to grab. I lifted my bags and headed towards the living room to set everything down. I did a double check that the confirmation for the hotel was in my purse. I heard the keys in the front door, and immediately, my stomach began tumbling at the thought of getting to see Athen in mere seconds. I hoped that feeling never went away. The door flew open, and both Cyril and Athen had bags of food in their hands.

"Holy cow, Arie! You weren't exaggerating!" I saw the tops of several chip bags sticking out of the grocery bags, and what looked like a case of Aquafina under Cyril's arm. "Looks like we'll be set for an eternity."

"Doubtful," Cyril piped up. "This should get us to Seattle though. I'm going to go put some of this in a cooler, and then we should be set to take off. Valet is bringing our car so they will give us a call when it's downstairs."

I couldn't get the smile off of my face. I was looking forward not only to this trip but to the car ride and being in such close quarters with Athen for hours. My day couldn't get any better. The phone rang disrupting my thoughts. Athen grabbed it, and I heard him telling valet we'd be down.

"Ok, everybody got everything?" Athen asked, looking only at me.

"Yep, I think so," I replied, looking over at Arie as she was hooking up Matilda's leash.

"Alright then, I'll grab the bags. Ana, you grab Matilda, and I think we are set." He leaned over and kissed me on my cheek, which got me all flustered yet again.

"Come on, Matilda." I grabbed her leash and out the door we all went.

As the elevator took us down to the lobby, I got more and more excited at the prospect of getting to see where Athen called home. They kept telling me it was my house too, but I didn't quite feel that way yet. Everything was so new, and it was a lot to take in, especially the what's mine is yours aspect.

We all walked over to the Valet desk, and the guy led us out to our car. I wondered which car from their many, we would be piling into. I wasn't disappointed to see Athen's X6 waiting for us. It had 5 seats, which got me that much closer to him regardless of which seat I was sitting in. The trunk opened up with the push of the key, and Cyril began arranging everything making a point to grab the first round of snacks out of the cooler. Matilda looked anxiously as the back filled up more and more. As I was trying to calculate where I would be sitting, I saw Athen tip the valet and wish him Happy Holidays. It must have been generous I thought as I saw the valet light up the way he did. Matilda jumped onto the back seat and planted herself right in the middle so she figured she was set to go.

I noticed Cyril head for the front passenger seat, so I took my cue and crawled in the back next to Matilda. Arie climbed in on the other side. Athen climbed in, and we were off for the day's travel. I knew it would take about 4 hours to drive to Seattle, give or take a little time at the border, and I was determined not to fall asleep. I didn't want to miss any of the trip. As we pulled out of the hotel circle, I noticed a guy sitting on the hotel's bench with a newspaper. Something told me to point him out.

"That would be one of them, Ana. Good eye. Not to worry, though, he is a young one. He would never dare to cross a family full of experience. We call those types posers."

"Glad you are so sure about that," I said to myself, more than anyone in particular. I was sure that creature had made an appearance and disrupted one of my many slumbering nights.

"Are they all over?" I inquired.

"Pretty much. There's a lot of evil in the world. Somebody's gotta keep it going. We have to do our best to stop it. Even the little things can add up. A low ranking one like that dabbles until they become more skilled in manipulation and fighting."

"What do you think that one was doing?" I imagined back to the scenario I encountered with Karen and wondered if it was something like that.

"Hard to tell. If we were close by, we could tell his motive pretty quickly."

"I hope it isn't dire."

"Not to worry, sweetie, very seldom does a newbie like that cause harm of any significance."

"So, when you say he is young, how does that work? Are they not all like us? It seems we've been around a long time, to say the least."

The air began filling in heavy in our little space, but this was something that seemed really important so I pressed on.

"Well?" I asked impatiently.

"It's pretty complex, almost incomprehensible. What I mean by a young demon is one that is newly created," Athen spoke in a low, almost inaudible hush.

I could feel the blood rushing out of my head, and the sickness begin to creep in.

"What do you mean created? You mean like demon possessed?"

"Well, partially. Except, it's one step beyond. When a human is possessed, there's still a chance that we can get them back. When the demon has fully succeeded, the human is no longer possessed, they just are..." He breathed out steadily, looking into my eyes through the rearview.

It hit me, "A demon...the hikers? The snowboarder? That's all related isn't it? What is going on?"

"We don't know yet, but yeah. It appears that's possibly the case."

"Is there no hope for them? Did they really turn into monsters?" My heartbeat slowed. Trying to comprehend the enormity of the situation seemed like an endless task. Am I a monster? I still came to existence in the same fashion as the others. Plus seeing Athen with that demon, who knows how easily swayed we are. Maybe, it's a finer line than any of us know. I trembled a little thinking of it, praying that it was only a figment of my imagination.

"We think they're building a legion. We won't know until we figure out if that's what happened." Cyril turned around to face me. "Whatever is going on isn't typical. We definitely have to keep a pulse on it. That being said, let's try to ensure that you have the best holiday season and get back into the swing of things. Shall we?"

I nodded completely exhausted again. As we turned onto the Sea to Sky highway, I fell asleep almost instantly.

***

We crossed the border into the U.S. fairly seamlessly. The wait was almost non-existent, probably because it was early in the week and in the early afternoon. I rearranged my pillow, trying not to bump into Arie who had immediately fallen back asleep after handing over her passport. I was excited to be heading back to Seattle. It had been a year since I had last been there, and next to Whistler, it was my favorite place. Arie was in dire need of a shopping fix, and I had to admit there were a few stores I wanted to venture into as well. I wanted to make sure to hit Karen's favorite handmade knits boutique.

Athen was glancing at me in the rear view mirror, my eyes catching his. My heart began to sing. There was something so captivating about him. I didn't know if it was the amused expression in his eyes or the ever-constant smirk, but I loved it. I had never experienced so much love before off of one look. I smiled back at him realizing this was what life was about. I couldn't wait to see the house on the water. My body filled with great joy right before falling asleep, dreaming about the wonderful possibilities that were waiting for Athen and I.

I awoke to Cyril teasing Athen about his driving ability in the city, and Arie scowling at the back of Cyril's head. Matilda looked amused at the whole situation, her tongue hanging out and panting up a storm. Even though I had only been awake a few moments, I quickly figured out that they missed the turn into the Westin Hotel's driveway. In this city getting lost in the maze of one-way streets meant doing circles for about 15 minutes. I met Athen's eyes in the rearview mirror, and for the first time ever, I saw a flash of embarrassment bounce off of him.

"It happens to the best of us," I interjected into Cyril's constant stream of jabs. "I think if we turn right at the next light, we should be good and can get into the parking garage."

I looked around the city in awe with how cheerful Seattle was despite the constant grey cloud cover. All of the trees had been decorated with lights and most of the main buildings had Christmas wreaths and decorations up. There was a mist in the air, but it helped Seattle maintain the ever-present coziness that surrounded the city year round. I was looking forward to walking down to the pier, possibly even squeezing in a holiday boat ride. It would be so fun to experience that with Athen. My plan was to treat this city as if I was a tourist, enjoying everything through the eyes of my newfound family. We pulled into the garage and immediately found a parking spot near the elevator. Perfect luck I thought to myself. Maybe, the change of scenery would allow me to forget my nightmares and the heaviness of what I am and should be. It was still hard to believe.

The guys grabbed our bags, and we piled into the elevator that led to the lobby. Matilda sat like a perfect little angel. As we moved up each floor, my excitement built more and more. I couldn't fathom what was in store for me this week. I looked forward to spending the beginning of the holiday season with Athen, Arie, and Cyril, regardless of location. The elevator doors spilled us into a magnificent lobby that already had holiday décor tucked in every crevice. To the right of the elevator were the banquet rooms, and the entire hallway leading to each door was covered with poinsettias and sparkly gold ribbon. To the left was the concierge and front desk with garlands and white lights hung on the cherry wood desk. The most spectacular sight was the large Christmas tree in the sitting area. It was completely blanketed in silver balls, icicles, and streaming silver ribbon woven throughout. Indeed, I would be enjoying the holidays this year. My emotional drought was finally over.

Arie and I went over to sit on the overstuffed couches near the tree to wait for Athen and Cyril to check in. I got very comfy as we heard the Christmas music rolling off of the grand piano in the corner. I was thoroughly enjoying the music and moment, absorbed in my own world, when I saw everyone staring at me - waiting for something. I came back to earth, remembering that I was the one who made the reservations. I hopped up as Athen and Cyril started laughing at me.

"I've got the confirmation number, guys," my voice echoed through the lobby. "Sorry about that."

The staff was wonderfully patient as I dug it out of my purse and slapped it on the counter along with my credit card and id. I noticed the woman who was at the far end of the counter coming down behind the desk pretty fast, which I thought was odd. I looked at her eyes once she was close enough, and I saw the darkness in them, realizing at that moment she was a poser, not a human. She must have been recently changed. Selfishly, I was relieved she wasn't the woman with the serpent eyes waiting to prey on Athen.

Arie told me that the evil ones had an inherent ability to detect when we were around. Often when I was in the village and sensed the uneasy feeling, I asked Athen about my assumptions, and he would affirm my observations. I was shocked to find out that the evil was lurking almost everywhere. I wondered why, back in Whistler, we would go to a coffee shop where apparently there was a presence, and that was when I was told their kind was everywhere. There was no avoiding it, but with that, our kind exists everywhere as well. I simply can't sense them yet. In the beginning of the reintroduction process, it was more important to be aware of the evil, more for self-preservation than anything. Athen assured me that in time I would be able to feel our kind. I hoped that would happen sooner rather than later . That certainly would make me feel better about things. I don't want to think the world is purely evil because right now that is what it feels like, even partly with myself.

We got the three keys for our suite and dispersed back towards the elevator as Athen squeezed my hand and whispered something I almost didn't hear as we climbed in the elevator.

"You were right, Ana. She was a tricky one too. Good job."

I wasn't sure why she would be considered tricky, but I was relieved to hear that maybe I was catching onto things a bit.

"Thanks," I exclaimed, "That makes me feel better. Our eye color certainly is prettier than theirs isn't it?"

"That's for sure," Arie chimed in.

For some reason with the protection of my family, I was not worried. I was beginning to understand the different threats that were lurking. Yet, I was pretty confident that with my family's presence, I would be safe. They seemed overly confident, even though there was a strong presence. I knew I needed to trust their judgment, otherwise I would go completely crazy. As each day went by, since the first night of the reintroduction process, my confidence grew exponentially. I was beginning to enjoy my new-old self.

As the elevator let us out on the 46th floor, I secretly hoped that maybe we wouldn't be using all three bedrooms in the suite. Arie swung open the door revealing a beautiful granite entry hall. The suite was overlooking Seattle with the lights twinkling brightly to welcome us all into our home for the next couple days. Athen flipped on the lights, and I looked around thrilled that the hotel suite was as grand as the lobby. Arie and Cyril claimed their bedroom before I could even find them all, which made me feel extremely uncomfortable as I looked at Athen hoping to judge his next move. I knew that he was probably listening to my thoughts, and I didn't even care. I wanted him to know that I wanted to share a room with him. I could feel myself getting warm, and thankfully, Arie recognized the awkwardness that was radiating from me.

"Come on Athen. Don't make her stand there," she said giggling, as Cyril carted the last bag into their bedroom. Matilda ran and jumped on the couch and made herself at home for the evening. It never took her long.

Athen grabbed my hand and led me around the sitting area to the two back bedrooms. He had my bag in his other hand, and I was anxiously awaiting to see where I landed. There was a door on each side of the flat screen, and I followed Athen into the room on the left. It was an elegant setting with a large goose down comforter spread on the bed with an orange coverlet. The room was very spacious and welcoming. The walls were a soft taupe. Athen placed my bag down at the end of the bed and pulled me closer. I was hoping this is where he would say it, but he didn't. He only shook his head.

"Athen, why not? I know you know what I'm thinking. You make it unbearably hard on me. I don't understand why we can't share the room?" I found myself pleading with him and couldn't understand his reaction.

Could it be her? The serpent-eyed demon flashing through me creating a self-consciousness I couldn't understand. From the short time working at the bar, I knew most guys would be falling over themselves to get into this situation. With Athen, however, who is supposed to be my soul mate, I can't even get him near me. It was hard not to take personally.

"Believe me, sweetie, I want to be with you. It's not the right time. It will all make sense for you when it happens. We can't jeopardize anything. There are a few more memories that need to occur. When those surface it will be the right time. You may not believe it, but this is probably harder on me. I still remember what it was like with you. I have been the one waiting for decades." His green eyes sparkled mischievously. I was instantly calmed. Serpent eyes had no chance. It was only a nightmare.

"Well, I doubt that. Now get out of my room." I threw a pillow at him - proud that I nailed him on his back as he was exiting.

"Get ready for dinner. Arie made reservations at one of her favorite spots. We won't want to keep her waiting," Athen yelled out from his room, and then I heard a tapping on the wall between us.

"Tapping the wall doesn't make you seem closer, Athen," I chirped back laughing.

I began unpacking some of my things, relieved that I had packed an assortment. I knew I had better grab the nicest outfit I put in my bag. Knowing Arie's taste, the place would be at the top of most people's lists. I looked in the mirror over the dresser, still startled at the image staring back at me. I wasn't sure if it was the green eyes that I wasn't used to seeing or my overall appearance. I was beginning to like this aspect of the change. It was hard to remember that I had looked so different. I picked out a simple black dress and a silver scarf to wrap around the top and felt as good as new. I was happy to get the evening started.

The car picked us up for dinner, which made me grateful that everyone was in the mood for a good time. That put me at ease knowing the seriousness of the week before might have been the worst of it, or I hoped it was. We piled into the back, and Arie began eagerly filling me in on the place we were headed, Canlis - a Seattle landmark. However, the conversation quickly turned serious.

"After losing you, Athen was so distraught. We couldn't come up with anything to distract him. The only thing that he looked forward to was the weekly dinner we had at Canlis because you two had been there together right before the incident. He vowed that as soon as you came back to us, we would start the tradition up again."

"Arie, you're making me sound insane." Athen was finally beginning to look a little embarrassed, a sight I didn't think I would see often. "Could you cool it a little bit, sis? We don't need to air out everything do we?"

"I kind of like it," I said, feeling a little in control of Athen's emotions finally. I could feel the blood running through my veins at a pace that was quickened only by the thought of our first encounter. I could hear Arie going on, but I couldn't concentrate on what she was talking about. I was getting a set of new images that I knew were a part of my past, and all I wanted to do was eat up every second. I saw Athen walk by me heading toward a lake. He didn't seem to recognize me. I got up from where I was sitting and followed him. I could feel the same excitement level that I feel now from being around him. He stopped on the trail to the lake, turning around only to smile at me, which stopped me in my tracks – exactly like at the pub. Another image flashed in my head of us together, wrapped in a blanket. I could feel the warmth of his skin, and the electricity coming from him. If only I could remember what led us to be in that position. His lips gliding down my neck towards my breast.

"Ana, are you okay?" Arie tapped me on my arm.

"Oh, yeah. Fine...Beginning to remember things," I said, feeling a bit sheepish.

"She sure is." Athen couldn't contain himself. He, of course, had to rub it in. His smile was so enduring that I let him get away with it. As long as he had that smile, it didn't matter what he said or that he kept eavesdropping into my thoughts. I was thankful it was only him who knew what I was thinking of though.

"Hey, was that good enough for you, Athen?" I whispered jokingly.

"You know it. We are getting closer, sweetheart. Not quite there yet." His grin was huge now. I knew what he was waiting for. I hoped it would happen sooner rather than later.

Our car pulled up to Valet to let us out, and we hurried inside to meet the roaring fire that awaited us. The restaurant was filled with a warm glow throughout. The lobby had a huge stone entryway and an imposing fireplace with people sitting and chatting as they awaited their seats, poinsettias lurking in every corner. There were stairs leading up to what I was guessing was private dining. I saw the lounge a few steps down. Familiar Christmas music was rolling through the air from the pianist. Arie was right. I couldn't think of a more perfect setting for our first Seattle meal.

"I'm amazed that this restaurant has been here long enough to have been in existence while I was still around the last time." I mused aloud.

"Yeah, this place is pretty incredible. It's still family owned and manages to keep the warmth and amazing menu year after year," Cyril piped in. He excused himself and went to check us in.

I looked around, thankful I had dressed up a bit. I scanned Athen and loved how great he looked in a jacket. He couldn't get it wrong. I hadn't seen him this dressed up yet. It was pretty impressive. The hostess led us to our table right by the window, overlooking the water. The view was enthralling with the twinkling lights out in the distance, as boats began making their way back to the docks for the evening.

As we were getting situated at the table, I noticed how busy the restaurant was, especially for a weeknight. There were many couples sprinkled throughout at the different tables, but the large tables seemed to be filled with mostly executives, who, I could only assume, were trying to impress their respective clients. Too bad they weren't here with their families, I thought to myself. The corporate world seemed so cold. In the far corner of the lounge, I was able to see the top of the Christmas tree peeking over, looking absolutely magical. I could tell that celebrating the holidays with my family was going to be magnificent.

"So guys, after recognizing the other type today in the hotel lobby at the counter, it made me realize how many questions I still had about this." I scanned Cyril, Arie, and Athen's face for some sign of resistance, and I saw none so I decided to keep on going. "I noticed that in the village you all were very protective of me. Was it the type that was up there versus down here?"

Athen grabbed my hand under the table, which I appreciated, and Arie began to fill me in as cryptically as she could without letting any of the neighboring tables overhear.

"Yes, in the village we were extremely protective of you because before your phasing began, you were very vulnerable. We were all so worried that we could lose you again before you had been reintroduced. Once that part was over, we were able to relax a little. There still a chance that a more developed one could still interfere with the process we've begun with you, so we'll continue to keep an eye out for sure," Arie said, winking at me trying to lighten the mood I assumed.

"So the one at the hotel front counter, why did I not feel threatened or worried?" I asked Athen.

"Many of them have their own agendas and are preoccupied with whatever they're set on. They could care less about us. Some, like the ones in the village, were most likely summoned to you by who we don't know yet, but it definitely lets us know to be fully aware while we are in Seattle. There is a directive on you possibly. We need to make sure that we are always with you in some capacity until it's over, or your process has finished. The one at the counter, however, clearly had no interest in you and is probably interested in turning tourists into minions or some such disgusting thing."

"Huh." I sighed on the verge of being more confused now than before I asked the question. "In the village then, you think they were summoned? Why would I be of so much interest to anyone or thing? I don't understand that part."

"As a family, we can do a lot of damage. Back in Whistler, we mentioned that we chose to be good. What we mean by that is that we truly fight for the good of humankind. If a demon is there to taunt a human, we try to step in to show the human the other side, the other choice. However, when one of our family members isn't with us, we spend our time trying to get them back. We are distracted, which is exactly what the other side likes to see, right? They don't want us to be able to step in with the human world. They want to keep us chasing after our loved ones so they can continue to damage humanity. Make a little more sense now?" Cyril chided.

"Oooh, it does. I never expected to hear that there was this level of good and evil playing in the world all the time that wasn't even remotely controlled by humans."

"If one of them had gotten to me before I phased, what would have happened?" I asked, afraid to hear the answer.

"We would have lost you again. You would never have remembered meeting us in the pub that night. We would have been wiped from your memory once more. You may have had to even start over in a new city. It just depends... Until the timing was right, and the process could begin again. Then hoping that you would sense us," Athen said in an almost whisper.

I looked up at him and caught that his eyes were brimming as were Arie and Cyril's. I quickly grabbed my napkin from my lap and started dabbing what was inevitably about to come pouring from my lids as well.

"Thanks for not telling me until now, guys," I uttered lowly, " I don't think I could have handled that too."

"We know, sweetie." Athen squeezed my hand once again under the table.

I don't think I was ever this excited to see a salad show up in my lifetime. The server began placing them in front of us. I think that was definitely all of the serious talk I could handle for the night. It would take me a while to recover from this bizarre world that I was reentering into. An underworld that wasn't completely mine for the taking. I needed to take small, baby steps.

A chill ran through me, and everyone at the table sensed it. I was having some sort of flashback. It was déjà vu. Athen and I were at this very restaurant sitting at a table that was set for two, placed directly in front of the window with both chairs facing the view. It suddenly occurred to me why Athen loved this restaurant so much. It was the last place we were together before the attack, literally.

All of a sudden, the salad that I was so excited about seconds ago didn't seem so appealing. The level of emotions that kept creeping up on me were overwhelming. I quickly excused myself to freshen up in the Ladies Room. I needed to regain some sort of composure. I quickly made my way through the lounge, moving through the crowd of people and up the stairs where I found the right door. I beelined right to the sink and reminisced back to the night at the Pub in Whistler when I first laid eyes on Arie and Cyril. Never would I have expected in such a short time to have my world flipped upside down. I hoped that I could handle this process. I took deep breaths hoping to fill the void in my chest that wasn't caused from lack of oxygen. As the faucet produced the constant stream of warm water, I glanced up at the mirror expecting to see the same disheveled face looking back at me as was in the pub. Instead, I saw a woman who was nothing like that night. My hair fell past my shoulders gracefully, framing my face in a softer way. Even though my eyes had been rimmed with tears several times tonight, they were beaming with a radiance and beauty that was no longer of this world. I turned the faucet off, finding myself sitting on the chaise to compose myself, slowly forcing myself to fall back into the happiness of being with my family. I took a deep breath in and began feeling Arie's energy winding its way towards me. I decided to step up the recovery process and cut her off at the door to avoid any more emotional elements thrown at me.

I swung the door open, barely missing her, and fully embraced Arie. We headed back to the table, and as we passed by the piano, one of my favorite songs came rolling off the piano.

"Wow, he certainly pays attention doesn't he, Arie?"

"He certainly does, sweetie. He requested it as soon as you left the table. *Cosmic Love* certainly is an ethereal song, huh? Who knew it came over the same on piano?" she said laughing as we sat back down at our table, rolling her eyes.

"Yeah, pretty fitting. I loved playing this song while Matilda and I were snuggling on the couch daydreaming. Florence and the Machine is pretty incredible."

I looked over at Athen thanking the heavens that everything was as it was. Like usual, my appetite didn't miss a beat. I began devouring my salad, much to everyone's amazement.

"I know what I have been meaning to ask you!" I couldn't believe I hadn't remembered to ask sooner. "When I was on the phone with Karen, I kept getting this needle-poking sensation run through my fingers. Then in person it happened ten times as bad. I knew out of the blue that she was up to something, and an image of a guy, who wasn't Justin, texting her popped into my head. I gave her my two cents immediately. She supposedly didn't continue down that path. Regardless, though, were the feelings that I kept getting connected to the behavior that she was exhibiting, or the choice she was about to make?"

"Wow, Ana. It usually takes months before any sort of feeling like that comes back. Maybe, it was because you were so connected to her prior to your reintroduction process. I think you intervened in a situation, helping her to choose the correct path. I'm amazed that you recognized that so early." Athen looked truly impressed and kind of proud.

"Yeah, Ana, that is pretty big. Soon, we'll get back to doing what we do best. I'm so proud of you. I can't believe you already experienced the visions too. To be able to see something as it's happening is huge. That's an important attribute. That is one of your gifts, Ana."

"Really? Thanks, I guess, but will I always feel the level of pain when I'm alerted to something that is about to take place?"

"Oh, heavens no. That is only in the beginning until your body can sense the nuances a bit more," Athen said laughing. "We aren't sadists."

"When you say I'm able to have premonitions or visions of the future, how will I know what is real and what is not? If I can see things as they're now, and also into the future, how can I tell the difference?" I asked Arie, avoiding Athen's eyes. I was determined not to give anything away or let my thoughts betray me.

"What do you mean?" Arie asked confused.

"Well, the nightmares I have been having for the last few months... How do I know those are only nightmares and not premonitions or vice versa?"

"As time goes on, you'll be able to distinguish the difference. Often as long as you don't recognize people or anything, you can just count on it being a normal dream. You know it's your mind trying to sort out the day's events or something. I would imagine if certain players kept entering your dreams, you would be able to conclude that those were visions instead."

I felt an emptiness.

"Huh, not quite as straightforward as I was hoping. For instance, that demon we saw on the way out of Whistler was a creature I had recognized from one of my nightmares. It wasn't good. It was part of a group. I don't remember what they were doing though." I was lying. They were with the hikers.

"My hunch is that it's a vision, Ana. If, as time goes on, you can remember what it is they were doing, it could prove really helpful. Baby steps, I know. But things will come - clarity will come." Athen touched my hand gently, the guilt filling my heart instantly for not telling him everything that very moment. It was too painful and would lead to me explaining all of my nightmares. I wasn't ready for that. I was afraid if I uttered anything out loud, it might make it true.

"I'll keep trying," I said, attempting to push the images of Athen's soul escaping into the clouds out of my head. I couldn't let him see that. I'm sure it wasn't a vision, only my imagination.

"The good news is that you have saved a lot of people with those visions of yours over the centuries. You have helped a lot of horrible decisions from ever being made. You'll see. Good will come of it all. I promise. Right now it's just a bit overwhelming trying to separate the truth from fiction, I'd imagine." He winked at me. I knew he was right. The possibilities were endless. I only hoped I would figure it out soon enough.

I felt immensely better, beginning to let the excitement build back up in every cell of my body as I thought about the good that I could do in the world once I got the hang of things.

"So what are the plans for tomorrow?" I inquired almost afraid to hear what Arie may have planned for such a short amount of time.

"Waterfront and shopping!" Arie exclaimed, my worries quickly drifting away as I enveloped myself in the warmth of my family.

CHAPTER 18

The sun woke me up before my alarm clock even rang, a strange sight for November in Seattle. Fortunately, Seattle was a dog friendly city. No way would Matilda want to be left in the hotel room all day. She's got places to see and sidewalks to explore. I grabbed the remote for the curtains, pressing the button commanding the sheer curtains to open up. I continued to lay in bed thinking back to the night before, reflecting about how many answers lead to more questions.

I was relieved I had a night full of blissful dreams, not the nightmares that I usually expected. One dream in particular that made me happiest of all was Athen cradling me tightly. We had just made love. We were on the beach. I could still feel his skin against mine. The cool dampness that was connecting our bodies was heavenly. I was in heaven. I only hoped that a new pattern of dreaming was emerging, more positive and less creepy. The dream was so vivid, and I could feel his every touch as he embraced me. That was my first dream of its kind. I couldn't wait for another. Being patient wasn't my best quality. I breathed in desperately, hoping to have the salty air from my dream run through me one last time before getting up.

I was listening intently for movement in the rest of the hotel suite so I didn't get out of bed too early; when all of a sudden, my bedroom door swung open to reveal Athen standing with a non-fat pumpkin spice latte from Starbucks in one hand and a Top Pot donut in the other.

"My word! You can't get any closer to perfection can you?" I asked, feeling the smile on my face unable to evaporate. Everyday Athen got kinder than the last, and I didn't even think that was possible. I sat up in my bed, secretly wishing I wasn't wearing the black t-shirt that Cyril bought me as a gift that read, "I DO ALL MY OWN STUNTS" blazing across the front with a stick figure biting the dust. I started to pat my hair down and then realized it was hopeless. It wasn't like anything was bound to happen at this rate anyhow, so I gave up.

"Hey now," Athen said laughing.

"For heaven's sake, that can be annoying. It will be nice when this whole mind reading thing doesn't happen all the time," I scolded him, grabbing my Top Pot donut.

"When did you get up? I thought I would have heard you."

"I wanted to surprise you, so I was pretty quiet. I'm glad it worked. I have a feeling with Arie in charge today, there'll be very little time to grab anything to eat. We should get what we can now." His beautiful eyes bringing me back to my wonderful dream from the night before.

"Are you kidding? Is she that serious about it?"

"Pretty much. We go along for the ride and try to help her carry her bags. That's about it."

"I hope Matilda can keep up." I looked over at Matilda who had a worried look in her big, brown eyes. She was a fit bulldog but, nonetheless, still a bulldog.

"I had a pretty incredible dream last night you know?" I teased him as best I could. "It almost seemed real. Maybe I just wanted it to be." My voice trailing and my grin unable to be hidden.

"Is that so?" Athen said, grabbing and holding me tightly against his chest. "Wanna share any details?" he asked gently, hugging my body back and forth with his.

Athen lifting me up and gently placing me on a boulder near the sea raced into my mind. He was frantically undressing me, as our lips became connected driving us both into a madness we had been without far too long.

"Absolutely not," I said, staring into his eyes. "Since you won't give me the real thing, I'm not going to give you the satisfaction of hearing the fun stuff I've got going on up here," I said, pointing to my temple, doing a double tap with my index finger.

"Fair enough." He kissed me on my forehead.

"Can't wait for the real thing though."

"Yeah, well, I'm barely able to look at you, let alone touch you at this point, sweetie, but it's the way it's got to be. You'll see."

I began hearing the others shuffling around in their room. I knew I'd better enjoy my donut pretty quickly, so I could hop in the shower to get ready for the day.

By the time we had made it downstairs to hit the streets of Seattle, it was about 10 am, which in Arie's mind was perfect timing, since that was when most of the shops opened up. The fog started to lift down the streets of Seattle allowing all of the Christmas decorations to be exposed on the lampposts. I had made clear the stores I needed to visit, Nordstrom's being first on the list. Much to my amazement, every store I had listed she, also, had planned on going to, plus some. It looked like today would be a whirlwind. Arie was a true shopper. Maybe, if I was lucky, she would want to keep on going, and Athen and I could sneak back to the hotel with Matilda or because of Matilda.

The streets were hustling with the typical business people, rushing off to who knows where, thinking things were far more important than they were, while in stark contrast witnessing the families who must have taken the holiday week off to be together. It was a truly friendly sight. All of the wreaths and holiday swags hung from building to building, hanging above the streets, creating a ceiling along 5th Avenue. The red, velvet ribbons were gently flapping in the light breeze reminding me how I was glad to have my jacket for the day's adventures. I began to get a little flutter in my stomach at the thought of beginning the holiday shopping experience with my family. Matilda began pulling on the leash in the direction of Nordstrom's and off we went. I was looking forward to seeing the holiday window displays there. They were always impressive. Seattle was known for great ones, but Nordstrom's really outdid the rest. The goal was to all take turns, since we were buying for each other, and stand post with Matilda outside each of the stores. So far, it had worked wonderfully.

***

We began hearing chatter that snow might come down to the lowlands, which made me think this might be the perfect time to head back to the hotel with Matilda and Athen. It was close to 5 pm, and the day had flown by so quickly with the guys taking turns watching Matilda as Arie and I went from store to store. I had gotten into the holiday spirit completely. I was thrilled to be marching through the aisles of scarves, knit caps, and gloves with the Christmas music serenading me throughout each department. I was beginning to realize how fun the holidays were. People were more relaxed, more kind and willing to chat a little longer. It made every environment a little bit more festive. I thought I had no more strength in my arms to carry the bags that I had accumulated and desperately needed to find the nearest Starbucks to crash. I explained my dilemma to Arie, and she completely understood. However, she wasn't planning on stopping. She apparently had several more stores on her list so Athen and I decided to head back to the hotel. My master plan was happening - alone time with Athen. As I hugged Arie goodbye, she whispered to me to ask Athen what he had planned for us tonight.

I looked over at Athen. He looked so innocent and casual. I wondered what he had up his sleeve this time. He grabbed my hand to prepare for the long walk back to the Westin; Matilda pulling us along excitedly. Athen's warmth was reaching me through his coat. I was elated to be next to him enjoying this experience. My thoughts were few as I enjoyed the moment until the words White Christmas came into my head. That was odd, I thought. That was one of my all time favorite Christmas movies, along with National Lampoon's Christmas Vacation and a

Christmas Story, but I wondered why White Christmas popped in. Before I knew it, I was humming White Christmas aloud.

He looked at me smiling with a contentment that made me realize something happened that he was hoping for. I'm sure it was another step in the infamous process. I didn't know the significance.

"You read my mind, Ana! It is starting to come to you slowly."

"What is?" I asked, not exactly sure what he was talking about.

He stopped on the sidewalk and hugged me while Matilda patiently waited for us to continue our march.

"I kept repeating White Christmas in my head hoping you would pick up on it. You did. Soon you'll be able to do that on more complete thoughts, and eventually, you'll be able separate ideas from many thoughts. Also, I know it's one of your favorites, and the 5th Avenue has a performance of White Christmas which we are going to tonight." I hoped I could someday repay him the happiness that he gave me daily. How could I ever thank him enough? His surprises were endless.

I squealed, dropping my bags. I jumped up grabbing him as hard as I could.

"Thank you so much. This day keeps getting better," I whispered in his ear. I didn't want to let go. I closed my eyes with happiness as he kissed my neck, only to see the serpent's eyes staring back at me smiling, as if he was kissing her.

CHAPTER 19

The moment had finally arrived! We were sitting in line at the ferry dock in Edmonds on our way to Kingston. We had arrived early since we had to pick up our turkey and ham that Arie had ordered from her favorite area meat shop, Bill the Butcher. They had, also, promised me that we would go extra early to walk around Edmonds before boarding the ferry. I was not disappointed. Edmonds was so cute. There were quaint little boutiques and antique shops with great cafes on every corner. I knew wholeheartedly that this would become a tradition before boarding the ferry to our home. I hadn't told them that news yet. I was finally able to think those words, our home. I hadn't been able to say the words aloud yet, but I could somewhat think them. The ferry worker began pointing at the lines of cars, directing us to inch forward to the loading dock. I hadn't been on a ferry for so long that I looked forward to it. Athen said it was a short ferry ride, but I was excited regardless. It would be a delightful trip, even with the fog that hovered thickly in the air.

Athen was following the ferry worker's direction as he pulled into the line on the second deck. He nudged as close to the car in front of us as possible so we didn't get a scolding from the ferry workers. My fingers started tingling. I couldn't wait to jump out of the car. I found my seat buckle and quickly unclipped it. I looked over at Cyril and Arie and noticed they weren't unfastening their belts.

"Are you guys staying in the car?" I pestered the group.

"Yeah, we've been on this a million times. Besides, the ride is over before you know it." Arie promised.

I wasn't going to take her word for it and hopped out of the car, kind of stunned that they would take this trip for granted, no matter how quick. Athen opened the front driver's door and climbed out. I was secretly relieved that it might be us two anyway. We snuck through the cars that were lined up in the tightly organized rows with only enough room to squeeze by. I followed Athen's trail and saw him heading towards the tiny, little doorway that led to the staircase. I saw the red life rings placed on the metal walls as I headed toward the stair well. Athen got there first, grabbing my waist quickly as he brought me towards him. I noticed that most everyone seemed to be staying in their cars. It wasn't only my carload of fuddy duds, at least. I reached for Athen's hand and instantly began to melt. The slight sound of the ferry churned through me as it began its journey across the sparkling Sound. The breeze began to make its way through the metal tunnels sending a shiver through me. The closeness was overwhelming.

As I touched Athen's hand, he whisked me into the base of the stairwell and fully wrapped his arms around me. I gazed up into Athen's eyes as he was looking out over the sound. His lustrous, green eyes taking everything in that he scanned. I sensed a distraction. He always had such an intensity surrounding him. That was a given. But I couldn't put my finger on what was causing it this time. I tried not to dwell on the feeling, and before I knew it, I could feel his breath on my neck as he grabbed my waist closer to his. Suddenly his lips were touching my skin, gliding over my lips, to my neck, and then collarbone. My heart began pounding as the electrical currents began chasing through my veins. All my worries from the moment before began to drift away. The excitement of the moment almost made it unbearable to stay standing, which I think he sensed as he lifted me up against the stair railing. The coldness of the metal walls shot through my clothing chilling me. I didn't mind one bit. It reminded me that this moment was indeed real.

To be in this moment with Athen, feeling his grasp around me as our lips touched each others, made my new world feel as if it was one big fantasy. I did not want to do anything to wake up from it. I wasn't sure what all we could pull off in a stairwell, but I was thrilled to find out. I wrapped my legs around him. Beginning to unfasten his buckle when his hand gently covered mine and held me back. The images of us together on the beach were flooding through me. I couldn't handle not being with him.

"Now's not the time, my love," he whispered softly in my ear. "We are almost to the dock."

"Please, tell me you are joking!" I glared at him but couldn't for a minute be upset with him.

He was laughing pretty hard by this time. I rolled my eyes as he helped me off the railing. The door at the top of the stairs opened bringing down a gentleman with a newspaper, probably a nightly commuter, but then I saw his fingernails. They were long and dark like the ones from the other night. I could feel myself freeze in place. I knew I had to act my hardest to show nothing was wrong. I still had no idea whether or not demons could read my mind as much as my family could.

"Well, that could have been embarrassing," I sighed to Athen.

"That's an understatement," Athen quickly shook his head, "I've got to watch myself with you."

Even though I had missed most of the ferry ride and the scenery it had to offer, I wasn't the least bit concerned because I knew in my heart that I would be traveling this route many times to come. Athen and I both situated ourselves back in the car, trying to act nonchalant as ever.

"The guy walking down the stairs on the ferry, where was he going? He didn't seem interested in me. What's up with him?" I asked.

"We took care of him before you got back to the car, Ana." Cyril sounded very serious and a bit distant.

"Can you give me a little more than that?" I asked a bit baffled.

"There was an Escalade about four cars behind ours, and that is where he was headed," Arie spoke up.

"Ok?" I asked, not letting up.

"Well, there was a man in the car, and his secretary was with him. They were on the way to his family home for Thanksgiving. Her family is on the east coast. Let's just say he had thoughts that were not in his family's best interest." Cyril let out slowly.

"He was going to cheat with his secretary on the ferry before going to his house where his wife and children wait? That is cold," I sighed.

"Yeah, it's pretty pathetic but not uncommon," Athen replied.

"Well, how did you guys stop it or dissolve the situation? Was that guy on the stairs involved?"

"Oh, most certainly, he was involved. He was the demon who had inserted the idea into the man's head while he sat above his Escalade on the ferry deck. The demon literally implanted the idea. The guy was beginning to act on the idea that was planted. He began by merely touching his secretary's leg. Then he abruptly stopped. The demon could sense interference so that is when he came down the stairs to see essentially what the problem was. It turned out that Arie was the problem." Cyril announced proudly. "Arie had collected images of his wife on their honeymoon and of her comforting him when he lost his mother and implanted those images of love and purity in his head as she walked by the Escalade. Her hope was that the good in him would see what he would be jeopardizing back at home before the demon could get to him to seal the deal so to speak. It was about the only way Arie could handle it without causing a commotion with the demon. Thankfully, the victim was a nice human who had a momentary lapse of judgment and was easily swayed."

"My word. That's intense. I had no idea we could change people's minds. I thought it was only us giving our opinions," I said in awe.

"Actually, it's not that we can change their minds. Humans are still independent beings, which is why sometimes the other side is the victor. It's that we can tap into their soul, in a sense, and try to guide them before they make the wrong choice. It's all about choices. They're still free beings. They could always choose the other side if the demons are more persuasive. Sometimes, it's as simple as the human making so many wrong choices that they feel that is the only option they have at that point. That is when the task gets far more difficult. We are always up for the challenge though," Arie said, trying to sound as light as she usually does.

"Interesting, I certainly hope I can excel at that one day." A sense of pride was swelling up in me realizing that I may have a chance to help someone choose goodness over evil.

"Will we ever know what happened to the hikers and the snowboarder?" I couldn't shake the thought of so many people all at once not only running into trouble but turning into something so evil. There had to be more to the story.

"Yeah, we'll know soon enough. It always comes out." Arie looked out the window as she spoke.

The rest of the ride home in the car took on a much more enchanting turn as we all tried to play catch up on memories I didn't quite have yet. I learned about a trip to Alaska where I thoroughly enjoyed a place called the Red Dog Saloon, which with a name like that I wanted proof. They guaranteed some.

As we pulled up to their home, I could see why they loved living down here. The home was sprawling. We drove up to it, and I was able to see that the home was perched on the bluff overlooking the Sound. It was most likely one of the homes I spied as we were sitting on the ferry. The home and view were beyond breathtaking. The architecture was very Northwest. Exposed beams and stonework were surrounding the home. There was a porch wrapping around the entire front of the house. I wouldn't be surprised if it wasn't wrapping the back to take advantage of the gorgeous view of the sound. From where we were, it almost looked like there was beach access as well. What a wonderful place to spend the holidays, I thought to myself.

Before I knew it, we pulled into the garage; three beautiful cars were parked in the other stalls. Quite a collection, I thought to myself. Then I noticed an orange Lotus, my favorite, not quite a practical snow car though.

"Nice, Lotus." I said, as we began piling out of the car.

"Thanks," Athen said, "I bought that last year for you. We'll be sure to hop in it before we leave."

"I don't think it holds much so don't go any place where you plan on bringing back any bags," Arie said. Her mind did seem to be on shopping quite a lot. I wonder if she ever got bored of it.

"No, she never gets bored of shopping." Athen, of course, answered my question.

"Wow, still not used to you doing that." I looked at him a little incredulous.

"You know, we can teach you how to avoid that, Ana. I'll make sure to do that before the holidays are up so you don't run away screaming from here," Arie said laughing.

"Thanks, I'd appreciate that."

The guys had finished grabbing our bags out of the back, and I tried to snag some of my shopping bags. I got the hint that presents were a pretty big part of the holidays, especially with Arie, so I did my best. I was hoping I'd gotten in the realm of her tastes. I peeked into the car, and Matilda was still sleeping. She didn't look like she wanted to move, but I knew I had to wake her up. She needed to venture inside to her next nesting spot.

"Come on, Matilda. I got ya." I gently picked her up, setting her on the garage floor, which was quite shiny, especially for a garage floor. She slowly began stretching, looking around before she began to move.

"What the heck is on the concrete that makes it shiny?" I asked.

"Oh, that was Athen and Cyril all the way. When we were having the house built, they demanded that we get the special coating so they could spray out the garage. Not that they have ever done that, of course." Arie tried to express exasperation, but it backfired, only showing off how fond of Cyril she truly was.

Matilda slowly made her way to the open door, leading us all into the home. I was nervous and excited to see what this home looked like on the inside. The outside was impressive and gorgeous, and I imagined the inside to be as grand. I could easily get used to this, I thought to myself.

I walked up a couple of stairs as I made my way in. It looked like I had landed in the mudroom. There were racks from floor to ceiling with canned goods. On the other side of the room was a bench with shelves next to it with shoes and coats. There was also a pile of dog beds and towels. The room was very spacious for being a mudroom. I wondered how big the other rooms were.

"You guys have a dog too?" I asked.

"No, those were for Matilda. We were expecting her and, of course, you."

"Ah, of course," I replied, too familiar with mind reading incidents to be surprised. "I'm going to leave some bags right here because my hands are tired. I'll come back and get them."

"Sure. I think I will too," Arie said, dumping her heaviest bags.

I continued walking through the mudroom, making my way into the kitchen, which was incredible. There were windows along one entire wall that overlooked the Sound from what I could tell, since it was evening, but I was able to see little lights off in the distance, along with what I think were ferry lights chugging away. The counters were all a dark granite with a beautiful, stone backsplash. There was a huge island that, alone, displayed more counter space than my entire kitchen up in Whistler. The refrigerator was enormous, but with Cyril and Athen around, I knew that was a must. The tones were all complimentary earth shades, but I could imagine how spectacular it was once it was daylight, and the green from everything outside would create a masterpiece in itself. Right past the breakfast bar, I saw the beginning to what I guessed was the family room. There was a huge, stone fireplace that went all the way up to the extraordinarily high ceiling, and on either side were more floor-to-ceiling windows. I couldn't imagine what this place looked like in the daylight if it was this captivating in the evening.

"Wow! Guys, this is incredible!" I exclaimed. I couldn't keep my awe inside anymore.

"I'm glad you like it. We got spoiled with the views, for sure. Hopefully, you'll like the room we picked out for you. We have two. I think you might like one more than the other. Feel free to let us know," she said with a smirk.

"Ok," I said, tentatively knowing that even the couch would be fine. "I know I'll love anything."

Matilda walked around like she owned the place and immediately started eyeing the couch in the family room. Although, I even had to admit that it looked pretty comfortable, especially after all of the travel. The overstuffed, red pillows that were tossed on it looked right up Matilda's alley. I kept following Arie as we made it through the family room and down a hallway, which led us to the stairs. I looked up and saw Athen coming down the stairs smiling. My God, he looked good. Great, and he probably heard that too. My cheeks did the scarlet turn, and he looked down at me and winked.

"I'm going to go grab your bags you left in the mud room. I'll be right up."

"Well, thanks. That's sweet of you."

"Of course," he said and pecked me on the cheek. "No sweat at all."

I heard Arie groan as Cyril appeared right behind us with her bags in hand. Arie seemed relieved that she wouldn't have to haul all of her bags up the stairs.

"I got 'em, honey. Once again, I beat the slacker Athen, but I'll go put them in the closet."

I walked up the stairs following Arie. Once we got to the top landing, more windows overlooked the Sound. In front of the windows a sleek, black velvet chaise was sitting. I'm sure that would become a favorite spot for Matilda. I wasn't sure which direction to go because there was a hallway in both directions. They both looked pretty long. Arie grabbed my hand and pulled me in the right direction.

"Ok, so Athen's wing is down this way along with one of the guest rooms. The other guest room is on our end, which is why I'm betting this one will be your favorite," she said laughing.

As we ventured down the hallway, she pointed out the linen closet, laundry room, a game room – which looked huge, a media room that had the large recliners, and what looked like a drop-down screen, and then a jaw-dropping bathroom that was pale blue with white marble and a claw-foot tub. It looked pretty fitting for being next to the ocean.

"Is that the bathroom I'll be using?"

"Well it can be, but you have one connected to your room. All the bedrooms here are like master suites, which is kind of nice. No sharing that way if we have guests."

"Do you have guests often?" I asked, realizing how nosey and almost worried I must have sounded. I was thinking of Athen with a guest, which sent shudders down me, a streak of jealously entered next. Then the woman with the serpent eyes entered my thoughts. Nausea was next.

"No, not really, but we do get them from time to time," she picked up on my worry and replied. "And not those kind of guests, Ana. He has only eyes for you. Has had forever. You will figure that out in time. I promise! We would usually get a family who was looking for a loved one themselves, just in transition from one place to the next really."

I tried to diminish the foolishness that was welling up especially in light of everything I had been told and witnessed in this short time, but being that everything was so new, it was still hard to believe. Once I could wrap my head around everything, it certainly would make it easier. I was getting tired of continually pinching myself and doubting everything.

"So, here is your room." She opened the door and flipped on the lights.

The large bedroom was a welcoming space. I couldn't have picked it out better if I had decorated it. The bed was right in the center of the wall between two windows that each had a window seat with pillows thrown all over. The walls were a brilliant pearl white, the curtains were a warm sage color, with flecks of color woven throughout. The comforter was white, but it had a coverlet draped across in the same hues as the curtains. It reminded me of the boulders up in Whistler. The bedside tables had an assortment of books on them. There was a sitting area that had French doors which led outside – possibly another water view.

"Holy smokes! This is mind blowing."

Athen walked in with my bags. "Wait until you see where those French doors lead."

I looked at him a bit confused, but my interest became quite peaked.

"Alright, I'm out," Arie hollered. "Time for me to freshen up after the drive."

I walked over to the other set of closed doors. One was the walk-in closet, which was huge and definitely highlighted that I didn't have nearly enough clothes to fill it. The second door led to the bathroom. Arie was right. It didn't disappoint and would be perfect. It, too, had a claw foot tub, displaying a perfect place for me to relax, especially after the horror filled nights I sometimes encountered.

"Ok, enough ogling at the bathroom. I want you to check out the deck."

Athen grabbed my arm, whisking me to the French doors. He flipped on the patio light and opened up the doors fully. I couldn't fathom what was making him so excited about this deck until we stepped out. It was wonderful, no doubt about that. I guess it worked in the winter since it was all under cover, but it seemed kind of cold for this time of year. The furniture was very pretty. Again, I didn't see any source of heat. I couldn't see because of the darkness, but I was guessing Puget Sound was off in the distance. But then I saw another set of French doors leading to Athen's bedroom. I realized that was what all the excitement was about. He pulled me to the other set of French doors, my stomach started to do flips. I felt a wave of excitement crashing into me. I had no idea why. It wasn't like anything was going to happen tonight. It never did. For crying out loud, I have my own room! It seemed like anything that had to do with one more part of exploring his life made me want to explode from the inside out.

He opened the doors, showing off a beautiful setting that I longed to be in, make mine. The light glowed out from the room and begged for me to enter. He stepped over the door and pulled me in. The layout was similar to my room, but the sitting area was larger. There were many framed pictures placed on the different pieces of furniture. I took a deep breath, secretly hoping I could possibly become that much closer to Athen by inhaling his personal space. In doing so, a wonderful woodsy scent crept through me. I suddenly knew this smell had always been with me. Athen had always been with me.

I tried to skim over looking at the bed. It was calling out to me. The goose-down comforter happened to look a little fluffier than mine or that was what I told myself. I saw a large, flat screen over his dresser, and in the far corner, I saw a fireplace with the same stone that I saw surrounding the fireplace in the family room.

"So, what do you think?"

"About which part?" I asked.

"The patio," Athen replied.

"Yeah, it's a pretty great.... The proximity and all. Pretty good thing," I said, shaking my head in approval.

"You are horrible at acting disinterested," Athen chided. Before I knew what was happening, Athen had wrapped his arms around my waist and effortlessly wrestled me to the bed.

CHAPTER 20

It was close to dinnertime, and Athen and I had been on his bed for who knows how long purely talking. I didn't want it to end, but I knew Arie would be excited to go out to dinner as a group. It would be nice to have dinner with everyone. Athen had rolled onto his back, and I nestled onto his chest for just a little longer.

"So how long would you have waited?" I asked.

"As long as it took. You are the only person for me. I would have thought you would have guessed it by now," he murmured, caressing my hair.

"Actually, I just like hearing it," I told him changing my gaze to meet his, not wanting to divulge my other reason for needing to hear it, "Even with everything, I still love to hear it."

I climbed on top of him, kissing him realizing that dinner could wait. I was hoping that this was what he had been waiting for, coming back to Kingston. I didn't think I could wait any longer. He began kissing me back as intently as I had begun. I made a promise that one way or another after tonight, we would be connected in all elements. His hands begin to linger over every inch of my body as he held me.

"Guys?" I couldn't believe what I was hearing. My body slumped on to Athen's. Arie's voice came ringing down the hall. Curse her, I thought and Athen started laughing.

"I guess you can hear what I'm thinking still, huh?"

"No, not this time. I was kind of thinking the same thing."

I crawled off of Athen grudgingly, but I knew we would get this time back again. It would only be a little later. I couldn't disappoint Arie.

"Hey, Arie," Athen and I yelled back in unison.

"Can we go get our tree before the lot closes down for the night? I kind of planned on it so we wouldn't lose any time for the holidays. There's a lot of things we have to do, in addition, like decorate the house, make cookies, you name it basically." Arie's voice was so excited and panicked; it would have been a form of torture for us not to comply. She opened the door as Athen grabbed his jacket that had fallen onto the floor, glaring back at her a bit.

"Oh sorry, oh geez, oh man. I'm so sorry." Arie looked truly mortified.

I jumped up and shook her lightly. "There's nothing to be sorry about. Let's get going."

***

We all piled into the Jeep while Athen grabbed some rope from one of the meticulously organized shelves in the garage to tie the Christmas tree to the top. I had buckled my seatbelt when Athen climbed in next to me, giving me a huge kiss, whispering thank you in my ear. I wasn't sure what for, but I grinned at him as if I did.

Cyril slowly began backing the Jeep out of the garage when something darted behind us in the mirror. It was so fast that I couldn't really see an image, only a dark shadow, if I had to guess anything. Cyril quickly stopped the Jeep. The tension in the air was thick. It must have been one of the creatures again. A demon hoping that I would be left alone on a balcony or on a walk in the woods, possibly.

"What was that?" I spurted out, not wanting to know the answer. Athen grabbed my hand, squeezing it gently. His eyes were edged with worry. There was no trace of cockiness like I had seen before.

"Why is this one worrying all of you more?" The pause from everyone was infuriating.

"Alright, if you guys expect me to be able to protect myself, even a little bit, you are going to have to start filling me in a little quicker." I removed my hand from Athen's for extra effect.

"That is one of the older demons who is out for fresh blood. He knows you are an easy target. Seems that he would be rewarded greatly, which tells us someone has definitely put a bounty on your head."

"Huh, what would they get if I was taken out again?" My skin was crawling with this information. I began to feel very clammy thinking that I was being placed as a target for some of these creatures.

"It will make more sense later. In short, they will get a get-out-of-jail free card. If one of them can eliminate their target, they're able to have their next foray overlooked. No matter how disturbing it is."

"So the demons can get punished by someone if their act is too evil? That is kind of odd."

"Well, it's not that it's too evil, more like calls attention to them or the underworld. If one of them brings you down, the next heinous thing they do will get overlooked. It's pretty awful how it works in the underworld. They are able to experience an interregnum from the underworld's authority."

"Yeah, that's an understatement. Certainly an incentive to not get caught in addition to the many reasons I can think of." I was afraid to ask the next set of questions, but I had to get them out.

"Can you guys stop them?'

"Yes. It takes more of us and a bit more concentration. Now that we know to be on the lookout for this type - that's half the battle," Cyril interjected.

"Did it get into our house?"

"That's doubtful. They don't tend to trespass where our spirits have been for extended period of times. Too much positivity, and they croak, in a way. They try to not hang out where a group of us have been."

Cyril reached for the radio and hit play on the SeaBear CD he had in the player. The Jeep began to back slowly out of the garage again. I took it to mean they weren't worried enough to stay put and fight.

"Should we fight it or should I worry?"

"No, it was casing us to see how many of us there are and if it had a chance. Clearly it doesn't, but until we get it taken care of it is best that there is always someone with you when you are outside the house." Athen did his best to comfort me as he spoke, but the situation itself seemed so bizarre that I was trying to wrap my brain around the newly-created images I now had floating around.

By the time we had reached the end of the driveway, the mood had instantly lifted. I was again in the holiday spirit, and the uplifting music was drifting through the car. Athen seemed to have relaxed as well, which was the only sign I needed. Arie seemed to be able to get back to her chipper self. She was absorbed in the tree hunt that was about to begin. There was a pause between songs when my stomach growled the loudest I had ever heard. I was immediately mortified, laughing as Arie whipped her head to the backseat.

"If I wasn't worried about the tree farm closing, I would suggest we eat dinner first, but they should have hot cocoa and cookies there too. Hopefully, that will quiet your stomach down until dinner," Arie laughed, as she shook her head and grabbed Cyril's hand that was resting on the center console.

"Some things never change."

"So where are we headed for dinner?" Athen asked, knowing I was wondering the same thing.

"The Main Street Ale House. They serve almost everything you can think of. They have a ton of microbrews on tap too."

"Sweet. Sounds awesome." I was relieved - a real place with real food. Now I couldn't wait to go tree hunting. "Wait, what about my id? It doesn't show the correct age for down here."

"Not to worry. That's all been taken care of." Athen grabbed a nice shiny id out of his wallet and handed it over.

"This won't count against us, will it?" I asked teasing.

We pulled down a long, dirt road where a sign had Christmas lights with an arrow pointing in the direction we were heading. I was getting excited about this adventure. I saw a little parking lot filled with cars, and families tying trees to the top of vehicles, and a little house on the corner of the lot that would no doubt serve the hot cocoa and cookies. I knew where I wanted to go right away.

Cyril pulled next to a family who was leaving. We all jumped out of the car; immediately Christmas carols reached us through the air from speakers that were set up on the porch of the house. I followed everybody up to the house and was relieved that it had to be our first stop regardless since that was where we pick up the saw to cut our tree down. Athen opened the front door, leaving me to smell the hot cocoa and apple cider that was displayed so proudly on the table in the foyer along with rows and rows of cookies. I was in heaven.

"I could stay here for dinner, guys," I exclaimed happily.

I rushed over to the table seeing all of the homemade cookies laid out. There were gingersnaps, chocolate peppermint patties, holiday decorated sugar cookies, and Russian tea cookies. I heard a man's gentle voice come from behind me.

"My wife makes those every morning and hates to see any leftover from the day. Don't be shy."

I turned around quickly to thank the owner, and I recognized him, but I wasn't sure why or from where.

"Thank you so much! These are my favorite in the world."

"Which one is?"

"All of them," I replied laughing, wondering where I had seen him before.

Athen poured me a cup of hot cocoa, and he poured a cup of hot cider for himself. Arie did the same for Cyril as he grabbed the saw and grabbed the map.

"I can't wait!" Arie exclaimed. "Let's hit it."

I grabbed Athen's hand, and we went tromping out the door to find our perfect tree. The reality of darkness hit me, and a sudden jolt of fear rushed over my body. If a creature was after me, I wasn't too sure that out in the middle of a forest of baby trees was the best place to be.

Athen must have seen my body tense and possibly overhearing what's running through my mind because I could feel his arm wrap around me even tighter than usual.

"We've got your back, sweetie." He kissed the top of my head like the first night I met him. I almost dropped to my knees.

"But who's got yours?" I looked up at him hoping for some words of encouragement that would assure me that nothing would ever happen to him. That wasn't what I received. I wondered if somehow he saw the images of my nightmares that I tried so hard to hide from him.

"There's always a way back." And he squeezed me tighter. Not what I wanted to hear.

The fear continued to spike through my veins. The Christmas tree hunt wouldn't go back to an innocent outing tonight. I couldn't stop thinking of a demon out and about trying to end me or my family. As we trudged through the slightly muddy terrain, my heart raced in spurts. Any odd breeze and my hands would begin to get clammy. A branch moving in the slightest way made me want to melt into my surroundings. My family was acting so carefree. I couldn't understand their ease with the circumstances. I was hoping it would come with time, or maybe they were good actors. As of now the constant rollercoaster of emotions was wearing me out, and I couldn't wait until it reached a fairly flat surface soon.

I noticed myself pointing at about any tree to get off the land and get back home when Arie caught onto my plan.

"Guys, I think we are misjudging Ana's comfort level right now. She is pretty freaked. I think one of us needs to do a little explaining so we can get a somewhat decent tree."

"I got it. I guess I thought our overwhelming strength would calm Ana," Athen joked, trying to get a laugh unsuccessfully. "Sorry. I don't mean to make fun of the situation."

I could sense that he was having trouble finding words, which was unusual for him. I reached out and grabbed his hand.

"Please be honest. Why aren't you guys as worried as back at the house?"

"Well, the tree farmers, for starters, are good guys. They're on our side. With those kind of numbers, no demon would dare try for you."

"Wow, I didn't catch it at all. Their eyes didn't strike me... They weren't green like ours."

"Uh, they aren't actually one of us. They are in the underworld, but they aren't a fallen angel or white demon or whatever you want to call us. They are messengers for the heavens. They have a direct line to above. The creatures who are after you certainly don't want to mess with the messengers because if it's spoken about, they will be banished from earth in a sort of constant purgatory."

"Huh, so you are telling me that demons can be wiped out for good? Does that mean we could be wiped out from earth as well? I thought we would continually be reintroduced or something?"

"No, you are right. Remember we are not black demons. We weren't sent here to wreak havoc on the humans. We can't get into heaven, at the moment anyway, because of actions our parents did. Also, we generally spend our time trying to intervene and make positive changes in the world with human interactions. That's got to count for something right? It would take something so heinous for us to be banished. I don't think it's in us to even commit that kind of act." Then why are you hanging out with serpentine eyes? I forced the question as quickly as it came from my mind. I hated this figment of my imagination who kept intruding leaving me with nothing but fear, self doubt, and jealousy.

The fear lifted from my soul as he spoke. The smile from earlier in the evening returned to my lips. I was going to be okay tonight.

"I guess that means I can begin enjoying the tree hunt after all," I was determined now to not let anything ruin my fun especially if I was on so called safe land. I began working my way through the Christmas trees again, "Alright, guys, let's get to it. By the way, can we just move here? I think my nerves would really appreciate it," I asked, only half joking.

Cyril and Arie had gone off in one direction, and Athen was trailing behind me as I was fighting my way through the branches in the other. Once again, a sense of delight washed over me. I hoped I would be able to wrap my head around so many of these marvels that I was learning about. It seemed unattainable.

"How about this one?" Athen's voice brought me back to reality.

I stopped abruptly, turning only to get my boot stuck in the mud and down I went. Athen grabbed me before I completely face planted. Thankful that only my socks were covered in mud, I tried to save face.

"Wow, you certainly are predictable aren't you?" Athen laughed at me with his wry grin.

"Alright, let's cut the chat. Which one are you spying?" I tried changing the subject as fast as I could. I was pretty sure being sexy didn't include being a full-time klutz.

He helped me walk through the slippery areas holding my waist, whispering directions as we made it through the miniature forest. I felt the chill in the air and was thankful for my goose-down jacket. Then I saw the most perfect tree towering directly in front of me. It was trimmed just right and had to be at least 3 feet taller than Athen.

"Oh, Athen! That's the tree! It's beautiful. We've got to get Cyril and the saw. It's got to be this one."

"Well, it certainly gets you as excited as before. I was hoping so." He gently pulled me towards him, lifting my head up as he began to softly kiss me. My entire body began to surge with the electricity that still came in full force. He lifted his lips from mine and stepped back.

"So I should go find Cyril, right?" He grinned his glorious grin, which made me quiver to my knees. I grabbed him and brought him back to me. He was mine.

I reached around his neck, kissing him uncontrollably. He had ignited the spark once more. There was nothing I wanted to do more than lay with him, feel his breath over every inch of me. His hands began running through my hair as his lips began running over my neck. My knees began trembling and, as if on cue, he caught me and laid me up against a fallen tree. I was hoping with all hope that this moment would be the one I was waiting for. I knew Cyril and Arie were around, but my hunch was that Arie had him on a goose chase. We had to have enough time for something. Athen's breath quickened as he rested me up against the tree. I pulled at his shirt trying to unbutton it as quickly as I could, but he stopped me.

"Just kiss me. It won't be long, I promise. I guarantee you they aren't very far away."

"Are you sure of that?" I asked unsure.

"Yeah, hollering distance. I swear."

My body went limp in his arms. I began laughing hysterically because crying wasn't very festive. I couldn't stop.

"Go ahead then. Let them know we found a tree." I hissed at him, shaking my head. I couldn't get the huge smile off my face, hoping at some point we would get to the next level.

"We will. I promise," he whispered back at me, before yelling out to Arie and Cyril.

The branches started snapping, and for once, I was relieved that I listened to Athen after all.

"You certainly were right. That could have been embarrassing," I said getting up, brushing myself off.

"Cyril is armed and ready." I heard Arie hollering through the tree.

"Awesome! Because I found the perfect tree. Well, Athen found it, but I think there isn't one finer around."

***

We all were snuggly in the car with the tree fastened down tightly on top with countless yards of twine. I snacked on another set of cookies I snagged from the office when we paid, while everyone buckled in and got situated.

"So are we off to dinner?" Cyril asked, as he adjusted the rearview mirror. Athen grabbed my hand. I looked over at him and filled up with gratitude at his level of understanding.

"Yeah, sounds good to us. We need a beer for our troubles." Athen responded as lightly as he could along with the much needed hand squeeze I got.

"Thank you," I mouthed to Athen.

"That's what I'm here for, sweetheart. I'll always protect you." I looked at him realizing his mouth was not moving. A chill went through my body. Did I hear his thought? An entire thought? Not just a word? I didn't know what to make of it. I didn't want to ask him in case I imagined it.

I was staring intently at Athen's face apparently trying to read it for some sign when he winked at me, letting me know that it did just happen.

"You heard correctly. You heard my thought." Athen was looking for a reaction. I couldn't give him that yet. I wasn't sure what I was feeling, fear or excitement. It was all kind of running together. Then I realized just how clearly he could hear my thoughts, all of them. My blood ran cold as I thought of his demise and serpent eyes. I wondered what he had pried from my mind so far.

"Wow." Was all that came out.

We drove to the pub in silence. I was staring out the window in awe wondering what was going to happen next with my abilities or lack of them.

"When will I be able to help people?" I blurted out.

Cyril looked at me in the rearview mirror, and Arie turned around in her seat.

"It won't be long, sweetie," Athen replied tentatively. "We'll start small after you see some of what we do. Maybe, next time we are up in Whistler?"

"Ok. I was only wondering."

"No, I get it entirely." He squeezed my hand as we pulled into the parking lot. As if on cue, my stomach growled. I was thrilled at the thought of a beer and a good old-fashioned cheeseburger.

We all got settled into the booth near the corner window, which was a nice view. The twinkling lights outside made the place even more festive and reminded me a bit of Whistler. I started to miss Whistler but was happy to be here with my family.

CHAPTER 21

I woke up from a wonderful sleep. There were no visitors and no catastrophes. I hadn't felt this rested in a long time. I looked at the end of my bed and saw Matilda snuggled in, as usual, completely melting my heart. I looked around the room taking in how breathtaking the setting was. I understood why this location was chosen for a home. The sheer curtains let the intense sparkle from the sun reflecting off the Sound into my bedroom. It was an astounding sight with the fir trees towering over the house canopying the perfect tunnel to look out through. I left my window open for the breeze, not realizing how cold it would get in the room. The hovering fir trees out back were providing enough shade to make the breeze blowing into the room a bit icy, but the view was worth it. I took a deep breath in, feeling the fresh air fill every cell of my body. Now if I could only get enough courage to grab a robe and brave the cold air in my room. I wouldn't be leaving the window open again. I was debating how best to shoot out of bed when the patio door opened, and Athen stood there proudly. Thank God!

"Is my timing impeccable or what?" he asked, his eyes twinkling with mischief.

"Yeah, it's pretty good. Have you been waiting?"

"I went downstairs and made some coffee and was drinking it up here on the patio. I have a thermos waiting for you too. It was so relaxing enjoying the view... Thanking the skies above for your return." His eyes gleamed as I noticed that the chair was pulled up to the French doors. I knew he wasn't referring to the view of the Puget Sound. I immediately blushed.

"Wow, well thanks. I could use something to warm up. It didn't occur to me how cold it could get." I spoke as he went to the window to shut it on his way to the bed.

"Well, this will warm you up. There's another pot brewing downstairs too. Since it's Thanksgiving, we have to keep a pot on all morning to keep Arie going."

"Oh no! Is she down there? I don't want to make her do all the work." I almost jumped out of the bed until the blast of cold air hit me.

"No, she hasn't made it down there yet. Cyril went for a walk and said she was still sleeping. You've got some time."

"Phew. Thanks for this," I said, moving my mug up towards him. I took a few sips, thinking I would bring up the demon that was apparently dashing around the property.

"Is that creature still out there?" I took Athen by surprise, but I generally got the most information when that happened, so I didn't mind.

"No, not directly. I don't think we should let our guard down, though. We are keeping our eyes open for sure. We'll keep you safe. We'll bring him down.

Hopefully, he doesn't have any minions though. If he does, we'll have to take care of those too."

"Minions?" I asked blankly. "Doesn't sound as romantic as Shakespeare's reference."

"Yeah, no minions of the moon here. You are right about that one. Minions, in this instance, are juvenile demons that tend to an older more mature demon's needs. Sometimes the more seasoned demon will send a minion or minions to test out the waters, a sort of judge for the battle kind of thing."

"Ah, great. Good to know," I said, shaking my head, "You know I think I'm set. I'm going to enjoy cooking the turkey today and put all this stuff out of my head."

He reached over and kissed my forehead.

"Good idea. Need a refill?"

I looked down to see my cup already empty.

"Nah, not yet. It warmed me up enough to hop in the shower. I'll grab some more downstairs."

"Sounds perfect. I'll let Matilda out while you get ready."

"I could get used to this you know," I said, as he was ushering Matilda through the door.

"Music to my ears," he said, closing the door.

I climbed down the stairs thankful for my fuzzy, white cashmere sweater when the wonderful smell of sautéing onions in butter hit me. Arie must have, somehow, beaten me to the kitchen. I scurried that much faster down the hall only to be welcomed by a wonderful sight in the kitchen of Cyril, Athen, and Arie, all in aprons, working together preparing the bird. Athen grabbed an apron and dangled it for me.

"Your turn. Come on. We've got a cutting board waiting for you." Arie sounded so excited. It got me thrilled to chop celery.

"After we get the bird in and then some of the sides started, we can start the decorating!" Arie exclaimed. I honestly thought I saw her lift off the ground with excitement.

"So chop faster is what you're telling me." I chipped in.

"Yeah, basically."

I was chopping the celery as fast as I could, while enjoying the view out the window. The sun was out which isn't as much of a novelty in the NW as some claim. The rays were bouncing off the Sound; all the while the ferry was chugging off in the distance. It was like a painting.

"It's still kind of chilly down here, isn't it?" Cyril asked, reaching for the fire remote before any of us could answer.

"That's great. Thanks, Cyril," I said relieved. I didn't want to be the chicken who mentioned I was turning into an icicle.

The guys were slicing a variety of meats, cheeses, and veggies for what I was assuming were snacks while we decorated. There were all sorts of empty puff pastries that looked like they were waiting to be filled. Cyril went to the fridge to grab something, and I saw how many trays of food existed in there already.

"Holy smokes! How did you get so many trays done so quickly?" I asked genuinely perplexed.

"Oh, I started last night. I couldn't sleep right away so I thought I'd get a head start." Arie piped up rather quickly. Everything about the holidays oozed happiness through her.

"You were on watch duty the first part of the night, and then Athen was the second. Got it," I said smiling. "It's okay to tell me like it is, guys. Actually, it's preferred. I swear."

"Sorry, Ana. We didn't want to freak you out any more than we had." Cyril tried to assure me. "It seems to be a theme."

"I appreciate that. I do, but I'd prefer to know. If that's alright with you." I looked around the kitchen at each of them and got a slow nod of agreement.

"Thanks! Now back to chopping. I've got to see what all Arie has planned for decorating."

***

Cyril lugged the last box of decorations into the family room, and Arie was quickly opening up each box. I'd never seen so many decorations before for a private residence, maybe for a hotel. There was one box with red satin covers spilling out from it along with silver rope. I had no idea what that was for. The next box had an assortment of at least forty different angels of various sizes and colors. Kind of ironic, I thought. The next box that was intriguing had items in it that looked like nothing but Christmas candy and cookies, but that couldn't be. There were pinwheels, gingerbread men, and gingerbread houses all glistening with rays of light bouncing in every direction. I walked over closer so that I could get a better look. What I saw was mesmerizing. What looked like actual cookies and candies were hundreds of hand blown glass ornaments with red tissue surrounding them all. Tiny specks of crystal representing sugar were sprinkled all over the tiny ornaments. The sunlight coming in through all of the windows caught the glass in such a way that they all sparkled with a great intensity; it was like a fairyland.

These were definitely my favorite decorations so far. I didn't want to put them back down. They seemed so familiar. The room became very silent. I wasn't sure why. I looked up and began to back away from the box. Everyone's eyes were filled with tears.

"What's up, guys?" I asked hesitantly.

I saw Athen move towards me with his eyes pushing back tears, a huge smile appearing.

"Those were yours," he told me.

"These were my favorite even back then?" I asked.

"Kind of. You created those. You made all of those ornaments."

I was completely shocked. I had no idea that I ever had a talent like this. I wonder if I could still pick it up. The delicate glass in front of me was so gorgeous. It was hard to believe that I had anything to do with creating something so intricate. I walked back over to the box, picking up the gingerbread and sure enough I saw my initials on it. My body went numb. I placed the ornament gently back in the box so nothing happened to it. My body slumped to the floor with the realization of an entire life that I was still learning to relive. I had no recollection of making these. No memories were flooding into my mind as in times before. I felt desperate for answers that I was not getting. I hoped I'd be able to remember creating these. Athen came up behind me, touching my shoulders gingerly.

"You'll remember in time, Ana. You will. It takes time."

I couldn't reply. I hoped he was right. I had to trust. Something I wasn't used to doing in my most recent of existences. I leaned back against him, admiring the tremendous view outside, which brought an overwhelming amount of tranquility.

"I'm so glad we are here for the holiday. It's the perfect place to be," I said, looking at everybody.

"It does have that effect," Arie said, as she patted Cyril's knee. Everyone had repositioned themselves in the family room. Cyril was sitting on the sectional. Arie was on the floor in front of him. Probably because they weren't sure what my reaction to the ornaments would be. I certainly had a lot of learning to do about my past, but it was refreshing to know that I had a family here to support me. The stone fireplace continued to throw off a nice amount of warmth, which Matilda found sometime during the process of bringing in all of the decorations. She was snoring hard so I knew she was at home. Cyril got up heading for the kitchen, rustling around. I was wondering what he was up to.

"Time to start the mulled cider. Don't you think? We've got a good thing we can add into it later if needed."

I looked around the room and saw the fluffy, green tree placed in between the corner windows. The boxes scattered everywhere exploding with tissue paper and ornaments added a sense of urgency. Unfortunately, the floor pillows looked so welcoming. I wondered why I was getting so tired all of a sudden. I glanced up at the wooden, framed clock that hung near the kitchen. It was a quarter to eleven. I had only been up a couple of hours. I wondered if more memories were trying to make their way back in or not. I figured I had a little time before the cider was going to be ready so I reached out for one of the extra-large red, velour pillows and wrapped my arms around it. I settled into my comfort only to match my breathing to that of Matilda's heading into a sleep far away from anything that I could relate to.

The imagery that was infiltrating every crevice of my mind was overwhelming. The memories were coming in faster than I had ever experienced before. I saw flashes of a stone building with what looked like a stone furnace. Then there was a field with a large home on it with a wraparound porch, with a bench. I saw several animals off in the fields, but I couldn't recognize what they were. I saw a flash of a horse carriage coming down a gravel road. A pain was surfacing similar to the one from the initial reintroduction process. It was gone in an instant. I saw Arie cooking in a kitchen that looked as if it was from the 40's. I couldn't understand why the different eras were being brought in so jumbled. I saw Arie collapsing in tears. Then the images went away. My mind went blank. I could feel Athen's hand caressing my hair, helping to wake me up gently.

My eyes were opening to awake my senses to the sweetness of mulled apple cider drifting in. Matilda was laying next to me on the floor. I began to feel very sheepish as it became apparent what must have happened. I saw Arie, Cyril, and Athen all on the sectional waiting. I thought I had been out for an hour, which made me feel even worse for taking time away from the planned decorating.

"Hey, sleepyhead," Athen said. "How are you doing?"

"How long was I out? It felt like ages."

"Actually, only about twenty minutes," Cyril replied, looking at his watch, "Barely enough time to let the cider warm up."

"Wow, that was intense," I said, as I tried to get back up without waking Matilda. "Believe it or not,

I'm ready to keep on trucking. I'm so sorry about that guys. I don't know where that came from."

"Don't apologize, Ana. This process isn't an overnight one. We know what to expect. We want to help you along the way."

"Well, thanks. It's a little embarrassing. Let's move on for now. I'm ready to get back at it."

"Are you sure? It's no big deal. We can wait." Arie promised.

"No, really. I think I'm ok, but I would like a cup of that awesome smelling cider now."

All three of them jumped off the sectional, making me laugh pretty hard. I began going through the boxes again, hoping not to find such a poignant treasure like before -enough surprises for the day. Cyril went into the kitchen to grab a mug of cider for me, while Arie went over to the stereo to plug in her iTunes with a pre-populated Christmas playlist, no doubt. Athen began rearranging some of the boxes, but he certainly was staying very close to me, which I appreciated deep inside.

The delicious smell of the turkey roasting reached every corner of the house, as did the Christmas music that Arie had picked out. Between the smells and the sounds, I couldn't wait for Thanksgiving dinner and was in awe at how much decorating we had accomplished in the short amount of time. Any surface that was bare now had a Christmas Angel, Nutcracker or Snowman on it. I was amazed at the several different types of table arrangements she had. Some were on the breakfast bar, end tables, and bookshelves. Pine garlands were thrown everywhere with little red berries peaking out from in between the branches. Even Scrooge would have had to come around to the Christmas spirit with Arie around. I was, also, informed that she had equally as many decorations awaiting us in Whistler.

The thought of Whistler made me wonder if I would be staying at my place or back at theirs. I was hoping it would be their place, not that I didn't love my place. Maybe by then Athen would stay over at my place. It didn't matter where I was as long as Athen was involved.

It was getting close to mealtime, but I suddenly became exhausted. This many hours of decorating seemed to take its toll.

"Hey, I think I'm going to go up and lay down for a little bit before dinner. I've gotten extremely tired." I grabbed Athen's hand as he was placing the last bit of garland around the entry mirror.

"Yeah, no problem. Want some company?" His eyes looked hopeful.

I didn't want to let him down, but I really needed rest, and who knows what my emotions would want me to do if he was laying next to me.

"No, I think I'm good. I'm gonna crash for a few. I'll be back before you know it." I winked at him as I moved up the stairs.

As I turned into my bedroom, I looked at my comforter with such longing. I couldn't wait to snuggle underneath it and rest for a few minutes, only a few minutes. I could barely keep my eyes open. Hopefully, I wasn't coming down with the flu or something. I called for Matilda to jump on up which she did without missing a beat. Before I knew it I was fast asleep welcoming more horrors into my life.

***

I woke up in a sudden panic. My heart was pounding. My head was burning. I had no idea what was happening. It was dark outside so I must have slept for a little longer than I thought. It's at least 3:45 pm or so since that was when it first gets dark. I tried to turn my head, but the pain was excruciating. I reached down for Matilda and found her with my hand. I knew I needed help but wasn't sure yelling would do much in a house this large. This was not a dream. This was real. The pain was far more debilitating than even the reintroduction process. The pain was getting worse by the second. My fingers began to lose feeling. The numbness began to creep up my hand and slowly began to spread to my wrist leaving a trail of coldness in its journey. I began to holler for Athen or anyone. Nothing would come out. I tried to move, but my body wouldn't budge. It was entirely numb. Matilda didn't seem disturbed, which gave me a little comfort, but my heart knew something was different. From my bed I stared straight ahead and saw out my window a dark reflection. I couldn't see a clear figure. I didn't really know what I was seeing. Was I even awake? It seemed like I was in a frozen dream state. How could I be seeing a something out my second story window?

The image was getting closer to the window, and as it did, my pain began to worsen. A sharpness was running through my veins as if someone was ripping a scalpel inside my body. This was the creature who had been on our property. The black swirl was becoming a little clearer. I began with all my might to scream. I wasn't sure what kind of noise was actually making it out, but I kept screaming with all my being. Matilda didn't move at all, which made my heart fall with the realization that no noise was coming from me. I wouldn't give up though. I kept yelling for help, in part, because I was in so much pain. I was certain that pure terror-filled screams were coming from me. I began to hear what sounded like a mumble coming from me, maybe a soft murmur. Even if someone happened to be walking by they wouldn't notice. The creature was now at my window. My fingers that were numb before now burned with an intense fire that I wouldn't wish on my worst enemy.

The creature in front of me began to look mostly human versus the quick black streak I'd seen briefly on our property. I'm sure if darkness wasn't surrounding him he would look like any other person walking down the street except for a few strange characteristics that I was pretty sure now were common traits among these demons. Partially because my fingers were in such pain I noticed his, and they were extremely pointy and long, but the most unnerving part was how long the creatures nails were. His jaw stuck out to me as well. It looked as if a grin was coming over his face. I kept up my screaming, but apparently, it was only for me to hear. His eyes were welcoming death.

Matilda's ears perked up. She could hear them running up the stairs. They were running down the hall. Somehow they made it to my bedroom, but in that instant, the image vanished from my bedroom's view.

"Ana, is everything ok?" Arie asked breathlessly. She looked around the room and saw that nothing seemed to be amiss.

"We felt that you were in pain," Cyril said, the last to reach my bedroom.

Athen came over to my side, gently touching my forehead.

"Ana, you are soaked. What happened? Did you have more memories? Is it from downstairs?"

Words weren't coming quite yet. I could only slowly shake my head. I tried to point out the window with my fingers. Everyone looked out my window and saw the very same thing I did, nothing.

"It's ok, sweetheart. These things can happen. The memories can be painful. I'm so sorry," Athen said, hugging me.

I shook my head. No words were coming. They didn't understand. I needed words. Now was the moment to see if I could manipulate my own thoughts to make sure that they could hear them.

I forcefully placed the thoughts in my head, their head. I attempted to give a step-by-step recap of what happened once I woke up. I looked up at them for any recognition that they intercepted my thoughts.

"Ana", Arie said gently, "I think that was part of a dream. The creature that we have been keeping watch on doesn't match that description. I think somehow the image you saw is from your memories from before."

I was so frustrated. I could feel the despair rising in me. I knew what I saw. It wasn't a memory. It was real. There was a creature outside my window. I looked at Athen hoping he would understand.

"You know, Arie, if it was a memory why can't she speak or move much?" He looked at both Arie and Cyril concerned.

"She is probably worn out still from earlier. That was a pretty big influx of memories she experienced."

I finally was able to shake my head and did as fast as I could. I began to describe the creature that I saw in my mind with hopes that it would prove something to them. Maybe they would be able to see it. I thought as hard as I could, 'The black bulbous, image became larger and larger as it got to the window. Once the creature was at the window, I could tell it was in human form. It had long, wrinkled, almost leathery fingers. Its fingernails were wretchedly long, tinged with brown. I could tell it was a male. It wore a burgundy shirt and black pants. The more pain it caused me, the more it would smile. Its eyes were cold and black, almost hollow. When it would open its mouth, all I could see was a dark cavern that seemed to go on forever. I didn't want to look at its mouth or into its eyes. It was as if I would get sucked in. Please believe me. It was after me. It wasn't a memory from earlier. I was worn out from trying to think my thoughts so loud.' I was drained from forcing those words to them all.

Athen grabbed my hand and turned to Cyril.

"It's not a minion. It's Azazel. He must have gotten to her from her window. This could be a bit more serious than we thought. We need to be prepared for a fight. I don't know why we are so interesting all of a sudden, but this is the real thing, again."

"Or there could be two of them." Arie finally got on board.

"You probably hit it on the head, sis. The first one probably was the minion. It looks like we'll need to be a bit more cautious than we realized until we take care of this. Apparently, someone decided to leave the desert."

"Well, if what you guys are saying is true, that means she was cast. We need to get her back to her old self. It's not going to happen on its own. Ana, I'm so sorry for not believing you. I never expected this."

I knew they would never want to cause me pain or hurt, but I certainly hoped that going forward they would begin to trust my instincts a bit more than up to this point. I gently shook my head and attempted a smile. I had no idea what was next, but I hoped we could get this chapter over with.

"We will." Athen kissed me on my head. Arie went downstairs to the kitchen to grab something. What, I had no idea, but I suddenly realized that the turkey didn't quite have the same level of intrigue as pre-nap. However, I didn't want to ruin Thanksgiving dinner for everyone.

CHAPTER 22

I made my way down for the holiday dinner and knew that there was going to be a much different tone than at a typical holiday meal. I could tell everyone was attempting to make it as normal as possible without throwing me over the edge, but somehow I had to convey to them that I needed the details to stay sane and in control. Athen was cutting the turkey, and Cyril was finishing up the mashed potatoes.

"Where's Arie?" I asked.

"She's in contact with some of the others explaining the situation. We haven't had this level of persistence for quite some time. She is hoping to find out something that may be floating through the channels. So far no one has heard of anything that would make us more of a target than usual."

"This is pretty intense. I had no idea how involved all of this would get." I mumbled a bit under my breath as I grabbed the breadbasket for the table.

"None of us could have predicted this one. We'll take care of it though. It or they will be a thing of the past by Christmas, guaranteed," Cyril boasted, from behind the mashed potatoes.

"I do admire your confidence, Cy," I said, grinning. I could feel my level of confidence brimming over the cup being back down here with my family.

Everyone began bringing the wonderful holiday delicacies to the table, spreading them out in between the plentiful holiday decorations. I could hear Arie bounding in from behind us, probably coming from the study.

"So what's the scoop, sis?" Athen asked, hopeful that she had uncovered the answers we needed to end it immediately.

"Well, it sounds like it might not only be Azazel. Apparently the demon we took care of in Whistler might be a minion of Asmodeus. He is here strictly for revenge. Possibly because we disturbed one of the minions belonging to him, but we don't know for sure.

Only time will tell."

"Why does that make a difference?" I asked clueless.

"Well, if he were sent to end one of us, and we ended him first, his memories will be cleared, and we are done. He won't come back after us. He'll go back to what he does once he re-introduces, which is preying on humans."

"So what is the history on Asmodeus?"

"We seem to be talking about all of the big guns of evil. He is an arch demon, and one of his specialties is revenge, along with jealousy and lechery."

"Geez, well I guess it's better to know than not. Let's hope there is no connection between any of this, and that these occurrences aren't connected," I said, trying to put everything out of my mind.

"But the question we are kind of not answering here is why was the one in Whistler after her? I hope he wasn't sent." Cyril and Athen traded glances while Arie lit the candles on the table.

"Alright, guys, enough shop talk," Arie said, bringing us all back to the innocence that only she was able to do.

The calm had settled over the dining room, and the dancing shadows from the fire in the family room added a nice touch. There were so many things laid out in front of me, I didn't even know where to begin. The sweet potato casserole was calling out to me though, and I dug into that first. Cyril grabbed the Bose stereo remote and turned on some wonderful holiday music. Nothing like Bing Crosby singing White Christmas to lift the mood instantly, I was truly in my element.

"So speaking of a White Christmas, what do you say once we get done with this little issue we head back up to Whistler. Do we want to spend Christmas up there or down here? We could go up there to get some skiing in." Cyril looked so excited at the mere thought of gliding down the powder. Everyone looked at me immediately.

"Whoa, guys, I don't want to be the one to choose. I'm cool with anything. I do love it down here, but I would love to see Whistler during the holidays for a little bit, since it has been my home for so long."

"Alright, we'll take care of the situation down here, spend a couple days more and then head up there for a couple weeks maybe? We could probably get back down here by the 20th and have plenty of time to enjoy things. Maybe your friend would want to come down for New Year's Eve?" Athen offered up.

So much had happened since we left Whistler, I hadn't even thought about Karen. I felt like such a horrible friend. Truthfully I probably was never that great of one anyway. I knew the right thing to do would be to invite her. I'm glad he mentioned it.

"Yeah, that would be good idea. Thanks, Athen. I tend to forget about life outside of our little circle lately," I said, as I plowed through the turkey and cranberry sauce that I had piled on my plate. This was the best tasting Thanksgiving without a doubt. I was having a bit of trouble understanding my appetite. One minute I think I'm about to die, and the next, I'm ravenous. Athen started to chuckle.

"You've always been like that, Ana," he said smiling.

"So Arie, when are you going to teach me that tip to keep some of my thoughts to myself?" I barked.

"Tonight! I promise," she exclaimed, throwing her napkin at Athen. "The fun will be over soon, Athen."

Everyone began on their second round of food, and I wondered how I would ever be able to fit in any of the desserts that we had made. I knew the pecan pie would win, but I wondered how many of the others would too.

I was dreaming about the desserts when a flash of the snowboarder came into my mind. I didn't know what was happening. I couldn't shake it. I knew it was the same guy as I saw in the picture back when I was with Athen at the grocery store. I saw the snowboarder walking to what looked like a yurt in the snow. There were people waiting for him inside the yurt.

"Ana? What's wrong? You look like you saw a ghost!" Arie put the pie dish down and stared intently.

"Athen, do you remember the missing snowboarder? Images of him are flashing in my head. Why would that be? I don't even know him? It's like a home movie is playing in my head only I don't know the ending."

"Ana, you've got to be kidding me. What do you see? I can't believe you are able to see things clearly."

"He's in the snow, looks like out in the wilderness. There is a yurt with a chimney that he is entering. He isn't alone. The inside of the yurt is pretty bare. There are about 3 people that I can see in there with him - except that their eyes..."

"What do you see, Ana?" Cyril pried.

"Their eyes are black. There is no essence of any human spirit within them. They're like the one that tried to attack me. They look like humans but must be demons."

"Can you see the snowboarder's eyes?" Athen asked.

"Not yet, they seem to all be heading to the table. There are maps, and all sorts of trinkets spread out on the table. It's like they're giving instructions."

"Keep focused on the his eyes, Ana."

"I am, I am... It looks like he is sitting down now, listening. I got it! His eyes, they aren't like the others."

Everyone began shrieking. I wasn't exactly sure why. Arie began running to the other room to make a call.

"What's going on? How do you know what I saw was accurate?" I asked emphatically.

"That was one of your true talents, Ana. You could find the missing and endangered. You could scope out the poor victims, and in many cases, we could get to them before it was too late. You can see visions just like the one with Karen and the guy texting her. It's like seeing the future, but rather it's the present. You can see what's happening in the moment. I didn't expect this to come back so early." Athen grabbed my hand. "Are you doing ok?"

"Yeah, I'm fine, but how can you be certain that I really saw him, and it wasn't just my imagination?"

"I just know. You used to get this look of concentration, and it appeared tonight while it was happening. I can guarantee what you told us tonight is happening at this very moment. Arie is calling some of our friends in Whistler to help since we are down here and have to deal with this other mess first. We've got to try to get him back. Go tell Arie everything you saw - the more detail the better. We need to track this kid down before it's too late."

"Alright. I'll go fill her in as best as I can." The thought that this all occurred while I was awake brought a wave of relief. Maybe those nightmares were just that – bad dreams, figments of my imagination, nothing more than that. Maybe my visions only happen when I'm awake. I hoped with all of my heart that was the case. My stomach became ill at the thought of the nightmares trying to make their way back into my conscious. I have fought against the images of Athen escaping into thin air a thousand times, and this gave me hope that maybe it was just a bad dream. Perhaps the demon with the serpentine eyes was only my subconscious reflecting my worst nightmares. Those images must be nothing more than tried and true nightmares, not premonitions. I followed after Arie to help her in any way I could.

***

It was pretty late in the evening, probably close to midnight, and we were all huddled around the fireplace in the family room. I had changed into my pjs and had my favorite fuzzy robe covering me up for extra warmth. Athen was near the fireplace, which was throwing a warm glow onto his skin, highlighting his yellow-green eyes. He was so hard to resist. He had changed into some flannel bottoms and a t-shirt, looking absolutely perfect.

"Well, Brenda and Rob think they may have some leads as to where this yurt might be. They're going to round up some others and head up there to see if they can find him. It sounds like our snowboarder hasn't been turned yet. We can only hope it's not too late. They told us they would keep us posted as soon as updates come in. In the meantime, we have to focus on our own little situation. We've got to get this resolved before we are of any help to what's going on in Whistler." Arie grabbed her cup of cider and sipped slowly.

"Switching gears...So the plan is to wait until he appears again. My guess is that he will be casing the house when we are away. I think we should all leave, and then Athen and I will bring him back to here and trap him. We'll take care of him that way." Cyril announced.

"Ok, but what if the minion is present?" Arie asked. I could detect a hint of worry in her voice.

"Aah, we can take care of it," Cyril said, his cockiness flooding the room.

246

"I know, I know. I think..." I cut her off before she could begin. I knew what she was feeling. We couldn't bear to lose them both at the same time.

"I want to be a part of this. I need to be. In fact, I insist. I can't be talked out of it. I know I'm no match for the demon's skill level, but there has to be a way to include me... We bring him into our trap, not fall into his. I can be the bait."

"She's right," Arie firmly agreed with me, and I could tell that our history must have included a lot of these types of chats, "We don't know his true skill level. If he detects your trance, he'll be waiting for you. We never want to be on the defensive, only the offensive."

The two guys looked at each other acknowledging defeat. They both sat back on the couch. I saw Athen begin to shake his head. I knew the fight was not entirely over.

"No, I'm not using you as bait. There's no way I can do that," Athen argued. "I've lost you once. I'm not going through that again, especially at my hands."

"It's true, Ana. I don't think I could go through another day, let alone a year, of having to deal with Athen's moping around. Plus, I missed you too. It's gotta be a no."

I could fell the fury building up inside me. I was being thrown aside and given no vote in any of this, and it was all involving me. I was not giving up.

"No, sorry. I'm not going to be on the sidelines anymore. That time has passed. We can all leave in that car together, but I guarantee you that Arie and I'll be back at the house waiting before you trance or whatever it is you're talking about. I won't take no as an answer. We'll have to come up with a solid plan, and I'll be a part of it. You'll be on your best performances to ensure nothing happens to me. Got it?" I didn't know where this assuredness was coming from, but I liked it. I looked over at Arie, and she nodded at me. I was on the right path. Maybe I wasn't the self-conscious Sally I'd grown to be on my own.

"That's my girl," Athen said, coming to sit next to me in the oversized chair. He squeezed in between the pillows and me, giving me a big hug, "You are quite right. I didn't ever want to get back to the stage where you were part of it, but I knew it would come sooner or later. You always wanted to be in the action. I guess I hoped that part of you wouldn't fully return like before. Apparently, I was wrong."

"Well, wait until I get my fighting skills up," I said, laughing with a pit in my stomach.

"Not so fast on that one," he said, kissing me on my forehead. "So what's our plan?"

CHAPTER 23

It was the Saturday after Thanksgiving. We had decided this would be the best day to lure the demon or demons to me. We didn't want it to look too eager in timing compared to his failed attempt. The butterflies had begun in my stomach, but a curious thing was beginning to happen as well. An excitement began building. I was part of something much bigger than myself. If I could master this small little task, it would help as I relearned the more complicated abilities. It was still hard to believe that someday, I would be fighting these creatures for the sake of mankind. The thought brought me a lot of happiness. I was completely fulfilled by my family. I was so fortunate to have a calling that would help the world, even if my part was a small one in the whole scheme of things. I had to keep focused on that aspect so I could fight the distaste of what my title was. I still resented that I could be classified in such a despicable group, regardless of what side I was on. I fought to keep the feelings at bay, not today.

I had finished putting on my oldest fair-isle sweater and had adjusted the t-shirt under it. The sweater was one that had seen a lot of use. The red coloring had faded in many spots, perfect for today's escapades. In case anything went wrong, I wouldn't be heartbroken if something happened to it. Not that I should be thinking of things like that, but in times like these, crazy thoughts happened.

We were pretty confident that the demon never left our property and was very aware of any of our movements when we were outside. Arie and Cyril went to the grocery store as a test run and sure enough the demon was lurking down the driveway. We decided to have the garage doors open and tables set up. Arie thought if it looked like we were making wreaths, it would give us all an excuse to be tromping around the woods near our house, collecting cedar and fir boughs. Then when we separate briefly, it shouldn't look too out of the ordinary. I was rather surprised that Arie had wreath-making equipment, but I was learning to not underestimate this family's many talents.

They told me not to talk about it at all and to follow our plans as exactly as possible. I met Arie, Athen, and Cyril down in the garage and sure enough the door was open, and the tables set up. She had the circular wreath crimper bolted to the table and a huge assortment of berries, twigs, and ribbons piled in two bins. I couldn't help myself from gazing out past the doors to see if I could see it, but I didn't and quickly looked down.

"Hey guys! I brought more hot cider to keep us hydrated. I'll plug the Crockpot in on the counter." I was hoping that my acting skills were on par.

"Thanks. Let me help you with that." Athen came over and grabbed the Crockpot, setting it on the workbench.

"Are we all ready to go gather the boughs?" Cyril asked, "I'm getting antsy to get this fun holiday task over with."

Arie playfully smacked him on his butt, "Very funny, Mr. Scrooge! Now get in the holiday spirit, or I'll make you."

"I'd like to feel that or I mean see that," Cyril exclaimed.

"Oh my word, that was corny," I said, rolling my eyes.

We all grabbed our garden clippers and headed out through the garage doors as planned. My nerves were starting to get the better of me. I knew I had to keep in control; otherwise, I would be endangering all of us. I followed Athen up the hill back towards the road. Arie and Cyril went down more toward the shore. There were downed limbs everywhere from the recent windstorms, so we were able to collect quite a few boughs right away.

"Ok, Athen, Arie said not to take any part on the limb that looked brown or grey. Do you think this counts?" I asked holding up a floppy looking Douglas fir limb. He must have known what I was feeling because he winked at me, which made me feel immensely better.

"Yeah, clip off the bottom, and we should be good."

"I bet we'll only have to go another thirty feet, and we'll have enough to take back to the garage," I said surprised. I never noticed how many limbs these trees dropped.

"True, but she said we needed a ton per wreath so we probably have many trips ahead of us." Athen tried to yell over the wind that was beginning to pick up.

"Hmm, alright," I said, realizing I was quickly losing enthusiasm. Not sure if it was over the task at hand or the larger picture.

Athen's cell phone rang. He placed his limbs on the large boulder that was next to us. I began to feel hot all over. That was not part of the plan.

"It's Cyril. That's weird." He touched the screen and put it on speaker.

"What's up?" Athen asked.

"It's Arie. She passed out. I don't know if the demon got to her. She isn't responding. Athen, I need your help now. We've got to get her inside."

Athen began running even before he hung up the phone.

"Ana. Stay put. We'll be coming back up this way. We'll need your help."

He was running at full speed. I yelled after him asking why I couldn't come with him, but he never responded. I began feeling my heartbeat's every thump. This was not part of the plan. My nerves were more on edge by the second. I wondered what happened to Arie. What seemed like an eternity was only a couple minutes, but I decided to walk over to the boulder and hop up on it. I laid my boughs on the boulder next to me, bewildered by what just happened. My senses began picking everything up – smells, sounds, sights. I was sitting for only a few more minutes before I began to hear the rustle behind me. The problem was that I didn't know if it was the creature or my family. There was no sense of familiarity whatsoever.

To my disgust, the brown tinged nails intertwined among my sweater fabric. My spirit became full of despair once the creature's fingers wrapped themselves around me. I looked down, filling up inside with fear like never before. My family was already supposed to be here. He must have gotten to Arie. I was never supposed to be alone. Cyril should've been in the trees right above me on the hill, and Arie near the garage. I didn't see any of this happening. Then my worst nightmare flashed in my mind. I had to shake it. It kept coming back. What if the demon got to all of them first? What would my fate be? Would I even care to go on? I might just rather go back to the numbness of before. Not knowing what you're missing was better than the alternative.

I heard no voice coming from the demon, rather a raspy breath speaking to me. "You are alone my angel. Isn't that what Athen likes to call you?" he asked, as he touched my cheek. "Looks like you are going away for a long time again."

I grabbed his hand and threw it back at him. I began to let my mind wander off to the nightmares. Could they have been real? Could I have lost my family? I knew I needed to fight regardless.

"Get your filth off of me," I howled at him. "Your presence does nothing to me. I have no feeling or regard for you one way or the other. You don't scare me. You make me laugh at your pathetic self."

If my family was gone, what do I care if I were saved or sacrificed? I turned to look into the demon's eyes only to see the nefarious gaze staring back at me. It was as if I was looking at the walking dead.

"I pity you," I whispered, as I lay back against the boulder. I would follow our family's plan even if they were already taken from me. I breathed out my last, long breath of despair.

I closed my eyes, and a jolt of familiar electricity shot through me. It took everything to keep my eyes shut, and the smile off my face. My family was alive. The plan was working, or more to the point, their plan was working. I could feel them. Once again, they left me out of the loop. They had to quit doing that. I was exhilarated. I continued to lay still on the boulder, eyes shut. The demon took his long finger and began to trace it along my cheekbone when a sudden burst of wind blew by me. I opened my eyes to see Cyril falling down, collapsing onto the demon. From the right, I saw Athen's body move under the demon, as if he was almost folding his form in half. Arie was creating a swirl of movement around the three beings. I could see clearly what was happening, but I didn't truly understand it. The demon was losing. The screeching bounced off the forest echoing into my ears, penetrating down to my soul. The sounds were pure and torturous, which made me almost giddy. I scolded myself for thinking such thoughts, even if it was a demon. The demon's black mist was continually escaping into the air and then reemerging. I never saw that in Whistler. This one seemed to be trying to regenerate.

I was able to make out bits and pieces of the creature. He was definitely on the losing end. Cyril and Athen were making sure this was extra painful and extra long. It almost looked as if every extremity was turning into dust; as if they were crushing every cell in his body. Athen and Cyril were dicing him so quickly that as parts of the demon regenerated the appendages were reattaching in the incorrect position. I knew I shouldn't be in awe over something like this, but it was truly incredible to watch. The evil was evaporating into the wind. The soulless creature was becoming smaller and smaller; until I finally knew he was gone. I had my family left next to me. They did it. They looked completely unscathed. It was over, for now.

CHAPTER 24

We had been through so much over Thanksgiving weekend, and I, for the first time in days, felt like I could take a deep breath in. Our trip to Seattle was so calming, as was our first evening in Kingston at the house, but then once the demon arrived, it became horrific. I understood this world a little bit better now, and my place in it. The dangers were becoming more apparent as were our strengths. I didn't participate in any of the actual combat this time around, but I was proud that I was able to help my family with the luring and rituals. I was looking forward to spending the next few days relaxing as much as possible, attempting to get some alone time with Athen snuck in there too. My long bath definitely helped get my mind and muscles relaxed. Part of me didn't want to leave the bathwater. I didn't realize how tense I had become during these last couple days.

I had forgiven them for not filling me in completely on their plans, I think, but I kind of wished they had told me because I really thought I had lost them, even let myself think it was okay if the demon took me. The fact the creature was able to touch me at all was more than I could handle. I sunk under the bath water commanding myself to let go of the images as I breathed out creating air bubbles for the demon's image to escape.

Cyril and Arie decided to go over to Edmonds and pick up some snacks for the remainder of our stay, which left Athen and me alone for the day. I was planning on taking full advantage. I was pretty thrilled at the idea. I heard my bedroom door open and was exhilarated at the thought that Athen was near.

"How are you doing?" Athen's voice reached me through the closed bathroom door.

"Better if you were in here. I'm getting out now." I told him, hoping it would provoke something to finally happen.

"We've got some free time, angel. My guess is that Arie is going to pull Cyril through all of Edmonds' shops, not just the bakery. I think that could be a good thing. How about you?" I could tell in his voice that his idea of good things was finally going to match mine.

"Uh, yeah!" I exclaimed, more excited than ever before, as I tried not to slip on the tile floor.

I grabbed a towel and quickly wrapped my hair and pulled my robe on. I couldn't wait to see what the rest of the afternoon had in store for me. The fear was completely drained from my body. I was back to my old self or maybe my new self. Regardless, I felt great. I grabbed my bracelet off the granite countertop and hopped to the door. I swung it open to see quite a surprising sight before me. There were ivory candles of every size lit all around my room; red and white rose petals were trailing from the door to the fireplace. He had placed the sheepskin blanket in front of the fire, and alongside it were two flutes with champagne and my favorite chocolate covered strawberries. I had no idea how he could have accomplished everything while I was soaking, but he always managed to take everything up a notch. Once my eyes followed the path of rose petals, I met his gaze, which still took my breath away. His brilliant, green eyes made my stomach flutter. They looked especially mischievous. It brought me back immediately to the night I saw him in the pub for the first time. That first night I was fumbling and nervous and oh so self-conscious. I don't even feel like the same person. The thought of even letting him see me without makeup, straight from the bath would never have happened with the old me. Now, I look in the mirror, and I'm so happy with what I see. Granted I feel as if I look better after the phasing, but Athen swears it's in my head, that I always looked like this. I have grown very fond of my own green eyes now, but they're still nothing compared to Athen's. His are incredible.

As I looked at him, his eyes were moving slowly up and down my body. I thought that was so cute being that I was completely covered up by a plush bathrobe. He was so stunning. The thought that he was mine made me feel like I was in heaven. He held out his hands, eyes twinkling. I couldn't resist.

"Come on over here, sweetheart. I have some champagne for us. We can finally relax and unwind. You've certainly been through a lot since coming into contact with us again, huh? Sorry about everything."

"I wouldn't take it back for anything, Athen. You have made my world complete. I have never been this confident, never had this much fun, I don't know how I existed before. I was like a zombie, just going through the motions."

I walked over and grabbed his hands. We settled down on the floor and held each other. It was wonderful, and for once I wasn't being overly eager. I was loving every second of what the afternoon had in store for me. I knew tonight would be the night. Like he said, the other times weren't right. Tonight would be perfect. I was going to let him be in charge. We spent hours laughing, catching up on memories I had no recollection of. I was so intrigued to hear details about my life.

Athen wanted to walk the beach, and I thought that sounded wonderful. I quickly got dressed and met him in the kitchen where he was preparing a plate of smore's ingredients. That made me chuckle.

"What are you giggling about?" he asked.

"Nothing. Sometimes it seems too perfect. Like I'm in a coma and will wake up at the worst moment."

"Nope. We belong together. Besides when you are together for as long as we have been, you don't sweat the small stuff. That's what people always get caught up in, but stretched over our lifetimes, most things are pretty inconsequential."

He grabbed the skewers, the Ziploc baggies full of goodies, and my hand as we left out the back door. I hadn't really gotten to visit the beach since I arrived.

I never noticed from the house, but they had little solar lights on the trail down to the beach, which was nice especially with my lack of coordination. The beach was amazing, not the typical sandy beaches that are on postcards, but rather shiny, multicolored pebbles with patches of sand and boulders encasing the path. Athen brought me to the largest patch of sand. Enough for a picnic or maybe sunbathing, not that there was ever that much warmth, I thought to myself. I looked over to the right and saw the ferry heading back to Edmonds, how special this place was. I was extremely lucky to be a part of it. The sun was gently saying its goodbyes for the evening, and I scanned the beach for Athen. Finally I spied him behind me gathering pieces of wood. I was wondering if it was for a bonfire or for a backup at the house. The twilight hours were so mind numbingly beautiful that it was easy to forget the chill that was hovering in the air.

"What are you doing? Is there anything I can help with?"

"I'm about to start a fire. It'll only take a second. I think I got it handled," he said beaming. I noticed how proud he was whenever he did something to make me happy. My insides immediately warmed. I felt so special, so very lucky.

"Oh yeah, the smores! How could I forget? I think I must be a little antsy," I laughed.

"Can't imagine what for," he said, with his eyes reflecting the moonlight that was beginning to show itself.

I sat on the blanket near the fire, purely in awe of everything. As the sun drifted away, we were left with nothing but darkness. The gentle lapping of the waves mixed with the crackling of the fire was so soothing. I looked over at the glow as it danced in the darkness. I leaned my head against Athen, soaking up everything that this day had brought to me so far. I knew it was coming to a close. I didn't want it to end. I looked up at Athen, wanting nothing more than him for all eternity. I knew he wanted the same.

"Thank you Athen. Thank you for everything." Then it hit me – the beach! My dream! This was my dream - this was the beach. Heaven was about to exist. I was certain of it.

Athen stood up, grabbed me from the blanket where we were sitting and cradled me in his arms. I could feel him moving, that he was taking me somewhere, but with the darkness I wasn't able to judge where we were going until he gently laid me down against a boulder. The coldness of the boulder mixed with the heat of my body was shocking. I looked into his eyes, with the darkness around us, I saw that his eyes had a gentle, green glow, very soft and sensual. I wondered if mine had the same. I saw the man who I had loved for centuries and would for centuries more, but at this moment in this lifetime, it was a first. He began lightly kissing my neck as I began unbuttoning his shirt. The quiet sound of the fire crackling brought me back to reality for a moment before I heard Athen begin speaking.

"Tonight's the beginning of our eternity, Ana. I'll not lose you again." His hand was lifting my sweater up, and I could feel his breath on me like never before. It hovered over every inch of my body, bringing me to a level of pleasure that I didn't think possible. I grabbed his neck and didn't ever want to let go. I could feel the strength of his arms as he continued to caress and kiss every inch of my body. With every crash of a wave, an insurmountable flood of desire ran through me. A love that I had longed a lifetime for was finally my reality. A partner who would carry me into eternity was finally with me. Nothing in my life was predictable any longer, and that was fine with me as long as I had Athen by my side.

My body moved rhythmically with his, never wanting this moment to end. I had tried so many times before, and Athen was right. This was the right moment. I could feel his hands gracing every part of my body with the lightest of touch as he cradled me in between him and the boulder. His kissing became more intense and passionate, stopping every so often to hold my head in his hands to look me in my eyes. I had never been more connected to him. This was perfection for me. I knew this was the life that was meant to be mine again. I grabbed his shoulders and began kissing his chest more intensely as he held me closer. He lifted me from the boulder, carrying me to the blanket that he had so carefully laid out for us near the fire. His warmth came through me again. I knew that this night would continue for as long as I wanted. I hoped the fire between us would never die down.

As I closed my eyes, my dream infected me like a disease. I have lived this before. With every thrust my fear became more tangible, more real. For every moment in this reality was a moment suspended in my dream. My ecstasy fell as I realized my dreams were also visions of the future. I could lose Athen, not once but twice. My fear began escaping, leaving a trail between our two bodies; my spirit sinking with the newfound information. The serpent eyes could get him.

CHAPTER 25

We were heading back up to Whistler to catch some skiing since the entire mountain was officially open. I did my best to push aside the darkness that dared to squash my most intimate moments. I made myself stop thinking about the night before and how glorious it was in every possible way. I wasn't sure how I would be able to make it through a day without feeling his embrace again, but I was going to have to. Reality still exists. Knowing the gravity of the situation made me restless. Realizing that my nightmares and dreams were foreshadowing the future made me sick. I wasn't sure how to stop the dreams from turning into reality, but I was going to have to figure it out. I couldn't let her win.

Athen had pretty much packed everything for us in Whistler. I loved the home here and couldn't wait to come back to it for the holidays, but I was looking forward to seeing Whistler in full-blown holiday swing. It sounded like we would stay for a couple weeks. Athen was helping me with my bags as I remembered the last few things I needed that were in the bathroom.

"So will those things be waiting for us up in Whistler?" I hollered from the bathroom as I tried to gather the last few hair accessories I could find.

"Um, wow, that's out of the blue again. I certainly hope not, but in all honesty, nothing would surprise me so as usual we all need to be watchful. You need to let us know of anything odd that you notice as well. Your senses are really coming back to you at an impressive rate. I don't think you should discount anything that you feel. Better to be safe than sorry. They haven't found the snowboarder yet. It looks as if they're on the move. They located a yurt that fit your description. They definitely saw that it had been inhabited recently, but nobody was there. They're on the run. The poor kid has no clue."

My stomach began to turn knowing how accurate he truly was about my senses. They were coming back, and I had to figure out what I was seeing, without anyone knowing. I pushed the thoughts of losing Athen away and focused only on the innocent bystander.

"Oh, that's a shame. It's getting really intense trying to balance everything. It makes me appreciate what I have even more. I love you. Thanks for being there. Thanks for making me wait too, by the way. It was pretty incredible." I told him, as I threw my stuff into my purse. Then I grabbed him lightly to reassure myself that he was still here and mine.

"Anytime," he said laughing.

"Now you say that?" I rolled my eyes.

He went over to the French door and jiggled it to make sure it was locked before we left our bedroom and headed downstairs.

"Everything all locked up?" Athen asked Cyril.

"Yep. We're good to go. I loaded the last of our bags. Thank goodness we are coming back down for Christmas. The thought of lugging all the shopping bags Arie bought up to Whistler was enough to make me boycott the season." Cyril ducked as instantly as he spoke to avoid Arie's purse from hitting him.

"I missed!" she exclaimed. "You are lucky."

Matilda ran out to the garage excited at the thought of a car ride so we quickly followed so she didn't have to stand in the cold garage. I began getting a feeling that I didn't recognize and thought I would let Athen know.

"Uh, guys? Something doesn't seem right. I can't put my finger on it, but something's up, I think."

Arie stopped dead in her tracks and called Matilda back to the mudroom. I was hoping that I didn't make too big of a deal out of this feeling I was getting. Athen grabbed my arm, ushering me back into the kitchen.

"You sensed exactly what we did. You can't formulate it yet. There is a creature out there again. Probably right near the garage door," Cyril whispered.

"Well, now what?" My heart was beating faster, and I was getting faint. "Should I be worried? Do we need to do something?"

Athen could sense my fear and wrapped his arms around my shoulder.

"Sweetie, we got it. This one I think is the leftover minion."

Cyril looked over at Athen who went dodging out as Matilda came running back in. I could see flashes of light, and before I knew it Cyril was back inside.

"Minions are the easiest," he told me as if this would explain everything.

"Aaah, I got it. I'll remember that for next time. Actually, I take that back. Let's hope there isn't a next time."

"True," Arie agreed, "Now let's try this again. The powder is calling."

CHAPTER 26

We arrived in Whistler with the familiar Inukshuk sculpture greeting us. The village was in full swing for the holidays. I was so glad to be back. We first stopped at my condo to make sure the contractors had finished putting everything back together from the first run in I had a short time ago. We all entered in as Matilda began running around the entire place as if she was making certain everything was as she left it. Sure enough, the contractors were finished. They had done a great job. While we were in Kingston, we decided to put this one up for rent. Then I would move into their larger condo. I was so excited to obviously be living with Athen, but there was a part of me that would miss this place since I had spent so much time here. I was glad it was still mine. I was only renting it out. I took the boxes we had brought into my bedroom and began putting in all of my clothes and things I didn't want to leave without.

Cyril and Arie were in the living room and kitchen cleaning those cupboards out and packaging those items up to take with us. I was grateful for their help. It made the process much faster. My goal was to do a little bit each week while we were up here and then get the process started to rent it.

Athen and I had, also, secretly discussed getting a house possibly outside of the village, a small one where we could be a little more secluded away from the hustle and bustle of the village. We would still want to keep both the condos in the village and maybe rent them as vacation rentals in between. It was too good of a spot to give up, but the idea of a house was pretty intriguing. We were going to bring it up to Cyril and Arie to see what they thought about the idea.

I was getting the last of the pictures off my dresser, and I saw one of the first ones of Athen and myself pre-phasing. I knew I finally had the proof I needed. I had changed since the whole reintroduction process. It wasn't only the eyes.

"Aha! I exclaimed to Athen.

"What is it?" he asked coming over to where I was sitting.

"I do look different than before. Look at the picture!"

"Sweetie, the only thing that changed is your confidence level and the color of your eyes. It just so happens the camera picked it up. But, honestly, you always took my breath away." He smooched me on my head and went back to whatever he was packing up for me.

"Huh."

We finished up and rang the bell captain to move the boxes down to our car. Our next stop was my new home for now. I was super excited to enter into the condo for the first time with the thought that I wasn't leaving. Sleeping in Athen's bed was even more miraculous. We decided to have dinner out somewhere after we brought everything up and then hit the sack early to start our first full day on the entire mountain. Plus, I knew that with sleeping next to Athen, I probably wasn't getting to bed quite that early.

We were at Araxi enjoying the wonderful truffle oil fries when Arie got a call on her cell phone. She excused herself, and I realized it must have been about the snowboarder.

"What do you think the news is?" I asked Athen.

"Last we heard the trail was a little cold. Are you sure you haven't had anymore visions?"

"Nothing." I was disappointed in myself. It seemed like I was leading everyone on a wild goose chase.

"We'll just see what she says when she gets back. You've done a lot more than you are giving yourself credit for." Cyril was trying to be supportive, but it didn't help how I was feeling. "Especially this early on in the game." Cyril winked at me trying to make me feel better. If only he knew about all of my visions.

Arie returned to the table, and her facial expression said it all.

"Well, the clothes you had described in your vision were dead on."

My heart fell to the floor. We were too late.

"They haven't found the snowboarder," she whispered, "But they found his clothes along with his other belongings he had the day he went missing. No other sign of him. They're on the run for sure."

"Do you think he has been turned?" I asked, my throat scratchy like sandpaper.

"I really don't think so, not yet anyway. I think they're enjoying toying with us," she said flatly.

"What about those hikers? What do you think has come of them? Is this related?" I asked, not sure why it mattered.

"Yeah. It certainly is related, but I don't know what the significance is yet," Cyril said, shaking his head in frustration.

Our entrees arrived, and as was becoming usual, we had to shake our previous conversation. It took some getting used to switching gears so often. It was exhausting mentally, but from what I could tell, the only way to maintain some normalcy was to be able to switch it off. I was getting the hang of it pretty quickly, all things considered. However, what I looked forward to most was falling asleep in Athen's arms and waking up in them the next morning. I noticed myself shoveling in the food that much quicker as these thoughts bounced around. I looked over at Athen and noticed he was shoveling it in at a pretty steady pace too, and I chuckled to myself.

***

The snow was breathtaking in the morning. The flakes were gently falling as they had been the entire night before, which made for incredible conditions. It's always great to get on the mountain when the first flakes of the season come down in November, but usually only the top part of the mountain was open. It satisfies the craving a bit, but barely long enough until the entire mountain was open. Then the real skiing can begin, like today. It was great that we were all at similar levels. I was enjoying myself so much, and the best part seemed to be that there weren't any creatures waiting for me. I thoroughly embraced the freedom around me.

It was getting close to noon when we decided that this would be our last run so we could go to the Longhorn and grab lunch. I was craving wings and a drink. We all made our way over to the entrance and propped our skis and poles in the storage area.

We walked past the diehards who were sitting outside eating and drinking next to the heat lamps and went inside to grab a place to sit.

"So everything seems pretty calm around here. That's a good thing, right?" I asked whoever would answer.

"Yep. So far so good. We need to keep an eye out," Cyril said, reaching for Arie's hand.

The waitress bounded over to get our drink order, and we all wanted the same thing, a hot peppermint patty. Beer didn't sound good compared to something warm for the first round.

Athen looked over at me. I could tell he wanted to bring up the topic of getting a house outside the village that we weren't able to discuss last night. I nodded my head.

"I know it may seem odd since we have a place in the village, but hear us out. We've been thinking about getting a house right outside the village. We can have more privacy and then use this one when we are skiing, but there are times in the summer when I think we would all enjoy some land to go along with the summer nights up here." Athen looked around trying to gauge Cyril and Arie's expression. I could tell he was gearing up for an argument and had his list of reasons ready for the firing. Instead he got an answer that completely took us by surprise.

"We've been thinking the same thing," Arie informed us, "Now that we are all together again, it seems fitting to have a little more room to roam. I think it's a great idea. We can always rent this one when we aren't using it."

"Wow, sis, I was expecting a bit of a fight or something, but this is great." Athen said sounding very relieved.

"I love looking at homes and have already compiled a list from some of the magazines I grabbed around the village last night on our way back from dinner. There is one that seems especially fitting, if you wanted to check it out," I mentioned.

"No, that sounds great. You certainly don't waste any time," Cyril said.

"It's back at the condo. I can show it to you when we get back." I was getting super excited. It would also give us more room for some of the stuff I had accumulated, too, from my condo. Thankfully, we all had the same decorating choices.

We scheduled a meeting with a realtor for that Tuesday, and when we pulled up to the driveway, we all knew this was the place. The home was spectacular. It had a large front porch that was covered in cobblestones. There were shingles and exposed beams on every corner, which was a favorite look of mine. Cyril pulled the car next to the realtor's, and we all hopped out of the Jeep. The towering trees that were kept on the lot greeted us as we walked up the driveway.

Athen took my hand, and I instantly squeezed it letting him know how happy I was with this place. We hadn't even gotten inside yet. The realtor opened the door as soon as we reached the last step. She looked very pretty. I sensed a familiarity about her, but dismissed it to her being a local Whistler resident. She was dressed in an off-white pantsuit with a red, silk scarf tied around her neck.

"Hi, I'm Stephanie and you are..." she said looking directly at me with a very calming smile, sticking out her hand.

"I'm Ana. I spoke with you on the phone," I said, shaking her hand, "This is Athen, Arie, and Cyril."

"Oh, yes. I think we have worked together, you own the condo at the Fairmont, right?" she asked looking at Athen.

That's when it hit me. She had brilliant green eyes. I looked over at Athen who nodded. Wow, this was truly an amazing world I belonged in. I don't know how I missed it for so long.

"So this foyer is two stories and to the right of us is considered the library. To the left is the dining room. It connects to the kitchen. Let's go have a look shall we?"

I loved this house. The layout was perfect. The house was filled with warmth, and we hadn't even moved in yet. We all walked into the family room, and I saw another set of stairs that were leading downstairs, which we followed and saw a cozy theater room, wine cellar, and little bar area. We came back up the stairs to the main floor, and I admired the view I had missed before. The snow was gently falling and graced the fir trees that were on the hill guiding the driveway back down the hill.

Cyril and Arie followed Stephanie upstairs, and we stayed down in the kitchen for a little while. I think Athen could sense the questions I had building up.

"She's one of us?" I whispered to Athen.

"She sure is," Athen replied.

"Are they all over? Is she in a family too? Like ours?"

"Yes, sweetie, she is. She is married to Joshua. They live here in the Winter and, believe it or not, they live in New Mexico in the Spring and Summer."

"So you guys are friends with them?"

"We've been friends with them for a few years. They know the situation, if that is what you are wondering."

"Yeah, I kind of gathered that," I said grinning.

"Aren't you something now?" Athen swatted at me, "Now let's go upstairs and check out the rest of the house."

We got to the landing. There was a little bonus room to the left. That was a nice feature I thought to myself. We heard Arie's voice and followed it down the hallway that went to the left. There was a smaller guest room, which looked plenty big, and then a master suite where Arie and Cyril were chatting with Stephanie.

"Well, this is a nice size, and it has a deck. That's great!" I exclaimed.

"And this is the smaller room," Cyril chipped in.

"Really? Let's go check out the other one, honey!" I said grabbing Athen's hand and pulling him with me.

As we got down the hall I heard Stephanie say, "Wow, she is certainly well adjusted for such a short time."

"Am I really?" I asked Athen.

"Yeah, you really are. It's a bit abnormal."

"Sweet," I said, before heading into the other master suite.

"Wow, this one is great! It has a deck too. The bathroom was bigger. I bet Cyril and Arie would like this one. I have to be honest. I kind of like the other one. It feels more cozy."

"I'm completely with you," Athen agreed.

We headed back to meet the others. I heard Stephanie telling them that if it was a cash offer, we could close in as little as two weeks.

"What a Christmas present that would be!" I exclaimed.

Athen came in and hugged my shoulders, "You guys think we should keep looking or do you think this is it?"

"I think we all know this is it!" Arie said, jumping up a little.

"Great. We'll go back to the office and submit the paperwork."

CHAPTER 27

It was a week before Christmas, and the village was bustling with people. There was the influx of tourists up to celebrate Christmas, along with all of the owners returning to their condos and timeshares. Lights were dangling everywhere. The snow was coming down so heavy it was hard for the heated pathways to stay clear. The village Christmas tree was especially touching this year. Every time my family and I passed it, I had to take a minute to stop and stare. Arie was making fun of me, for how many pictures of us by it I had taken so far.

We had all decided to go to Dublin Gate for a Guinness so we could map out the plans for the next day. We wanted to get some snowboarding in since we had been skiing so much since we arrived. Athen wanted to try out the half pipe. There was no way I was touching that. I was planning on only watching that part.

The Dublin Gate was fluttering with activity. The bar was completely full, and there was only one table in the corner that looked like it was meant for two people comfortably, but we made a beeline and squished on the bench to make it work. Who knew when the next table would open up. A wave of happiness rushed through me as I remembered the last time we were here. I was in heavenly bliss dancing with Athen that night. It all had seemed like such a dream. What transpired after that, I would never have guessed in a million years. I hugged onto Athen's arm extra hard. I was pretty sure that he knew what I was thinking back to. He kissed my forehead, and the familiar electricity ran through my veins. I looked at my family unable to understand how I got so lucky.

"Do you think the movers finished moving the rest of Ana's things to the house today?" Cyril asked, as he was flagging down the server.

"They said they would be able to," Arie said, "We should go check tomorrow. You know I was kind of thinking that since we bought this place that maybe we should change our plans and stay up here for the rest of the holidays?"

"Wow, Arie! I think that would be a great idea. We could get situated and you could decorate yet again," I laughed.

"Great! What do you guys think?" she asked Athen and Cyril.

"We are game for whatever you all want," Cyril said, smooching Arie on her lips.

"This is awesome, plus we can have a second Christmas down south!" She almost squealed with delight.

"Oh brother. Really?" Athen asked, and he kissed me so gently on my lips I almost didn't realize what was happening. Always a competition with these guys, I thought happily.

Arie broke free from Cyril to announce the one thing that took all of us by surprise.

"I kind of guessed you guys would be game for that so I sent out invitations for an Open House slash Christmas party. Won't that be fun?"

I think we were all in shock being that we had barely left a conversation about the movers still moving our items into the home. Leave it to Arie to want to entertain, regardless of the moment.

"Do you think we can pull this off?" I asked Arie, puzzled that she would do this without consulting us first.

"Don't mind her," Athen said, giving me a little hug. "She's got it all under control. Don't you?"

"Of course! It isn't going to be anything big. I wanted to invite some of Ana's friends and some of our friends so we can all get introduced a bit."

"Well, judging by the real estate agent, I have a feeling your guests are going to be a whole lot more interesting than mine will be. How did you know who to invite?" I asked suspiciously.

"Oh, Ana! That was the easiest part. I asked Karen to come up with the list," she said beaming.

"Right, well that ought to be something."

The server came over and got our drink orders. I found myself drifting off about this party. I wondered first of all, who Karen would possibly invite being that she was my one actual friend, the rest were acquaintances. But what was more intriguing was to find out who all would be there that Arie invited. I'm sure they weren't all going to be other worldlies, but I could be wrong. I wondered if I would be able to recognize them all. I honestly didn't think there were any others in Whistler so even the real estate agent took me by surprise. Obviously, I was wrong. I wasn't feeling the usual angst over having a get together, which made me relieved. Usually my stomach became queasy at the thought of one, and I tried to think of any excuse to get out of it. Maybe those feelings would arrive a little closer to the event, or maybe my family and Athen made the difference. As I came back to reality, I heard Athen, Cyril, and Arie all rattling off names of people she sent the invites to, and so far, it sounded like Cyril and Athen were in agreement.

"With everything that has been going on back at the other house and here in Whistler, I think it's good to get together with everyone and keep them filled in on the events. We all need to be watching out for each other, because I think we are the beginning."

Hearing those words frightened me. I still couldn't fully comprehend what was going on being that I had nothing in my memories yet to compare. I wasn't sure why they could tell these attacks were representing a larger picture, but I'm sure I would figure that out soon enough. If my dreams didn't tell me, I was sure my family would.

"You believe this is the beginning of something? I thought, at first, you guys assumed it was to distract us since I was so new again?" I responded in a statement that turned into a question.

"That is the typical turn of events, but there have been some things that don't line up with that thought anymore. The fact that Azazel and Asmodeus are involved escalates the situation right off the bat. Also, the fact that the creatures keep coming is something that doesn't usually occur either. There seems to be a legion or legions building up forces around here. It forces us to look at all alternatives, very bleak alternatives."

"I reached out to some of the other families, and they had mentioned that they had noticed more of a presence of the demons in their immediate areas now. They consistently mentioned that nothing had happened. Rather they caught them lurking more and causing insignificant human contact. This is different than their normal patterns, and we have to find out why and make sure that we are all safe, but I think the larger our network, right now, the better. So we found out quite a bit this morning. The hikers weren't exactly hikers. They were involved in some pretty horrific dealings on a human level. They had connections with a cult down in the states and had been walking a fine line for quite some time. The press left that out. They were all friends from high school, and a couple of them hit it big doing some dirty work for a large gang, and all the friends shared the wealth. I highly doubt they were just hiking up in the mountains."

Cyril had a complete look of disgust. "I could keep going on, but let's just say they were headed down that path for a long time, and they presented themselves to the underworld as best as one can. They were ready for the taking."

"Yikes, that certainly isn't what I was expecting to hear. That sounds gruesome. With everything I read in the papers, I thought they were just friends who were at the wrong place at the wrong time. What about the snowboarder?"

"Honestly, that one doesn't make sense. It doesn't fit the same circumstances as the other group, that's for sure. I'm waiting to hear back from some of our friends on that one. They're closer to it than we were. It is like he went off the map. Last I heard there were no leads, other than what you saw in your visions."

"Huh, will it come up at the party? Will we be covering this after my friends leave, of course?"

"Oh, most definitely. We've got a lot to cover that evening. We'll be trying to fit in as much as we can."

"Do they all know about me? Everyone that is coming to the party, that is?"

"Geez, Ana! You think they didn't notice Athen sulking ever since they met him up here? Yeah, they're very up to speed on things. I'm sure they will be relieved to see Athen actually demonstrating communication skills again," Cyril piped up.

"Oh, come on. I wasn't that bad," Athen said, tossing his napkin at Cyril, which didn't have much of an impact since we were all sitting so close together.

"Don't be nervous," Arie chided in, "Everyone is nice. They care about you. Anyone that goes through what you have been through kind of makes us all realize that it isn't that far off of a reality. If anything they will put you on a pedestal."

"Exactly what I have always wanted," I responded, rolling my eyes.

CHAPTER 28

It was the evening of the party in our new home, and guests would be arriving soon. I had finished curling my hair and decided I could go ahead and slip on my dress. I shouldn't get it too messed up by the time everyone arrives. Matilda was gently snoring in our bedroom in front of the fireplace. I loved our new home. The exposed dark beams and stone throughout were beautiful, especially with the garland hung everywhere. I was amazed at how quickly we were able to organize everything. Arie, of course, was able to get all of the Christmas decorations up in between us all hitting the slopes. She had a large tree up in the family room and a smaller one in the living room to greet the guests. It made me miss the one we so valiantly picked out down in Kingston. Hopefully, it wouldn't be completely dead by the time we got back to it.

I was thankful she catered everything. It took the heat off of this event. Especially since I was so worried about meeting so many new people. It had never been my specialty, but it certainly had gotten easier with the arrival of my family. I heard Athen coming down the hall and wondered if he was going to pop in to get his change of clothes on.

"Hey, sweetie, you look ravishing." His voice lifted me up to the heavens and made me feel instantly better.

"Not so bad yourself," I told him, swatting him on his butt.

"Do you think the combination of everyone will be okay tonight?" I asked Athen innocently, which led him to laugh uncontrollably.

"What?" Giving him my best shot at an evil eye.

"Honey, we have been existing among humans since the beginning. Don't you think we've got the hang of it?"

"True. I only remember how you all made me feel that first night."

"Well, that was only because we were testing the field so to speak. That doesn't happen to humans. We were trying to find out if you sensed us yet."

"What about Karen? Why did she feel so horrible? Remember she had to leave that night? I took over her table."

"I didn't say we couldn't do that to humans, but it doesn't happen by us merely being in the same room together. We have to provoke it. We had a plan that night and couldn't afford to miss our chance because we got sat in the wrong section, so in that case, yes, Arie used her powers in that way. It won't be coming out tonight though," he said still chuckling.

I was in disbelief. They actually made Karen ill so I would serve them that night. Pretty clever, but wrong on so many levels.

Athen walked into the closet, and I backed up a few steps so I could get a glimpse of him changing. He was so irresistible. I had to get my fill when I could. I saw him grabbing a nice pair of corduroys and a navy sweater, which I'm sure he would make look incredible.

I heard a car pulling up into the driveway and knew that was my signal. Our first guests had arrived.

The evening was in full swing, and Athen was right. There was nothing abnormal about the evening at all. I was so thrilled to see Karen and her boyfriend Justin. Everything seemed wonderful with both of them so I was relieved about that. I'm not sure how much influence I had over that situation, but it made me proud. In between the many introductions with all of my new 'friends', it felt as if Karen and I were able to connect again as we had before all of the crazy changes.

Karen did a good job of inviting people on my behalf. It was mostly people from the pub that I had worked with. It was great to catch up with my favorite bartender Tim, and of course, my boss Don. I was touched that they took the time to show up. Sabrina, who was always so perky, came with her fiancé. They were newly engaged, and I could relate to her happiness at long last. She clung onto about every word her fiancé spoke, and I thought it was sweet since he did the same with her.

I met several of Arie and Cyril's friends. There was Gloria, who owned a restaurant in the town below Whistler in Squamish, and she was stunning. Her brown hair complimented her green eyes or the other way around. She seemed genuinely excited to meet me. Although I had a feeling we had met several times before. Vanessa and Trina were sisters who came up to the village every winter, and Arie and Cyril had known them for years. They seemed so very kind as well and very familiar too. I probably had been serving them all this time and obviously had no idea. One thing that struck me was how many of the friends seemed to be Arie and Cyril's, and so few were Athen's. I made a mental note to ask Arie about that later.

I was able to sneak over to Karen, and she filled me in on how well things were going at the pub, picking up crazy hours due to the holidays, but still able to enjoy her other favorite pastime, which was jewelry making. Her pieces were always so intricate, and I was honored that she had chosen to give me a piece for the holidays. It was a sterling silver, pendant angel that seemed more fitting now than ever. I was able to present my gift to her as well, a cashmere scarf, hat, and glove set that I picked up down in Seattle at her favorite sweater boutique. It was well after midnight before they took off, and not one of the other guests from my family's list had left.

Arie's playlist of Christmas music finally hit the repeat mark, which was impressive being that it had been playing for well over five hours. She hopped over to our Bose system and switched it over to non-holiday music. It was kind of a nice reprieve after noticing how similar so much of the holiday music was no matter who sung the song. Rudolph and Frosty can only be sung about in so many ways.

I noticed most of the guests were starting to gather in the family room, drinks in hand, and a quiet hush came over everyone. Death Cab for Cutie was playing softly from the other room, but other than that, the mood had changed pretty swiftly. Athen came up behind me and wrapped his arms around my waist.

"We are going to discuss a few of the iniquitous occurrences with everyone before they all leave," he whispered in my hair.

"Oh, the real reason for the party."

Cyril began with a toast to everyone for coming up for our holiday open house, and everyone responded back in a loud, "Cheers!"

"We have some business to quickly get out in the open too. As you know there have been occurrences. We initially attributed them to the re-phasing of Ana. However, they have become more frequent, persistent, and candidly rough. It seems Azazel is involved and possibly Asmodeus. It has been pretty calm since we have been back to Whistler, but before we left we had noticed increased activity. We had a couple of run-ins that we were able to thwart. Once we got down to Washington, their presence was much more pronounced. I think there may be a movement going on, a building of legions. I don't know why or if it's over anything specific, but I think we all need to be a little bit more cognizant of our surroundings and make sure our network is strong. We need to be vigilant in our methods of communicating any threats that may be lurking out there to one another for the time being, no matter how big or small."

Jordan, who I met only briefly at the front door, began to speak up.

"Cy, it's not only your family who has been targeted. We have had run-ins similar to your family. The presence around us is much more than we have ever experienced for no specific cause. Many are low level demons, posers, with very little experience, but all the same." His voice trailed off.

A woman stepped through the crowd. I had not met her yet. Her mate was right behind her holding her hand as they made way to be able to speak.

"That's Jessica," Athen whispered. "She has been in Whistler with her husband longer than any of us."

Jessica began speaking.

"We, too, have experienced unexpected interference, far more than usual when stepping in with humans. We have had several situations in the last few weeks while we are working with our targets, and the creatures would vanish only to bring in a new set. We honestly dismissed the occurrences. But hearing some of your stories makes me reconsider. What struck me as worrisome was that on even minor infractions, the demons were persistent, where they normally would retreat. They've lingered on infidelity scenarios and everything. Usually we try our persuasion a little, and they flee. It hasn't been that way."

Our front door opened, and a breeze began drifting though the entire house. I couldn't see who was at the door. I hoped it wasn't one of my friends returning for something. I began to sense an uneasiness infiltrate the room. The crowd was completely quiet as the stranger made his way into the family room. I saw his bright green eyes look up at us all. It was the snowboarder. How could he be one of us, and my family miss it or my vision be so wrong? There was an awkward silence throughout the entire room as he made his way to the center of our family room.

"Is Ana here?" his voice uttered the words I least expected.

Athen tightened his grip around me a littler harder.

"You are going to have to explain the significance of all of this to me later," I whispered to Athen.

"I honestly don't know the significance."

My heart plummeted and confusion set in.

I had no idea who this person was, and the fact that my family didn't either made me worried. Arie stepped forward.

"I'm Ana."

What was she doing? My body stiffened at the notion that she was putting herself in jeopardy. I noticed the mood in the room shift from awkward silence to anticipation. I began seeing bodies around the room shift and ready themselves for what was about to begin. They were preparing for a fight, but I couldn't understand why they would be fighting one of our own. There was a feeling unlike any that I had encountered thus far. A restless stirring just daring the being to make a move was hovering in the air. Athen slowly moved my body back into the crowd's protection. That's when I realized the snowboarder was a demon, an imposter posing as one of us. He had been taken.

This demon was sent into our den to masquerade as one of us. He was probably created on the mountain just for this very occurrence. His masters fully knew that he wouldn't come out in the same form he went in. He was being sacrificed as a message to us. The legions were building, and we were the targets, not just our human companions.

Before I knew it, the demon leapt for Arie who crouched down as graceful as a swan while Cyril leapt over her capturing his neck by one hand in a quick, fluid motion as I had seen many times before. From every angle the white demons collapsed onto the imposter tearing every piece of him to shreds. As

288

the black cloud began to surface, it traced its way back out the front door. I collapsed onto the floor in a sitting position in utter disbelief. From this moment on, I had no shame for what I was, only pride.

I was proud to be a white demon, a fallen angel. I now fully understood the difference. I would never again feel the shame that haunted me from that first night of my reintroduction process. We were all intertwined, somehow, and had to fight for the common goal. I looked up at Athen and whispered I love you to him as he helped me up.

The silence in the room began turning into a flurry of activity. I heard Arie continue speaking, letting them know the specifics of our occurrences that she had attempted to tell everyone before we were interrupted. We were in this together. That was apparent. To what degree, we didn't know, but we definitely had to build up our forces. I squeezed Athen's hand, so thankful for him.

I suddenly wanted everyone to leave. I needed time to absorb what was going on, hoping that my imagination was much more active than what reality could hold. I learned quickly that my reality was far beyond what my imagination ever dreamed. I wasn't sure how much time had passed, but while I was trying to wrap my head around things, Arie had finished up, and everyone was beginning to gather their coats and other items, trickling out the front door. I followed Athen to the foyer to say goodnight to everyone. Amidst the many hugs and cheek kisses, I began feeling stronger, more secure with what might be lurking out there against us. We had a strong community, and this was only a tiny portion of it.

Athen and I made our way up to bed. Matilda decided to stay downstairs. Sometimes she enjoyed the thought of not moving more than being tempted to snuggle with us.

"So what did you think of tonight?" Athen asked, as we hugged under the covers trying to warm up.

"I had my reservations for sure, but I'm happy Arie did this. It makes me feel not so alone in this, whatever this is. I can't believe one of them showed up in our house though. I thought they wouldn't trespass in our area and the green eyes?" Athen squeezed me, and I cozied up even more.

"We have a strong network out there. We have to dial into them all and let the word spread. As for the uninvited visitor... It's a shame. The demons knew what they were doing. He is only weeks old. He was just sent in, not even knowing his own fate. As for the green eyes, laughable as it may seem, green contacts do wonders."

"I can't believe he was turned. It makes me sad we couldn't get to him. His poor family."

"Well, that would explain why I didn't sense him as one of us. I'm surprised I didn't catch that he was one of them, however. I was so shocked that I was looking at the same person as in the pictures and then when he asked for me by name, I was at a loss."

"Yeah, it was a trigger for us, but as you saw he didn't have a chance. We've got to figure out why the demons are moving and taunting us so much. We have got to find out what their motive is sooner rather than later. We'll get it, though. Don't you worry."

"I have to admit I was comforted a little to hear that the others were noticing things too. It makes me feel like it isn't me the creatures are out to get."

Athen nodded, "I know.   But don't get too comfortable."

We laid in bed quietly holding each other until morning let us know it had arrived. Then we finally fell asleep. Christmas was only a few days away.

CHAPTER 29

I was back at the house putting dishes away when I began to feel Athen's aura tense up. I was thankful that I was finally beginning to be in tune with my family's whereabouts and their feelings without being directly with them. Being so new to it made it hard to distinguish the different level of consciousness, unfortunately. He was out with Matilda so I wasn't sure why this was coming over me. Hoping that the negative vibes that were disseminating around my body were false, I told myself that I was over reacting. I tried frantically to rid the fear that began to take hold. I left the kitchen and went over to the family room to look outside where I last saw Athen and Matilda in the woods. I scanned quickly and didn't see anything. The feeling began getting stronger, but I convinced myself that I was getting overly paranoid. That was the problem with still trying to gauge the emotions of others. These skills were not easy to pick up.

I talked myself out of my panic attack, going back to the kitchen to finish putting the items away from the dishwasher. I saw Matilda's reflection in the window running towards the house without Athen, and then suddenly his voice entered through my veins, "I will follow your soul wherever that leads me. We'll never be apart again for as long as we were, but my immediate time might be ending. Ana, bring Cyril, quickly."

The plate I was holding crashed to the floor. Arie came running down the stairs, and Cyril dashed in from the deck. They already knew. This wasn't a false alarm. I didn't need to say a word. I was seeing the present. Athen was surrounded by six black demons. They didn't have the human form that I was used to seeing, but they didn't have the image right before their death either. Athen had summoned me up. This wasn't like before. He was the target, not I. He had the complete disadvantage. This was like my dream. Why didn't I tell anyone? If the demons couldn't get me they would get the next best thing to split our family apart and stop us from trying to do good in the world. The first legion had announced itself. Now it was our time to fight for Athen.

I ran as fast as I could following Arie and Cyril out the door. Our bodies darted through the woods as spirits did in the otherworld. I no longer had the restraints of earth or nature keeping me in check. We were mere seconds into our journey and almost to Athen, but it felt like an eternity. I knew in my heart this time was different. The images bothered me the most. I could see them in my mind just swirling around Athen, teasing him. This had been one big game to the demons thus far. This was my nightmare. I wouldn't let this end the way it had in my nightly dance of good and evil. I had to get to him. We had to save him. I cursed myself for not telling anyone of the horrible demons that ate at me in my dreams.

The level of confidence and cockiness that Cyril had exhibited last time was nowhere to be found. I knew Athen was strong, quick and smart with his fighting ability. I, also, knew at this moment, he was in trouble. He was outnumbered for one, and I was helpless to save him unless we were there. Everything was a blur as I sped up even faster. I could see Athen crouching down. I couldn't tell why he was doing that. I was concentrating so hard on my visions, I realized I hadn't shared any of them still.

"He's crouching. There are six black images surrounding him, Cyril. I don't know what it means," I screamed, my lungs out of air.

"We are almost there, just focus." Arie planted the words directly in my head.

The trees and homes were unrecognizable shapes and colors on the backside of the village. Everything was a blur. I knew I had to get to Athen. Time was not on my side. There was no way I could lose him. We had barely found each other again. I didn't understand why this was happening. Why was our family the target?

I saw Arie and Cyril slow down up on top of the hill. They had found Athen. I could see Athen look up at them in my vision in recognition before I met the others. As I tried my hardest to get there even faster, I cursed myself for not being up to their level of speed. I finally arrived at my destination. Meeting their gaze as I saw what was before us. It was not one creature. It was several just like my nightmare, and unfortunately, my eyes were far more developed than before. I could see that Athen was losing. It was my nightmare.

There were six black beings wrapping themselves through Athen, swirling in such a manner that was frightening beyond belief. I wasn't sure if it was the pure number of demons or the advanced skill level that they possessed, but they were all over. Screams and crashes echoed out in between shrill laughter coming directly from the legion members. I knew this might not have an ending that I could live with. It might end like my nightmare. I forced myself to quit thinking those thoughts and concentrate on what was before me. All I could see of him was his white and green energy trying to hold them off. He was at his end. He was crouching, jetting one leg out, and reaching with his right arm. I saw him grab one of the demons and rather than it turn to air like I imagined, the demon only stiffened into a serpent and dropped to the grass. Could it be her?

My spirits lifted seeing him defeat that being. But witnessing his reaction as he did it made me realize that he had obviously been holding them off for some time, and then I watched the demon slither away and regenerate. One against six was unimaginable, and they were regenerating. Athen was exhausted. His spirit was diminishing. These were definitely not minions. These were well-developed demons. I saw Cyril leap into the mess and then Arie. As I began to position myself to jump in, Arie screamed out to stay put; that I was needed on the outside of the circle. I couldn't fathom what she was talking about. Athen needed my help. We obviously needed numbers and watching on the sidelines was only going to quicken his demise. I was witnessing my true love be defeated because of me, and now I'm told not to move. I wasn't going to listen. I was going to act.

"Ana, I love you. I'll see you soon. I promise. Please listen to Arie and learn. This is how a white demon dies. Remember, it can be beautiful." I heard

Athen's voice radiating over to me. I fell to my knees. I knew what this meant but refused to accept it. I continued to witness the spectacle as it escalated. The black and white images began to wrap themselves and release much faster. It looked like Arie and Cyril were able to annihilate two of the demons as soon as they jumped in. There was hope. My nightmare was wrong.

I saw Cyril grab another one of the black demons and crush it. It fell to the grass lifeless. I was beginning to feel invigorated as I saw Athen begin to get a reprieve, until I realized there were still six demons. They were still regenerating. Another one darted from the sky in an instant as a loud thunderous clap occurred.

Tears began streaming down my face as high pitch sounds began screeching through the air making sounds my ears were barely capable of hearing, followed by another loud cracking boom, and that was it. That was when I knew it was over. Athen was gone. There was a green burst of light. Then I saw his white spirit begin to spiral up towards the sky. I dropped my head to the ground screaming. It was my fault. I was afraid to stop watching his spirit as if by tracking it I could stop the process. The black spirits vanished immediately leaving Cyril and Arie in their full form. They both came running over to hold me. I kept looking up into the sky, screaming. I could no longer separate his image from the clouds. My body began to uncontrollably shake. To have found love and lost it so quickly was more than I could handle. I closed my eyes and prayed to be taken with Athen. I could have stopped it.

"Ana, Ana, listen to me! Listen to me!" Arie was shaking me. I didn't even know how much time had passed on the hill or how long she had been yelling at me. I didn't care. I wanted Athen. I did nothing to stop the demons, and now Athen was gone. I didn't know how long it would be before I would ever see him again. My head began pounding. I wasn't sure how much longer I would be able to sit upright.

"It was just like my nightmare. It was just like my nightmare. I can't go on. Please, this was my fault. If only I had said something. I just can't. Please leave me be."

"Ana, we can bring him back. Ana, you have to focus. This is the time that we should be planning. Come on, Ana! Don't waste time. The sooner we start, the better our chances to get him back sooner. We don't have time to worry about that stuff right now. We must begin the Awakening."

I looked at Arie and finally realized what her words meant. I was wasting time. I needed to do whatever they said. I needed to quit feeling sorry for myself. Athen did it for me. I need to gain courage and do this for him. They knew how to bring him back. I didn't. I had to be strong. Cyril and Arie helped me up, and we began speeding back to the house. I knew I would do anything it took to get him back as quickly as possible. I cringed at the thought of how long it took them to reconnect with me this last time. We had to start the Awakening, whatever that entailed.

By the time we got back to the house, I could barely hold myself together. I looked to Arie hoping she would begin explaining things to me, but she didn't. She went straight to the study. Cyril dashed upstairs leaving me to my own misery not knowing what to do or what was expected. The tears began welling up again. I knew I had to follow Arie to find out what she was doing, if for nothing else then my own sanity.

"What are you doing? How can I help?" I muttered to Arie.

"I'm reaching out to the other families to let them know to be aware. The legions have begun their formation. There is a movement to destroy us, and we seem to be the family they started on. Once I do that, we'll hope that enough time has settled. We need to track him. Get him before his complete immersion. It's a balancing act. We do it too soon, we'll find him, but we'll miss our chance because he won't be ready. He won't recognize us. We do it too late, and we won't be able to locate him for a long time. We need to begin the Awakening, and you must follow our instructions, Ana. The Awakening is the most crucial part of the entire process."

"The Awakening? So how long are you talking in generalities? Hours? Days?"

My heart was beating so fast I couldn't even fathom everything that was going on. Too soon, too late – I had no idea what this meant.

Arie turned to look at me, her eyes red with tears, "This evening will be our best shot." She grabbed my hand. "But, sweetie, it's no guarantee. Trying to disrupt the process this way is a very painful event for the one connected to him intimately. More so than anything you have faced thus far."

"I don't care."

"I know you don't, but I wanted to warn you. Regardless of whether our timing is right or not, the process is still the same. Go rest up as best you can. I've got to get the word out. Cyril's up doing the same. I know this isn't easy, but we'll do our best to call him back tonight. We've got one shot. If we don't do the Awakening right, it could be decades."

"Will I see him tonight if we do everything perfectly?" I asked with the little energy I had left.

"Oh no, Ana. I didn't mean to imply you would see him tonight. It's just the process that is starting. If we are lucky, we'll see him in a few months at the earliest. The Awakening basically calls out to his spirit so his senses aren't locked up completely. Hopefully, he'll be aware of us more easily when the time comes." I knew she was doing her best at acting positive for me, but it fell flat.

I let go of her hand and was leaving the study when I turned around to ask her one last question.

"So when I was taken, the whole one shot thing.... It was missed with me?"

"Yeah, it was missed with you. We went in too early. We tried to tell Athen to wait, but he was so full of rage and despair he wouldn't listen. And we got to you too early. He started the Awakening too early, almost immediately actually. His emotions got the better of him. You hadn't even fully regenerated yet. You had no time to settle in. You had no recollection of us. We probably only got to you a few hours too soon, but it was enough to have to make us wait decades. That's what we are hoping to avoid tonight."

"I see... If only I had said something. I don't think I could live with these nightmares for eternity. I just didn't want to believe they could be true..."

Every part of my body ached. If they weren't able to get the timing right, how could we possibly make it work when I didn't even know what I was doing. I trudged over to the couch in the family room and snuggled with Matilda. My world was once again turned upside down. All I could do was wait and see the process unfold. Do as I was told when I was told. I needed to ensure that I did what I needed to bring Athen home soon. It was the least my beloved Athen deserved. I didn't know that I could last decades without him. I didn't feel as strong as he was. It might be better if I'm taken too so I don't have to live without him. At least in the other form, I didn't remember him.

I had fallen asleep on the couch and was awoken by Cyril and Arie who were dressed in what looked like very old-fashioned, velvet robes. Cyril's was a dark royal blue with black trim. Arie's was black with silver trim and embroidery on the sleeves. She had another one draped over her arm. I assumed it was mine. They helped me up and began getting my current outfit stripped down. They placed me in the heavy robe and in a different situation, I would be able to appreciate the beauty of these robes, but now I was only doing what I was told.

"Arie, we are going to go out back and get things ready. Give us twenty minutes. We'll have everything in its place. It will be the perfect part of night to begin the awakening. Make sure you make it out on time."

I nodded and still had no idea what was expected of me, but I had learned to trust my family. If they chose not to tell me certain things, there was always a good reason. I had to trust this was another time like that as well. As they left the family room, I began to feel a glimmer of hope build through my body. I hadn't felt Athen's presence once since I saw his spirit leave the hillside; an empty void was left for me to deal with, but I began to feel that was all about to change if only I trusted. I began to feel life come through me again. I had to make sure I was fully aware and able to perform whatever duties were asked of me. I knew I could I get Athen back soon, possibly sooner than months. What was in my favor was my ignorance. I had to trust Arie and Cyril with all of the details -the ritual, the timing, everything. I had no way to rush anything as Athen had done with me. He knew the process and followed his emotions rather than trusting the ritual. I had that in my favor. I trusted the ritual. I breathed in, closing my eyes gently only to see a horror facing back at me. The woman with the serpent eyes was caressing Athen's arm. I saw her lips moving. She was looking directly at me. Uttering the words, "I win. He is mine." She was smiling callously as she did in my other dreams. She seemed so sure of herself. As if she knew she had won him - like he was a trophy. I forced the images out of my mind. I was determined not to let these creatures succeed with whatever it was they were trying to do. I wasn't prepared for them to invade my mind like they were, but I had to get strong and flush these thoughts out.

I took a deep breath and opened the French doors to meet Cyril and Arie. I knew I had no other choice but to trust. I couldn't let my mind wander. I could not let the serpentine eyes sway me. I needed hope. Athen was full of hope.

The cold air hit my face bringing me to confront another uncertain reality. I was fighting to get Athen back, and I wouldn't stop my journey until he was in my arms again. The night awaiting me beyond the doors embraced me yet offered little comfort. There was no sign of life, only silence. What had happened to me, to my life? This new existence had been more captivating than I could ever have imagined. I had loved and lost more in this short period of time. I knew it was only the beginning, if I could only survive for him. I heard the whispers from the others and retreated to what I knew was expected of me. The Awakening was to begin.

LEGIONS

Book 2 of The Watchers Trilogy

Excerpt

I noticed him from afar. My heart began beating a little faster. He was bent over a long, wooden table with books spread around him. He was touching his forehead the way he did when he was concerned about something. My mind flashed to the night that he came to pick me up from the bar when the stranger was lurking. His beautiful eyes glistened, but they lacked that familiar green glow. It was hard to not go running over to him and jump on his lap. Hiding as best I could, I slowly walked to a bookcase that had art history books stacked neatly.

I snuck another glance at him. His pull was so hard to resist. I couldn't jeopardize the process, being here was bad enough. Cyril and Arie would kill me if they knew I was even here checking on him. We had a plan. I promised I would follow it, and apparently my word didn't mean anything to me any longer. I didn't know how I got this close. I felt that I was in control of the situation - everything would be ok. Plus, after hearing he wasn't alone at the Starbucks made me think of all kinds of horrible scenarios. I just had to double check... Make sure she hadn't completely gotten to him yet.

He was taking notes feverishly. I was puzzled over what in the short time he had in this new existence would compel him to research something so frantically. I made a mental note to myself to figure out what books he was looking at. I pretended to be looking for something in the stack of art books as I tried to come up with my exit plan. I got my Athen fix and he was alone, which made me feel a million times better. That's all I needed for now. As I did my best to pretend to be interested in the stack of books, I accidentally knocked the top book off the pile. As it was about to crash to the floor I caught it but not before causing enough of a commotion to get a group of guys to look over at me from the table across from Athen. One of them winked at me, which made me cringe. In normal circumstances he was probably good looking. However, nobody compared to Athen. Other men were on the verge of being repulsive.

Before I knew what was happening, I felt a singeing pain coming from behind me. I quickly spun around to see Athen staring right at me. Our eyes locked. I opened my mouth to speak, nothing would come out. It was like the first time I saw him at the Pub in Whistler.

Concern washed over his face, his body became rigid, his eyes distant. I couldn't understand why. Was I seeing recognition or fear in his eyes? He quickly grabbed his coat and notebook, giving me one last look and darted out before I could say anything, leaving a pile of books in his wake.

I knew what I did was wrong. I never should've come to get a glimpse of Athen. I had to be reminded of his presence. I couldn't stay away. The wait had been excruciating, and I wanted to make sure he was okay. Thanks to my clumsiness, I wasn't sure if he was. I found my way quickly over to the table where he was sitting to see what he was researching. As I got closer to the table my hands began to shake. I wasn't sure what I was expecting, maybe historical or technical books or how about comics? There were seven books laid out all over the table, some open and others in tidy piles. My gut became snarled as I approached the first book he left open. I recognized it instantly.

The book was a dictionary on Angels and Demons. The same one we had in our collection back in Whistler.

Chills began at the base of my spine running quickly through the rest of my body. Why would he be interested in this topic? I began quickly shuffling through all of the books. Every one of them was on either one or the other subject. I had no idea what this meant. Recognizing that the only people who would know what this signifies would be infuriated that I was even at the library - let alone making eye contact with him. The industrial, dull metal clock on the wall was ticking away my fate as my insides twisted with fear at the prospect of having to come clean with Arie and Cyril. A sigh escaped as I headed out the way I came in; only this time there was not excitement building - just fear and disappointment.

ABOUT THE AUTHOR

Karice Bolton lives in the Pacific Northwest with her awesome husband and two wonderfully cute English Bulldogs. She enjoys the fact that it rains quite a bit in Washington and can then have an excuse to stay indoors and type away. She loves anything to do with the snow and seeks out the stuff whenever she can.

CPSIA information can be obtained at www.ICGtesting.com
Printed in the USA
LVOW081619170712

290453LV00001B/33/P